Through Five Republics on Horseback

G. Whitfield Ray

Contents

THROUGH FIVE REPUBLICS ON HORSEBACK

BY

G. Whitfield Ray

PREFACE

The ***Missionary Review of the World*** has described South America as THE DARKEST LAND. That I have been able to penetrate into part of its unexplored interior, and visit tribes of people hitherto untouched and unknown, was urged as sufficient reason for the publishing of this work. In perils oft, through hunger and thirst and fever, consequent on the many wanderings in unhealthy climes herein recorded, the writer wishes publicly to record his deep thankfulness to Almighty God for His unfailing help. If the accounts are used to stimulate missionary enterprise, and if they give the reader a clearer conception of and fuller sympathy with the conditions and needs of those South American countries, those years of travel will not have been in vain.

"Of the making of books there is no end," so when one is acceptably received, and commands a ready sale, the author is satisfied that his labor is well repaid. The 4th edition was scarcely dry when the Consul-General of the Argentine Republic at Ottawa ordered a large number of copies to send to the members of his Government. Much of it has been translated into German, and I know not what other languages. Even the ***Catholic Register*** of Toronto has boosted its sale by printing much in abuse of it, at the same time telling its readers that the book "sold like hot cakes." A wiser editor would have been discreet enough not to refer to "Through Five Republics on Horseback." His readers bought it, and--had their eyes opened, for the statements made in this work, and the authorities quoted, are unanswerable.

Seeing that there is such an alarming ignorance regarding Latin America, I have, for this edition, written an Introductory Chapter on South America, and also a short Foreword especially relating to each of the Five Republics here treated. As my portrayal of Romanism there has caused some discussion, I have, in those pages, sought to incorporate the words of other authorities on South American life and religion.

That the following narratives, now again revised, and sent forth in new garb, may be increasingly helpful in promoting knowledge, is the earnest wish of the author.

G. W. R.
Toronto, Ont.

INTRODUCTION

Through Five Republics on Horseback" has all the elements of a great missionary book. It is written by an author who is an eye-witness of practically all that he records, and one who by his explorations and travels has won for himself the title of the "Livingstone of South America." The scenes depicted by the writer and the glimpses into the social, political and religious conditions prevailing in the Republics in the great Southern continent are of thrilling interest to all lovers of mankind. We doubt if there is another book in print that within the compass of three hundred pages begins to give as much valuable information as is contained in Mr. Ray's volume. The writer wields a facile pen, and every page glows with the passion of a man on fire with zeal for the evangelization of the great "Neglected Continent." We are sure that no one can read this book and be indifferent to the claims of South America upon the Christian Church of this generation.

To those who desire to learn just what the fruits of Romanism as a system are, when left to itself and uninfluenced by Protestantism, this book will prove a real eye-opener. We doubt if any Christian man, after reading "Through Five Republics on Horseback," will any longer conclude that Romanism is good enough for Romanists and that Missions to Roman Catholic countries are an impertinence. We trust the book will awaken a great interest in the evangelization of the Latin Republics of South America.

Of course, this volume will have interest for others besides missionary enthusiasts. Apart from the religious and missionary purpose of the book, it contains very much in the way of geographical, historical and scientific information, and that, too, in regard to a field of which as yet comparatively little is known. The writer has kept an open mind in his extensive travels, and his record abounds in facts of great scientific value.

We have known Mr. Ray for several years and delight to bear testimony to his ability and faithfulness as a preacher and pastor. As a lecturer on his experiences in South America he is unexcelled. We commend "Through Five Republics on Horseback" especially to parents who are anxious to put into the hands of their children inspiring and character-forming reading. A copy of the book ought to be in every Sunday School Library.

J. G. Brown.
626 Confederation Life Building, Toronto.

A PRELIMINARY WORD ON SOUTH AMERICA

The Continent of South America was discovered by Spanish navigators towards the end of the fifteenth century. When the tidings of a new world beyond the seas reached Europe, Spanish and Portuguese expeditions vied with each other in exploring its coasts and sailing up its mighty rivers. In 1494 the Pope decided that these new lands, which were nearly twice the size of Europe, should become the possession of the monarchs of Spain and Portugal. Thus by right of conquest and gift South America with its seven and a half million miles of territory and its millions of Indian inhabitants was divided between Spain and Portugal. The eastern northern half, now called Brazil, became the possession of the Portuguese crown and the rest of the continent went to the crown of Spain. South America is 4,600 miles from north to south, and its greatest breadth from east to west is 3,500 miles. It is a country of plains and mountains and rivers. The Andean range of mountains is 4,400 miles long. Twelve peaks tower three miles or more above ocean level, and some reach into the sky for more than four miles. Many of these are burning mountains; the volcano of Cotopaxi is three miles higher than Vesuvius. Its rivers are among the longest in the world. The Amazon, Orinoco and La Plata systems drain an area of 3,686,400 square miles. Its plains are almost boundless and its forests limitless. There are deserts where no rain ever falls, and there are stretches of coast line where no day ever passes without rain. It is a country where all climates can be found. As the northern part of the continent is equatorial the greatest degree of heat is there experienced, while the south stretches its length toward the Pole Quito, the capital of Ecuador, is on the equator, and Punta Arenas, in Chile, is the southernmost town in the world.

For hundreds of years Spain and Portugal exploited and ruled with an iron hand their new and vast possessions. Their coffers were enriched by fabulous sums of gold and treasure, for the wildest dream of riches indulged in by its discoverers fell infinitely short of the actual reality. Large numbers of colonists left the Iberian peninsula for the newer and richer lands. Priests, monks and nuns went in every vessel, and the Roman Catholicism of the Dark Ages was soon firmly established as the only religion. The aborigines were compelled to bow before the crucifix and worship Mary until, in a peculiar sense, South America became the Pope's favorite parish. For the benefit of any, native or colonist, who thought that a purer religion should be, at any rate, permitted, the Inquisition was established at Lima, and later on at Cartagena, where, Colombian history informs us, 400,000 were condemned to death. Free thought was soon stamped out when death became the penalty.

Such was the wild state of the country and the power vested in the priests that abuses were tolerated which, even in Rome, had not been dreamed of. The priests, as anxious for spiritual conquest as the rest were for physical, joined hands with the heathenism of the Indians, accepted their gods of wood and stone as saints, set up the crucifix side by side with the images of the sun and moon, formerly worshipped; and while in Europe the sun of the Reformation arose and dispelled the terrible night of religious error and superstition, South America sank from bad to worse. Thus the anomaly presented itself of the old, effete lands throwing off the yoke of religious domination while the younger ones were for centuries to be content with sinking lower and lower. [History is repeating itself, for here in Canada we see Quebec more Catholic and intolerant than Italy. The Mayor of Rome dared to criticize the Pope in 1910, but in the same year at the Eucharistic Congress at Montreal his emissaries receive reverent "homage" from those in authority. No wonder, therefore, that, while the Romans are being more enlightened every year, a Quebec young man, who is now a theological student in McMaster University, Toronto, declared, while staying in the writer's home, that, as a child he was always taught that Protestants grew horns on their heads, and that he attained the age of 15 before ever he discovered that such was not the case. Even backward Portugal has had its eyes opened to see that Rome and progress cannot walk together, but the President of Brazil is so "faithful" that the Pope, in 1910, made him a "Knight of the Golden Spur."]

If the religious emancipation of the old world did not find its echo in South America, ideas of freedom from kingly oppression began to take root in the hearts of the people, and before the year 1825 the Spanish colonies had risen against the mother country and had formed themselves into several independent republics, while three years before that the independence of Brazil from Portugal had been declared. At the present day no part of the vast continent is ruled by either Spain or Portugal, but ten independent republics have their different flags and governments.

Since its early discovery South America has been pre-eminently a country of bloodshed. Revolution has succeeded revolution and hundreds of thousands of the bravest have been slain, but, phoenix- like, the country rises from its ashes.

Fifty millions of people now dwell beneath the Southern Cross and speak the Portuguese and Spanish languages, and it is estimated that, with the present rate of increase, 180 millions of people will speak these languages by 1920.

South America is, pre-eminently, the coming continent. It is more thinly settled than any other part of the world. At least six million miles of its territory are suitable for immigrants--double the available territory of the United States. "No other tract of good land exists that is so large and so unoccupied as South America." [Dr. Wood, Lima, Peru, in "Protestant Missions in South America."] "One of the most marvellous of activities in the development of virgin lands is in progress. It is greater than that of Siberia, of Australia, or the Canadian North-West." [The Outlook, March, 1908.] Emigrants are pouring into the continent from crowded Europe, the old order of things is quickly passing away, and docks and railroads are being built. Bolivia is spending more than fifty million dollars in new work. Argentina and Chile are pushing lines in all directions. Brazil is preparing to penetrate her vast jungles, and all this means enormous expense, for the highest points and most difficult construction that have ever been encountered are found in Peru, and between Chile and Argentina there has been constructed the longest tunnel in the world. [One railway ascends to the height of 12,800 feet.]

Most important of all, the old medieval Romanism of the Dark Ages is losing its grip upon the masses, and slowly, but surely, the leaven is working which will, before another decade, bring South America to the forefront of the nations.

The economic possibilities of South America cannot be overestimated. It is a continent of vast and varied possibilities. There are still districts as large as the German Empire entirely unexplored, and tribes of Indians who do not yet know that

America has been "discovered."

This is a continent of spiritual need. The Roman Catholic Church has been a miserable failure. "Nearly 7,000,000 of people in South America still adhere, more or less openly, to the fetishisms of their ancestors, while perhaps double that number live altogether beyond the reach of Christian influence, even if we take the word Christian in its widest meaning." [Report of Senor F. de Castello] The Rev. W. B. Grubb, a missionary in Paraguay, says: "The greatest unexplored region at present known on earth is there. It contains, as far as we know, 300 distinct Indian nations, speaking 300 distinct languages, and numbering some millions, all in the darkest heathenism." H. W. Brown, in "Latin America," says, "There is a pagan population of four to five millions." Then, with respect to the Roman Catholic population, Rev. T. B. Wood, LL.D., in "Protestant Missions in South America," says, "South America is a pagan field, properly speaking. Its image-worship is idolatry. Abominations are grosser and more universal than among Roman Catholics in Europe and the United States, where Protestantism has greatly modified Catholicism. But it is *worse* off than any other great *pagan* field in that it is dominated by a single mighty hierarchy--the mightiest known in history. For centuries priestcraft has had everything its own way all over the continent, and is now at last yielding to outside pressure, but with desperate resistance."

"South America has been for nearly four hundred years part of the parish of the Pope. In contrast with it the north of the New World-- Puritan, prosperous, powerful, progressive--presents probably the most remarkable evidence earth affords of the blessings of Protestantism, while the results of Roman Catholicism *left to itself* are writ large in letters of gloom across the priest-ridden, lax and superstitious South. Her cities, among the gayest and grossest in the world, her ecclesiastics enormously wealthy and strenuously opposed to progress and liberty, South America groans under the tyranny of a priesthood which, in its highest forms, is unillumined by, and incompetent to preach, the gospel of God's free gift; and in its lowest is proverbially and habitually drunken, extortionate and ignorant. The fires of her unspeakable Inquisition still burn in the hearts of her ruling clerics, and although the spirit of the age has in our nineteenth century transformed all her monarchies into free Republics, religious intolerance all but universally prevails." [Guiness's "Romanism and Reformation."]

Prelates and priests, monks and nuns exert an influence that is all- pervading. William E. Curtis, United States Commissioner to South America, wrote: "One-fourth of all the property belongs to the bishop. There is a Catholic church for every 150 inhabitants. Ten per cent. of the population are priests, monks or nuns, and 272 out of the 365 days of the year are observed as fast or feast days. The priests control the government and rule the country as absolutely as if the Pope were its king. As a result, 75 per cent. of the children born are illegitimate, and the social and political condition presents a picture of the dark ages." It is said that, in one town, every fourth person you meet is a priest or a nun, or an ecclesiastic of some sort.

Yet, with all this to battle against, the Christian missionary is making his influence felt.

La Razon, an important newspaper of Trujillo, in a recent issue says: "In homage to truth, we make known with pleasure that the ministers of Protestantism have benefited this town more in one year than all the priests and friars of the Papal sect have done in three centuries."

"Last year," writes Mr. Milne, of the American Bible Society, "one of our colporteurs in Ayacucho had to make his escape by the roof of a house where he was staying, from a mob of half-castes, led on by a friar. Finding their prey had escaped, they took his clothes and several boxes of Bibles to the plaza of the city and burnt them."

It was not such a going-back as the outside world thought, but, oh, it was a deeply significant one, when recently the leading men of the Republic of Guatemala met together and solemnly threw over the religion of their fathers, which, during 400 years of practice, had failed to uplift, and re-established the old paganism of cultured Rome. So serious was this step that the *Palace of Minerva*, the goddess of trade, is engraved on the latest issue of Guatemalan postage stamps. Believing that the few Protestants in the Republic are responsible for the reaction, the Archbishop of Guatemala has promised to grant one hundred days' indulgence to those who will pray for the overthrow of Protestantism in that country.

"Romanism is not Christianity," so the few Christian workers are fighting against tremendous odds. What shall the harvest be?

PART I.
THE ARGENTINE REPUBLIC

The country to which the author first went as a self-supporting missionary in the year 1889.

And Nature, the old nurse, took
The child upon her knee,
Saying, "Here is a story book
Thy Father hath written for thee."

"Come, wander with me," she said,
"Into regions yet untrod,
And read what is still unread
In the manuscripts of God."

And he wandered away and away
With Nature, the dear old nurse,
Who sung to him night and day
The rhymes of the universe.

--Longfellow.

THE ARGENTINE REPUBLIC

The Argentine Republic has an area of one and a quarter million square miles. It is 2,600 miles from north to south, and 500 miles at its widest part. It is twelve times the size of Great Britain. Although the population of the country is about seven millions, only one per cent, of its cultivable area is now occupied, yet Argentina has an incomparable climate.

It is essentially a cattle country. She is said to surpass any other nation in her numbers of live stock. The Bovril Co. alone kills 100,000 a year. On its broad plains there are *estandas*, or cattle ranches, of fifty and one hundred thousand acres in extent, and on these cattle, horses and sheep are herded in millions. Argentina has over twenty-nine million cattle, seventy-seven million sheep, seven and a half million horses, five and a half million mules, a quarter- million of donkeys, and nearly three million swine and three million goats. Four billion dollars of British capital are invested in the country.

Argentina has sixteen thousand miles of railway. This has been comparatively cheap to build. On the flat prairie lands the rails are laid, and there is a length of one hundred and seventy-five miles without a single curve.

Three hundred and fifty thousand square miles of this prairie is specially adapted to the growing of grain. In 1908-9 the yield of wheat was 4,920,000 tons. Argentina has exported over three million tons of wheat, over three million tons of corn, and one million tons of linseed, in one year, while "her flour mills can turn out 700,000 tons of flour a year." [Hirst's Argentina, 1910.]

"It is a delight often met with there to look on a field of twenty square miles, with the golden ears standing even and close together, and not a weed nor a stump of a tree nor a stone as big as a man's fist to be seen or found in the whole area."

"To plant and harvest this immense yield the tillers of the ground bought nine million dollars of farm implements in 1908. Argentina's record in material progress rivals Japan's. Argentina astonished the world by conducting, in 1906, a trade valued at five hundred and sixty million dollars, buying and selling more in the markets of foreign nations than Japan, with a population of forty millions, and China, with three hundred millions." [John Barrett, in Munsey's Magazine]

To this Land of Promise there is a large immigration. Nearly three hundred thousand have entered in one single year. About two hundred thousand have been going to Buenos Ayres, the capital, alone, but in 1908 nearly five hundred thousand landed there. ["Despite the Government's efforts, emigration from Spain to South America takes alarming proportions. In some districts the men of the working classes have departed in a body. In certain villages in the neighborhood of Cadiz there arc whole streets of deserted houses."- Spanish Press.] In Belgium 220 people are crowded into the territory occupied by one person in Argentina, so yet there is room. Albert Hale says: "It is undeniable that Argentina can give lodgment to 100,000,000 people, and can furnish nourishment, at a remarkably cheap rate, for as many more, when her whole area is utilized."

Argentina's schools and universities are the best in the Spanish- speaking world. In Buenos Ayres you will find some of the finest school buildings in the world, while 4,000 students attend one university.

Buenos Ayres, founded in 1580, is to-day the largest city in the world south of the equator, and is "one of the richest and most beautiful places of the world." The broad prairies around the city have made the people "the richest on earth."

Kev. John F. Thompson, for forty-five years a resident of that country, summarizes its characteristics in the following paragraph: "Argentina is a *land of plenty*; plenty of room and plenty of food. If the actual population were divided into families of ten persons, each would have a farm of eight square miles, with ten horses, fifty- four cows, and one hundred and eighty-six sheep, and after they had eaten their fill of bread they would have half a ton of wheat and corn to sell or send to the hungry nations."

CHAPTER I.
BUENOS AYRES IN 1889.

In the year 1889, after five weeks of ocean tossing, the steamer on which I was a passenger anchored in the River Plate, off Buenos Ayres. Nothing but water and sky was to be seen, for the coast was yet twenty miles away, but the river was too shallow for the steamer to get nearer. Large tugboats came out to us, and passengers and baggage were transhipped into them, and we steamed ten miles nearer the still invisible city. There smaller tugs awaited us and we were again transhipped. Sailing once more toward the land, we soon caught sight of the Argentine capital, but before we could sail nearer the tugs grounded. There we were crowded into flat-bottomed, lug-sailed boats for a third stage of our landward journey. These boats conveyed us to within a mile of the city, when carts, drawn by five horses, met us in the surf and drew us on to the wet, shingly beach. There about twenty men stood, ready to carry the females on their backs on to the dry, sandy shore, where was the customs house. The population of the city we then entered was about six hundred thousand souls.

After changing the little gold I carried for the greasy paper currency of the country, I started out in search of something to eat. Eventually I found myself before a substantial meal. At a table in front of me sat a Scotsman from the same vessel. He had arrived before me (Scotsmen say they are always before the Englishmen) and was devouring part of a leg of mutton. This, he told me, he had procured, to the great amusement of Boniface, by going down on all fours and *baa-ing* like the sheep of his native hills. Had he waited until I arrived he might have feasted on lamb, for my voice was not so gruff as his. He had unconsciously asked for an old sheep. I think the Highlander in that instance regretted that he had preceded the Englishman.

How shall I describe the metropolis of the Argentine, with its one- storied, flat-roofed houses, each with grated windows and centre *patio*? Some of the poorer inhabitants raise fowls on the roof, which gives the house a barnyard appearance, while the iron-barred windows below strongly suggest a prison. Strange yet attractive dwellings they are, lime-washed in various colors, the favorite shades seeming to be pink and bottle green. Fires are not used except for cooking purposes, and the little smoke they give out is quickly dispersed by the breezes from the sixty-mile-wide river on which the city stands.

The Buenos Ayres of 1889 was a strange place, with its long, narrow streets, its peculiar stores and many-tongued inhabitants. There is the dark-skinned policeman at the corner of each block sitting silently on his horse, or galloping down the cobbled street at the sound of some revolver, which generally tells of a life gone out. Arriving on the scene he often finds the culprit flown. If he succeeds in riding him down (an action he scruples not to do), he, with great show, and at the sword's point, conducts him to the nearest police station. Unfortunately he often chooses the quiet side streets, where his prisoner may have a chance to buy his freedom. If he pays a few dollars, the poor *vigilante* is perfectly willing to lose him, after making sometimes the pretence of a struggle to blind the lookers-on, if there be any curious enough to interest themselves. This man in khaki is often "the terror of the innocent, the laughing-stock of the guilty." The poor man or the foreign sailor, if he stagger ever so little, is sure to be "run in." The Argentine law-keeper (?) is provided with both sword and revolver, but receives small remuneration, and as his salary is often tardily paid him, he augments it in this way when he cannot see a good opportunity of turning burglar or something worse on his own account. When he is low in funds he will accost the stranger, begging a cigarette, or inviting himself at your expense to the nearest *cafe*, as "the day is so unusually hot." After all, we must not blame him too much--his superiors are far from guiltless, and he knows it. When Minister Toso took charge of the Provincial portfolio of Finance, he exclaimed, "C-o! Todos van robando menos yo!" ("Everybody is robbing here except I.") It is public news that President Celman carried away to his private residence in the country a most beautiful and expensive bronze fountain presented by the inhabitants of the city to adorn the principal *plaza*. [Public square.] The president is elected by the people for a term of three years, and invariably retires a rich man, however poor he may have been when entering on his office. The laws of the country may be described as model and Christian, but the carrying out of them is a very different matter.

Some of the laws are excellent and worthy of our imitation, such as, for example, the one which decrees that **bachelors shall be taxed**. Civil elections are held on Sundays, the voting places being Roman Catholic churches.

Both postmen and telegraph boys deliver on horseback, but such is the lax custom that everything will do to-morrow. That fatal word is the first the stranger learns--manana.

Comparatively few people walk the streets. "No city in the world of equal size and population can compare with Buenos Ayres for the number and extent of its tramways." [Turner's "Argentina."] A writer in the **Financial News** says: "The proportion of the population who daily use street-cars is **sixty-six times greater in Buenos Ayres than in the United Kingdom**."

This **Modern Athens**, as the Argentines love to term their city, has a beautiful climate. For perhaps three hundred days out of every year there is a sky above as blue as was ever seen in Naples.

The natives eat only twice a day--at 10.30 a.m., and at 7 p.m.--the common edibles costing but little. I could write much of Buenos Ayres, with its **carnicerias**, where a leg of mutton may be bought for 20 cts., or a brace of turkeys for 40 cts.; its **almacenes**, where one may buy a pound of sugar or a yard of cotton, a measure of charcoal (coal is there unknown) or a large **sombrero**, a package of tobacco (leaves over two feet long) or a pair of white hemp-soled shoes for your feet--all at the same counter. The customer may further obtain a bottle of wine or a bottle of beer (the latter costing four times the price of the former) from the same assistant, who sells at different prices to different customers.

There the value of money is constantly changing, and almost every day prices vary. What to-day costs $20 to-morrow may be $15, or, more likely, $30. Although one hundred and seventy tons of sugar are annually grown in the country, that luxury is decidedly expensive. I have paid from 12 cts. to 30 cts. a pound. Oatmeal, the Scotsman's dish, has cost me up to 50 cts. a pound.

Coming again on to the street you hear the deafening noises of the cow horns blown by the streetcar drivers, or the ***pescador*** shrilly inviting housekeepers to buy the repulsive-looking red fish, carried over his shoulder, slung on a thick bamboo. Perhaps you meet a beggar on horseback (for there wishes **are** horses, and beggars **do** ride), who piteously whines for help. This steed-riding fraternity all use invariably the same words: *"Por el amor de Dios dame un centavo!"* ("For the love of God give me a cent.") If you bestow it, he will call on his patron saint to bless you. If you fail to assist him, the curses of all the saints in heaven will fall on your impious head. This often causes such a shudder in the recipient that I have known him to turn back to appease the wrath of the mendicant, and receive instead--a blessing.

It is not an uncommon sight to see a black-robed priest with his hand on a boy's head giving him a benediction that he may be enabled to sell his newspapers or lottery tickets with more celerity.

The National Lottery is a great institution, and hundreds keep themselves poor buying tickets. In one year the lottery has realized the sum of $3,409,143.57. The Government takes forty per cent. of this, and divides the rest between a number of charitable and religious organizations, all, needless to say, being Roman Catholic. Amongst the names appear the following: Poor Sisters of St. Joseph, Workshop of Our Lady, Sisters of St. Anthony, etc.

Little booths for the sale of lottery tickets are erected in the vestibules of some of the churches, and the Government, in this way, repays the church.

The gambling passion is one of Argentina's greatest curses. Tickets are bought by all, from the Senator down to the newsboy who ventures his only dollar.

You meet the water-seller passing down the street with his barrel cart, drawn by three or four horses with tinkling bells, dispensing water to customers at five cents a pail. The poorer classes have no other means of procuring this precious liquid. The water is kept in a corner of the house in large sun-baked jars. A peculiarity of these pots is that they are not made to stand alone, but have to be held up by something.

At early morning and evening the milkman goes his rounds on horseback. The milk he carries in six long, narrow cans, like inverted sugar-loaves, three on each side of his raw-hide saddle, he himself being perched between them on a sheepskin. In some cans he carries pure cream, which the jolting of his horse soon converts into butter. This he lifts out with his hands to any who care to buy. After the addition of a little salt, and the subtraction of a little buttermilk, this **manteca** is excellent. After serving you he will again mount his horse, but not until his hands have been well wiped on its tail, which almost touches the ground. The other cans of the **lechero** contain a mixture known to him alone. I never analyzed it, but have remarked a chalky substance in the bottom of my glass. He does not profess to sell pure milk; that you can buy, but, of course, at a higher price, from the pure milk seller. In the cool of the afternoon he will bring round his cows, with bells on their necks and calves dragging behind. The calves are tied to the mothers' tails, and wear a muzzle. At a **sh-h** from the sidewalk he stops them, and, stooping down, fills your pitcher according to your money. The cows, through being born and bred to a life in the streets, are generally miserable-looking beasts. Strange to add, the one milkman shoes his cows and the other leaves his horse unshod. It is not customary in this country for man's noble friend to wear more than his own natural hoof. A visit to the blacksmith is entertaining. The smith, by means of a short lasso, deftly trips up the animal, and, with its legs securely lashed, the cow must lie on its back while he shoes its upturned hoofs.

Many and varied are the scenes. One is struck by the number of horses, seven and eight often being yoked to one cart, which even then they sometimes find difficult to draw. Some of the streets are very bad, worse than our country lanes, and filled with deep ruts and drains, into which the horses often fall. There the driver will sometimes cruelly leave them, when, after his arm aches in using the whip, he finds the animal cannot rise. For the veriest trifle I have known men to smash the poor dumb brute's eyes out with the stock of the whip, and I have been very near the Police Station more than once when my righteous blood compelled me to interfere. Where, oh, where is the Society for the Prevention of Cruelty to Animals? Surely no suffering creatures under the sun cry out louder for mercy than those in Argentina?

As I have said, horses are left to die in the public streets. It has been my painful duty to pass moaning creatures lying helplessly in the road, with broken limbs, under a burning sun, suffering hunger and thirst, for three consecutive days, before kind death, the sufferer's friend, released them. Looking on such sights, seeing every street urchin with coarse laugh and brutal jest jump on such an animal's quivering body, stuff its parched mouth with mud, or poke sticks into its staring eyes, I have cried aloud at the injustice. The policeman and the passers-by have only laughed at me for my pains.

In my experiences in South America I found cruelty to be a marked feature of the people. If the father thrusts his dagger into his enemy, and the mother, in her fits of rage, sticks her hairpin into her maid's body, can it be wondered at if the children inherit cruel natures? How often have I seen a poor horse fall between the shafts of some loaded cart of bricks or sand! Never once have I seen his harness undone and willing hands help him up, as in other civilized lands. No, the lashing of the cruel whip or the knife's point is his only help. If, as some religious writers have said, the horse will be a sharer of Paradise along with man, his master, then those from Buenos Ayres will feed in stalls of silver and have their wounds healed by the clover of eternal kindness. "God is Love."

I have said the streets are full of holes. In justice to the authorities I must mention the fact that sometimes, especially at the crossings, these are filled up. To carry truthfulness still further, however, I must state that more than once I have known them bridged over with the putrefying remains of a horse in the last stages of decomposition. I have seen delicate ladies, attired in Parisian furbelows, lift their dainty skirts, attempt the crossing--and sink in a mass of corruption, full of maggots.

In my description of Buenos Ayres I must not omit to mention the large square, black, open hearses so often seen rapidly drawn through the streets, the driver seeming to travel as quickly as he can. In the centre of the coach is the coffin, made of white wood and covered with black material, fastened on with brass nails. Around this gruesome object sit the relatives and friends of the departed one on their journey to the *chacarita*, or cemetery, some six miles out from the centre of the city. Cemeteries in Spanish America are divided into three enclosures. There is the "cemetery of heaven," "the cemetery of purgatory," and "the cemetery of hell." The location of the soul in the future is thus seen to be dependent on its location by the priests here. The dead are buried on the day of their death, when possible, or, if not, then early on the following morning; but never, I believe, on feast days. Those periods are set apart for pleasure, and on important saint days banners and flags of all nations are hung across the streets, or adorn the roofs of the flat-topped houses, where the washing is at other times dried.

After attending mass in the early morning on these days, the people give themselves up to revelry and sin at home, or crowd the street- cars running to the parks and suburbs. Many with departed relatives (and who has none?) go to the *chacarita*, and for a few *pesos* bargain with the black-robed priest waiting there, to deliver their precious dead out of Purgatory. If he sings the prayer the cost is double, but supposed to be also doubly efficacious. Mothers do not always inspire filial respect in their offspring, for one young man declared that he "wanted to get his mother out of Purgatory before he went in."

A Buenos Ayres missionary writes "There are two large cemeteries here. From early morn until late at night the people crowd into them, and I am told there were 100,000 at one time in one of them. November 1 is a special day for releasing thousands of souls out of Purgatory. We printed thousands of tracts and the workers started out to distribute them. By ten o'clock six of them were in jail, having been given into custody by a 'holy father.' They were detained until six in the evening without food, and then were released through the efforts of a Methodist minister."

The catechisn reads: "Attend mass all Sundays and Feast days. Confess at least once a year, or oftener, if there is any fear of death. Take Sacrament at Easter time. Pay a tenth of first-fruits to God's Church." The fourth commandment is condensed into the words: "Sanctify the Feast days." From this it will be seen that there is great need for mission work. Of course Romanism in this and other cities is losing its old grip upon the people, and because of this the priest is putting forth superhuman effort to retain what he has. *La Voz de la Iglesia* ("The Voice of the Church"), the organ of the Bishop of Buenos Ayres, has lately published some of the strongest articles we have ever read. A late article concludes: "One thing only, one thing: OBEY; OBEY BLINDLY. Comply with her (the Church's) commands with faithful loyalty. If we do this, it is impossible for Protestantism to invade the flowery camp of the Church, Holy, Catholic, Apostolic and Roman."

Articles such as this, however, and the circulation of a tract by one of the leading church presses, are not calculated to help forward a losing cause. The tract referred to is entitled, "Letter of Jesus about the Drops of Blood which He shed whilst He went to Calvary." "You know that the soldiers numbered 150, twenty-five of whom conducted me bound. I received fifty blows on the head and 108 on the breast. I was pulled by the hair 23 times, and 30 persons spat in my face. Those who struck me on the upper part of the body were 6,666, and 100 Jews struck me on the head. I sighed 125 times. The wounds on the head numbered 20; from the crown of thorns, 72; points of thorns on the forehead, 100. The wounds on the body were 100. There came out of my body 28,430 drops of blood." This letter, the tract states, was found in the Holy Sepulchre and is preserved by his holiness the Pope. Intelligent, thinking men can only smile at such an utter absurdity.

An "Echoes from Argentina" extract reads: "Not many months ago, Argentina was blessed by the Pope. Note what has happened since:--The Archbishop, who was the bearer of the blessing and brought it from Rome, has since died very suddenly; we have had a terrible visitation of heat suffocation, hundreds being attacked and very many dying; we have had the bubonic pest in our midst; a bloody provincial revolution in Entre Rios; and now at the time of writing there is an outbreak of a serious cattle disease, and England has closed her ports against Argentine live stock. Of course, we do not say that these calamities are the **result** of the Pope's blessing, but we would that Catholics would open their eyes and see that it is a fact that whereas Protestant countries, **anathematized** by the Pope, prosper, Catholic countries which have been blessed by him are in a lamentable condition."

BUENOS AYRES AT THE PRESENT TIME.

Perhaps no city of the world has grown and progressed more during this last decade than the city of Buenos Ayres. To-day passengers land in the centre of the city and step on "the most expensive system of artificial docks in all America, representing an expenditure of seventy million dollars."

To this city there is a large emigration. It has grown at the rate of 4,000 adults a week, with a birthrate of 1,000 a week added. The population is now fast climbing up to 1 1-2 millions of inhabitants. There are 300,000 Italians, 100,000 Spaniards, a colony of 20,000 Britishers, and, of course, Jews and other foreigners in proportion. "Buenos Ayres is one of the most cosmopolitan cities of the world. There are 189 newspapers, printed in almost every language of the globe. Probably the only Syrian newspaper in America, *The Assudk*, is issued in this city." To keep pace with the rush of newcomers has necessitated the building of 30,000 houses every year. There is here "the finest and costliest structure ever built, used exclusively by one newspaper, the home of *La Prensa*; the most magnificent opera house of the western hemisphere, erected by the government at the cost of ten million dollars; one of the largest banks in the world, and the handsomest and largest clubhouse in the world." [John Barrett, In Munsey's Magazine.] The entrance fee to this club is $1,500. The Y.M.C.A. is now erecting a commodious building, for which $200,000 has already been raised, and there is a Y.W.C.A., with a membership of five hundred. Dr. Clark, in "The Continent of Opportunity," says, "More millionaires live in Buenos Ayres than in any other city of the world of its size. The proportion of well- clothed, well-fed people is greater than in American cities, the slums are smaller, and the submerged classes less in proportion. The constant movement of carriages and automobiles here quite surpasses that of Fifth Avenue." The street cars are of the latest and most improved electric types, equal to any seen in New York or London, and seat one hundred people, inside and out. Besides these there is an excellent service of motor cabs, and *tubes* are being commenced. Level crossings for the steam roads are not permitted in the city limits, so all trains run over or under the streets.

"The Post Office handles 40,000,000 pieces of mail and 125,000 parcel post packages a month. The city has 1,209 automobiles, 27 theatres and 50 moving picture shows. Five thousand vessels enter the port of Buenos Ayres every year, and the export of meat in 1910 was valued at $31,000,000. No other section of the world shows such growth." [C. H. Furlong, in The World's Work.]

The city, once so unhealthy, is now, through proper drainage, "the second healthiest large city of the world." The streets, as I first saw them, were roughly cobbled, now they are asphalt paved, and made into beautiful avenues, such as would grace any capital of the world. Avenida de Mayo, cut right through the old city, is famed as being one of the most costly and beautiful avenues of the world.

On those streets the equestrian milkman is no longer seen. Beautiful sanitary white-tiled *tambos*, where pure milk and butter are sold, have taken his place. The old has been transformed and PROGRESS is written everywhere.

CHAPTER II.
REVOLUTION.

South America, of all lands, has been most torn asunder by war. Revolutions may be numbered by hundreds, and the slaughter has been incredible. Even since the opening of the year 1900, thirty thousand Colombians have been slain and there have been dozens of revolutions. Darwin relates the fact that in 1832 Argentina underwent fifteen changes of government in nine months, owing to internal strife, and since then Argentina has had its full share.

During my residence in Buenos Ayres there occurred one of those disastrous revolutions which have from time to time shaken the whole Republic. The President, Don Juarez Celman, had long been unpopular, and, the mass of the people being against him, as well as nearly half of the standing army, and all the fleet then anchored in the river, the time was considered ripe to strike a blow.

On the morning of July 26, 1890, the sun rose upon thousands of stern-looking men bivouacking in the streets and public squares of the city. The revolution had commenced, and was led by one of the most distinguished Argentine citizens, General Joseph Mary Campos. The battle-cry of these men was "Sangre! Sangre!" ["Blood! Blood!"] The war fiend stalked forth. Trenches were dug in the streets. Guns were placed at every point of vantage. Men mounted their steeds with a careless laugh, while the rising sun shone on their burnished arms, so soon to be stained with blood. Battalions of men marched up and down the streets to the sound of martial music, and the low, flat-roofed housetops were quickly filled with sharpshooters.

The Government House and residence of the President was guarded in all directions by the 2nd Battalion of the Line, the firemen and a detachment of police, but on the river side were four gunboats of the revolutionary party.

The average South American is a man of quick impulses and little thought. The first shot fired by the Government troops was the signal for a fusilade that literally shook the city. Rifle shots cracked, big guns roared, and shells screaming overhead descended in all directions, carrying death and destruction. Street-cars, wagons and cabs were overturned to form barricades. In the narrow, straight streets the carnage was fearful, and blood soon trickled down the watercourses and dyed the pavements. That morning the sun had risen for the last time upon six hundred strong men; it set upon their mangled remains. Six hundred souls! The Argentine soldier knows little of the science of "hide and seek" warfare. When he goes forth to battle, it is to fight--or die. Of the future life he unfortunately thinks little, and of Christ, the world's Redeemer, he seldom or never hears. The Roman Catholic chaplain mumbles a few Latin prayers to them at times, but as the knowledge of these *resos* does not seem to improve the priest's life, the men prefer to remain in ignorance.

The average Argentine soldier is a man of little intelligence. The regiments are composed of Patagonian Indians or semi-civilized Guaranis, mixed with all classes of criminals from the state prisons. Nature has imprinted upon them the unmistakable marks of the savage-- sullen, stupid ferocity, indifference to pain, bestial instincts. As for his fighting qualities, they more resemble those of the tiger than of the cool, brave and trained soldier. When his blood is roused, fighting is with him a matter of blind and indiscriminate carnage of friend or foe. A more villainous-looking horde it would be difficult to find in any army. The splendid accoutrements of the generals and superior officers, and the glittering equipments of their chargers, offer a vivid contrast to the mean and dirty uniforms of the troops.

During the day the whole territory of the Republic was declared to be in a state of siege. Business was at a complete standstill. The stores were all closed, and many of them fortified with the first means that came to hand. Mattresses, doors, furniture, everything was requisitioned, and the greatest excitement prevailed in commercial circles generally. All the gun-makers' shops had soon been cleared of their contents, which were in the hands of the adherents of the revolution.

That evening the news of the insurrection was flashed by "Reuter's" to all parts of the civilized world. The following appeared in one of the largest British dailies:

"BUENOS AYRES, July 27, 5.40 p.m.

"The fighting in the streets between the Government troops and the insurgents has been of the most desperate character.

"The forces of the Government have been defeated.

"The losses in killed and wounded are estimated at 1,000.

"The fleet is in favor of the Revolutionists.

"Government house and the barracks occupied by the Government troops have been bombarded by the insurgent artillery."

That night as I went in and out of the squads of men on the revolutionary side, seeking to do some acts of mercy, I saw many strange and awful sights. There were wounded men who refused to leave the field, although the rain poured. Others were employed in cooking or ravenously eating the dead horses which strewed the streets. Some were lying down to drink the water flowing in the gutters, which water was often tinged with human blood, for the rain was by this time washing away many of the dark spots in the streets. Others lay coiled up in heaps under their soaking *ponchos*, trying to sleep a little, their arms stacked close at hand. There were men to all appearances fast asleep, standing with their arms in the reins of the horses which had borne them safely through the leaden hail of that day of terror. Numerous were the jokes and loud was the coarse laughter of many who next day would be lying stiff in death, but little thought seemed to be expended on that possibility.

Men looted the stores and feasted, or wantonly destroyed valuables they had no use for. None stopped this havoc, for the officers were quartered in the adjacent houses, themselves holding high revelry. Lawless hordes visited the police offices, threw their furniture into the streets, tore to shreds all the books, papers and records found, and created general havoc. They gorged and cursed, using swords for knives, and lay down in the soaking streets or leaned against the guns to smoke the inevitable *cigarillo*. A few looked up at the gilded keys of St. Peter adorning the front of the cathedral, perhaps wondering if they would be used to admit them to a better world.

Next day, as I sallied forth to the dismal duty of caring for the dead and dying, the guns of the Argentine fleet [British- built vessels of the latest and most approved types.] in the river opposite the city blazed forth upon the quarter held by the Government's loyal troops. One hundred and fifty-four shots were fired, two of the largest gunboats firing three-hundred and six- hundred pounders. Soon every square was a shambles, and the mud oozed with blood. The Buenos Ayres ***Standard***, describing that day of fierce warfare, stated:

"At dawn, the National troops, quartered in the Plaza Libertad, made another desperate attack on the Revolutionary positions in the Plaza Lavalle. The Krupp guns, mitrailleuses and gatlings went off at a terrible rate, and volleys succeeded each other, second for second, from five in the morning till half-past nine. The work of death was fearful, and hundreds of spectators were shot down as they watched from their balconies or housetops. Cannon balls riddled all the houses near the Cinco Esquinas. In the attack on the Plaza Lavalle, three hundred men must have fallen."

"At ten a.m. the white flag of truce was hoisted on both sides, and the dismal work of collecting the dead and wounded began. The ambulances of the Asistencia Publica, the cars of the tram companies and the wagons of the Red Cross were busily engaged all day in carrying away the dead. It is estimated that in the Plaza Lavalle above 600 men were wounded and 300 killed. Considering that the Revolutionists defended an entrenched position, whilst the National troops attacked, we may imagine that the losses of the latter were enormous."

"General Lavalle, commander-in-chief of the National forces, gave orders for a large number of coffins, which were not delivered, as the undertaker wished to be paid cash. It is to be supposed that these coffins were for the dead officers."

"When the white flags were run up, Dr. Del Valle, Senator of the Nation, sent, in the name of the Revolutionary Committee, an ultimatum to the National Government, demanding the immediate dismissal of the President of the Republic and dissolution of Congress. Later on it was known that both parties had agreed on an armistice, to last till mid-day on Monday."

Of the third day's sanguinary fighting, the ***Standard*** wrote:

"The Plaza Libertad was taken by General Lavalle at the head of the National troops under the most terrible fire, but the regiments held well together and carried the position in a most gallant manner, confirming the reputation of indomitable valor that the Argentine troops won at the trenches of Curupayti. Our readers may imagine the fire they suffered in the straight streets swept by Krupp guns, gatlings and mitrailleuses, while every housetop was a fortress whence a deadly fire was poured on the heads of the soldiers. Let anybody take the trouble to visit the Calles

[Streets] Cerrito, Libertad and Talcahuano, the vicinity of the Plazas Parque and Lavalle, and he will be staggered to see how all the houses have been riddled by mitrailleuses and rifle bullets. The passage of cannon balls is marked on the iron frames of windows, smashed frames and demolished balconies of the houses.

"The Miro Palace, in the Plaza Parque, is a sorry picture of wreckage: the 'mirador' is knocked to pieces by balls and shells; the walls are riddled on every side, and nearly all the beautiful Italian balconies and buttresses have been demolished. The firing around the palace must have been fearful, to judge by the utter ruin about, and all the telephone wires dangling over the street in meshes from every house. Ruin and wreckage everywhere.

"By this time the hospitals of the city, the churches and public buildings were filled with the wounded and dying, borne there on stretchers made often of splintered and shattered doors. Nearly a hundred men were taken into the San Francisco convent alone." Yet with all this the lust for blood was not quenched. It could still be written of the fourth day:

"At about half-past two, a sharp attack was made by the Government troops on the Plaza Parque, and a fearful fire was kept up. Hundreds and hundreds fell on both sides, but the Government troops were finally repulsed. People standing at the corners of the streets cheering for the Revolutionists were fired on and many were killed. Bodies of Government troops were stationed at the corners of the streets leading to the Plaza, Large bales of hay had been heaped up to protect them from the deadly fire of the Revolutionists.

"It was at times difficult to remember that heavy slaughter was going on around. In many parts of the city people were chatting, joking and laughing at their doors. The attitude of the foreign population was more serious; they seemed to foresee the heavy responsibilities of the position and to accurately forecast the result of the insurrection.

"The bulletins of the various newspapers during the revolution were purchased by the thousand and perused with the utmost avidity; fancy prices were often paid for them. The Sunday edition of *The Standard* was sold by enterprising newsboys in the suburbs as high as $3.00 per copy, whilst fifty cents was the regulation price for a momentary peep at our first column."

Towards the close of that memorable 29th of July the hail of bullets ceased, but the insurgent fleet still kept up its destructive bombardment of the Government houses for four hours.

The Revolutionists were defeated, or, as was seriously affirmed, had been sold for the sum of one million Argentine dollars.

"Estamos vendidos!" "Estamos vendidos!" (We are sold! We are sold!) was heard on every hand. Because of this surrender officers broke their swords and men threw away their rifles as they wept with rage. A sergeant exclaimed: "And for this they called us out--to surrender without a struggle! Cowards! Poltroons!" And then with a stern glance around he placed his rifle to his breast and shot himself through the heart. After the cessation of hostilities both sides collected their dead, and the wounded were placed under the care of surgeons, civil as well as military.

Notwithstanding the fact that the insurgents were said to be defeated, the President, Dr. Celman, fled from the city, and the amusing spectacle was seen of men and youths patrolling the streets wearing cards in their hats which read: *"Ya se fue el burro"* (At last the donkey has gone). A more serious sight, however, was when the effigy of the fleeing President was crucified.

Thus ended the insurrection of 1890, a rising which sent three thousand brave men into eternity.

What changes had taken place in four short days! At the Plaza Libertad the wreckage was most complete. The beautiful partierres were trodden down by horses; the trees had been partially cut down for fuel; pools of blood, remnants of slaughtered animals, offal, refuse everywhere.

Since the glorious days of the British invasion--glorious from an Argentine point of view--Buenos Ayres had never seen its streets turned into barricades and its housetops into fortresses. In times of electoral excitement we had seen electors attack each other in bands many years, but never was organized warfare carried on as during this revolution. The Plaza Parque was occupied by four or five thousand Revolutionary troops; all access to the Plaza was defended by armed groups on the house-tops and barricades in the streets, Krupp guns and that most infernal of modern inventions, the mitrailleuse, swept all the streets, north, south, east and west. The deadly grape swept the streets down to the very river, and not twenty thousand men could have taken the Revolutionary position by storm, except by gutting the houses and piercing the blocks, as Colonel Garmendia proposed, to avoid the awful loss of life suffered in the taking of the Plaza Libertad on Saturday morning.

At the close of the revolution the great city found itself suffering from a quasi-famine. High prices were asked for everything. In some districts provisions could not be obtained even at famine prices. The writer for the first time in his life had to go here and there to beg a loaf of bread for his family's needs.

A reporter of the *Argentine News*, July 31st of that same year, wrote:

"There is a revolution going on in Rosario. It began on Saturday, when the Revolutionists surprised the Government party, and by one on Sunday most of the Government buildings were in their hands. It is now eight in the morning and the firing is terrible. Volunteers are coming into the town from all parts, so the rebels are bound to win the stronghold shortly. News has just come that the Government troops have surrendered. Four p.m.--I have been out to see the dead and wounded gathered up by the ambulance wagons. I should think the dead are less than a hundred, and the wounded about four times that number. The surprise was so sudden that the victory has been easy and with little loss of life. The Revolutionists are behaving well and not destroying property as they might have done. The whole town is rejoicing; flags of all nations are flying everywhere. The saddest thing about the affair is that some fifty murderers have escaped from the prison. I saw many of them running away when I got upon the spot. The order has been given to recapture them. I trust they may be caught, for we have too many of that class at liberty already. * * * * It is estimated that over 100,000 rounds of ammunition were fired in the two days. * * * The insurgents fed on horse-meat and beef, the former being obtained by killing the horses belonging to the police, the latter from the various dairies, from which the cows were seized."

In 1911 the two largest Dreadnoughts of the world, the *Rivadavia* and the *Moreno*, were launched for the Argentine Government. These two battleships are *half as powerful again* as the largest British Dreadnought.

CHAPTER III.
THE CRIOLLO VILLAGE.

The different centres of trade and commerce in the Argentine can easily be reached by train or river steamer. Rosario, with its 140,000 inhabitants, in the north; Bahia Blanca, where there is the largest wheat elevator in the world, in the south, and Mendoza, at the foot of the Andes, several times destroyed by earthquake, five hundred miles west--all these are more or less like the capital.

To arrive at an isolated village of the interior the traveller must be content to ride, as I did, on horseback, or be willing to jolt along for weeks in a wagon without springs. These carts are drawn by eight, ten, or more bullocks, as the weight warrants, and are provided with two very strong wheels, without tires, and often standing eight and ten feet high. The patient animals, by means of a yoke fastened to their horns with raw-hide, draw these carts through long prairie grass or sinking morass, through swollen rivers or oozing mud, over which malaria hangs in visible forms.

The *voyager* must be prepared to suffer a little hunger and thirst on the way. He must sleep amongst the baggage in the cart, or on the broader bed of the ground, where snakes and tarantulas creep and the heavy dew saturates one through and through.

As is well known, the bullock is a slow animal, and these never travel more than two or three miles an hour.

Time with the native is no object. The words, "With patience we win heaven," are ever on his lips.

The Argentine countryman is decidedly lazy.

Darwin relates that he asked two men the question: "Why don't you work?"

One said: "The days are too long!" Another answered: "I am too poor."

With these people nothing can succeed unless it is begun when the moon is on the increase. The result is that little is accomplished.

You cannot make the driver understand your haste, and the bullocks understand and care still less.

The mosquitoes do their best to eat you up alive, unless your body has already had all the blood sucked out of it, a humiliating, painful and disfiguring process. You must carry with you sufficient food for the journey, or it may happen that, like me, you are only able to shoot a small ring dove, and with its entrails fish out of the muddy stream a monster turtle for the evening meal.

If, on the other hand, you pass a solitary house, they will with pleasure give you a sheep. If you killed one without permission your punishment would perhaps be greater than if you had killed a man.

If a bullock becomes ill on the road, the driver will, with his knife, cut all around the sod where the animal has left its footprint. Lifting this out, he will cut a cross on it and replace it the other side uppermost. This cure is most implicitly believed in and practised.

The making of the cross is supposed to do great wonders, which your guide is never tired of recounting while he drinks his *mate* in the unbroken stillness of the evening. Alas! the many bleaching bones on the road testify that this, and a hundred other such remedies, are not always effectual, but the mind of the native is so full of superstitious faith that the testimony of his own eyes will not convince him of the absurdity of his belief. As he stoops over the fire you will notice on his breast some trinket or relic--anything will do if blessed by the priest--and that, he assures you, will save him from every unknown and unseen danger in his land voyage. The priest has said it, and he rests satisfied that no lightning stroke will fell him, no lurking panther pounce upon him, nor will he die of thirst or any other evil. I have remarked men of the most cruel, cutthroat description wearing these treasures with zealous care, especially one, of whom it was said that he had killed two wives.

When your driver is young and amorously inclined you will notice that he never starts for the regions beyond without first providing himself with an owl's skin. This tied on his breast, he tells you, will ensure him favor in the eyes of the females he may meet on the road, and on arrival at his destination.

I once witnessed what at first sight appeared to be a heavy fall of snow coming up with the wind from the south. Strange to relate, this phenomenon turned out to be millions of white butterflies of large size. Some of these, when measured, I found to be four and five inches across the wings. Darwin relates his having, in 1832, seen the same sight, when his men exclaimed that it was "snowing butterflies."

The inhabitants of these trackless wilds are very, very few, but in all directions I saw numbers of ostriches, which run at the least sign of man, their enemy. The fastest horse could not outstrip this bird as with wings outstretched he speeds before the hunter. As Job, perhaps the oldest historian of the world, truly says: "What time she lifteth herself up on high, she scorneth the horse and his rider." The male bird joins his spouse in hatching the eggs, sitting on them perhaps longer turns than the female, but the weather is so hot that little brooding is required. I have had them on the shelf of my cupboard for a week, when the little ones have forced their way out Forty days is the time of incubation, so, naturally, those must have been already sat on for thirty-three days. With open wings these giant birds often manage to cover from twenty-five to forty-five eggs, although, I think, they seldom bring out more than twenty. The rest they roll out of the nest, where, soon rotting, they breed innumerable insects, and provide tender food for the coming young. The latter, on arrival, are always reared by the male ostrich, who, not being a model husband, ignominiously drives away the partner of his joys. It might seem that he has some reason for doing this, for the old historian before referred to says: "She is hardened against her young ones as though they were not hers."

As the longest road leads somewhere, the glare of the whitewashed church at last meets your longing gaze on the far horizon. The village churches are always whitewashed, and an old man is frequently employed to strike the hours on the tower bell by guess.

I was much struck by the sameness of the many different interior towns and villages I visited. Each wore the same aspect of indolent repose, and each was built in exact imitation of the other. Each town possesses its plaza, where palms and other semi-tropical plants wave their leaves and send out their perfume.

From the principal city to the meanest village, the streets all bear the same names. In every town you may find a *Holy Faith street*, a *St. John street* and a *Holy Ghost street*, and these streets are shaded by orange, lemon, pomegranate, fig and other trees, the fruit of which is free to all who choose to gather. All streets are in all parts in a most disgraceful condition, and at night beneath the heavy foliage of the trees Egyptian darkness reigns. Except in daylight, it is difficult to walk those wretched roads, where a goat often finds progress a difficulty. Rotten fruit, branches of trees, ashes, etc., all go on the streets. A hole is often bridged over by a putrefying animal, over which run half-naked urchins, pelting each other with oranges or lemons--common as stones. When the highways are left in such a state, is it to be wondered at that, while standing on my own door-step, I have been able to count eleven houses where smallpox was doing its deadly work, all within a radius of one hundred yards?

Even in the city of La Plata, the second of importance in Argentina, I once had the misfortune to fall into an open drain while passing down one of the principal streets. The night was intensely dark, and yet there was no light left there to warn either pedestrian or vehicle-driver, and ***this sewer was seven feet deep***.

Simple rusticity and ignorance are the chief characteristics of the country people. They used to follow and stare at me as though I were a visitor from Mars or some other planet. When I spoke to them in their language they were delighted, and respectfully hung on my words with bared heads. When, however, I told them of electric cars and underground railways, they turned away in incredulity, thinking that such marvels as these could not possibly be.

Old World towns they seem to be. The houses are built of sun-baked mud bricks, kneaded by mares that splash and trample through the oozy substance for hours to mix it well. The poorer people build ranches of long, slender canes or Indian cornstalks tied together by grass and coated with mud. These are all erected around and about the most imposing edifice in the place--the whitewashed adobe church.

All houses are hollow squares. The ***patio***, with its well, is inside this enclosure. Each house is lime-washed in various colors, and all are flat-roofed and provided with grated windows, giving them a prison-like appearance. The window-panes are sometimes made of mica. Over the front doors of some of the better houses are pictures of the Virgin. The nurse's house is designated by having over the doorway a signboard, on which is painted a full-blooming rose, out of the petals of which is peeping a little babe.

If you wish to enter a house, you do not knock at the door (an act that would be considered great rudeness), but clap your hands, and you are most courteously invited to enter. The good woman at once sets to work to serve you with **mate**, and quickly rolls a cigar, which she hands to you from her mouth, where she has already lighted it by a live ember of charcoal taken from the fire with a spoon. Matches can be bought, but they cost about ten cents a hundred. If you tell the housewife you do not smoke she will stare at you in gaping wonder. Their children use the weed, and I have seen a mother urge her three-year-old boy to whiff at a cigarette.

Bound each dwelling is a **ramada**, where grapes in their season hang in luxuriant clusters; and each has its own garden, where palms, peaches, figs, oranges, limes, sweet potatoes, tobacco, nuts, garlic, etc., grow luxuriantly. The garden is surrounded by a hedge of cacti or other kindred plants. The prickly pear tree of that family is one of the strangest I have seen. On the leaves, which are an inch or more in thickness, grows the fruit, and I have counted as many as thirteen pears growing on a single leaf. When ripe they are a deep red color, and very sweet to the taste. The skin is thick, and covered with innumerable minute prickles. It is, I believe, a most refreshing and healthful food.

Meat is very cheap. A fine leg of mutton may be bought for the equivalent of twelve cents, and good beef at four cents a pound. Their favorite wine, **Lagrimas de San Juan** (Tears of Holy John), can be bought for ten cents a quart.

All cooking is done on braziers--a species of three-legged iron bucket in which the charcoal fire is kindled. On this the little kettle, filled from the well in the **patio**, is boiled for the inevitable **mate**. About this herb I picked up, from various sources, some interesting information. The **mate** plant grows chiefly In Paraguay, and is sent down the river in bags made of hides. From the village of Tacurti Pucu in that country comes a strange account of the origin of the **yerba mate** plant, which runs thus: "God, accompanied by St. John and St. Peter, came down to the earth and commenced to journey. One day, after most difficult travel, they arrived at the house of an old man, father to a virgin young and beautiful. The old man cared so much for this girl, and was so anxious to keep her ever pure and innocent, that they had gone to live in the depths of a forest. The man was very, very poor, but willingly gave his heavenly visitors the best he could, killing in their honor the only hen he possessed, which served for supper. Noting this action, God asked St. Peter and St. John, when they were alone, what they would do if they were Him. They both answered Him that they would largely reward such an unselfish host. Bringing him to their presence, God addressed him in these words: 'Thou who art poor hast been generous, and I will reward thee for it. Thou hast a daughter who is pure and innocent, and whom thou greatly lovest. I will make her immortal, and she shall never disappear from earth.' Then God transformed her into the plant of the yerba mate. Since then the herb exists, and although it is cut down it springs up again." Other stories run that the maiden still lives; for God, instead of turning her into the mate plant, made her mistress of it, and she lives to help all those who make a compact with her, Many men during "Holy week," if near a town, visit the churches of Paraguay and formally promise to dedicate themselves to her worship, to live in the woods and have no other woman. After this vow they go to the forest, taking a paper on which the priest has written their name. This they pin with a thorn on the mate plant, and leave it for her to read. Thus she secures her devotees.

Roman Catholicism is not "Semper Idem," but adapts itself to its surroundings.

Mate is drunk by all, from the babe to the centenarian; by the rich cattle-owner, who drinks it from a chased silver cup through a golden *bombilla*, to his servant, who is content with a small gourd, which everywhere grows wild, and a tin tube. Tea, as we know it, is only to be bought at the chemist's as a remedy for *nerves*. In other countries it is said to be bad for nerves.

Each house possesses its private altar, where the saints are kept. That sacred spot is veiled off when possible--if only by hanging in front of it a cow's hide--from the rest of the dwelling. It consists, according to the wealth or piety of the housewife, in expensive crosses, beads, and pictures of saints decked out with costly care; or, it may be, but one soiled lithograph surrounded by paper flowers or cheap baubles of the poorer classes; but all are alike sacred. Everything of value or beauty is collected and put as an offering to these deities--pieces of colored paper, birds' eggs, a rosy tomato or pomegranate, or any colored picture or bright tin. Descending from the ridiculous to the gruesome, I have known a mother scrape and clean the bones of her dead daughter in order that *they* might be given a place on the altar. Round this venerated spot the goodwife, with her palm-leaf broom, sweeps with assiduous care, and afterwards carefully dusts her crucifix and other devotional objects with her brush of ostrich feathers. Here she kneels in prayer to the different saints. God Himself is never invoked. Saint Anthony interests himself in finding her lost ring, and Saint Roque is a wonderful physician in case of sickness. If she be a maiden Saint Carmen will find her a suitable husband; if a widow, Saint John will be a husband to her; and if an orphan, the sacred heart of the Virgin of Carmen gives balsam to the forlorn one. Saint Joseph protects the artisan, and if a candle is burnt in front of Saint Ramon, he will most obligingly turn away the tempest or the lightning stroke. In all cases one candle at least must be promised these mysterious benefactors, and rash indeed would be the man or woman who failed to burn the candle; some most terrible vengeance would surely overtake him or his family.

God, as I have said, is never invoked. Perhaps He is supposed to sit in solitary grandeur while the saints administer His affairs? These latter are innumerable, and whatever may be their position in the minds of Romanists in other lands, in South America they are distinct and separate gods, and their graven image, picture or carving is worshipped as such.

When religious questions have not arisen, life in those remote villages has passed very pleasantly. The people live in great simplicity, knowing scarcely anything of the outside world and its progress.

At the Feast of St. John the women take sheep and lambs, gaily decorated with colored ribbons, to church with them. That is an act of worship, for the priest puts his hand on each lamb and blesses it. A *velorio* for the dead, or a dance at a child's death, are generally the only meetings beside the church; but, as the poet says:

> "'Tis known, at least it should be, that throughout
> All countries of the Catholic persuasion,
> Some weeks before Shrove Tuiesiday comes about,
> The people take their fill of recreation,
> And buy repentance ere they grow devout,
> However high their rank or low their station,
> With fiddlling, feasting, dancing, drinking, masking,
> And other things which may be had for asking."

Carnival is a joyous time, and if for only once in the year the quiet town then resounds with mirth. Pails of water are carried up to the flat roofs of the houses, and each unwary pedestrian is in turn deluged. At other times flour is substituted, and on the last day of the feast ashes are thrown on all sides. At other seasons of the year the streets are quiet, and after the rural pursuits of the day are over, the guitar is brought out, and the evening breeze wafts waves of music to each listening ear. The guitar is in all South America what the bag-pipes are to Scotland-the national musical instrument of the people. The Criollo plays mostly plaintive, broken airs--now so low as to be almost inaudible, then high and shrill. Here and there he accompanies the music with snatches of song, telling of an exploit or describing the dark eyes of some lovely maiden. The airs strike one as being very strange, and decidedly unlike the rolling songs of British music.

In those interior towns a very quiet life may be passed, far away from the whistle of the railway engine. Everything is simplicity itself, and it might almost be said of some that ***time itself seems at a standstill***. During the heat of the day the streets are entirely deserted; shops are closed, and all the world is asleep, for that is the ***siesta*** time. "They eat their dinners and go to sleep--and could they do better?"

After this the barber draws his chair out to the causeway and shaves or cuts his customer's hair. Women and children sit at their doors drinking mate and watching the slowly drawn bullock-carts go up and down the uneven, unmade roads, bordered, not by the familiar maple, but with huge dust-covered cactus plants, The bullocks all draw with their horns, and the indolent driver sits on the yoke, urging forward his sleepy animals with a poke of his cane, on the end of which he has fastened a sharp nail. The ***buey*** is very thick-skinned and would not heed a whip. The wheels of the cart are often cut from a solid piece of wood, and are fastened on with great hardwood pins in a most primitive style. Soon after sunset all retire to their trestle beds.

In early morning the women hurry to mass. The Criollo does not break his fast until nearly mid-day, so they have no early meal to prepare. Even before it is quite light it is difficult to pass along the streets owing to the custom they have of carrying their praying- chairs with them to mass. The rich lady will be followed by her dark- skinned maid bearing a sumptuously upholstered chair on her head. The middle classes carry their own, and the very poor take with them a palm-leaf mat of their own manufacture. When mass is over religion is over for the day. After service they make their way down to the river or pond, carrying on their heads the soiled linen. Standing waist- high in the water, they wash out the stains with black soap of their own manufacture, beating each article with hardwood boards made somewhat like a cricketer's bat. The cloths are then laid on the sand or stones of the shore. The women gossip and smoke until these are dry and ready to carry home again ere the heat becomes too intense.

In a description of Argentine village life, I could not possibly omit the priest, the "all in all" to the native, the temporal and spiritual king, who bears in his hands the destinies of the living and the dead. These men are the potentates of the people, who refer everything to them, from the most trivial matter to the weightier one of the saving of their souls after death. Bigotry and superstition are extreme.

Renous, the naturalist, tells us that he visited one of these towns and left some caterpillars with a girl. These she was to feed until his return, that they might change to butterflies. When this was rumored through the village, priest and governor consulted together and agreed that it must be black heresy. When poor Renous returned some time afterwards he was arrested.

The Argentine village priest is a dangerous enemy to the Protestant. Many is the time he has insulted me to my face, or, more cowardly, charged the school-boys to pelt and annoy me. In the larger towns the priest has defamed me through the press, and when I have answered him also by that means, he has heaped insult upon injury, excluded me from society, and made me a pariah and a byword to the superstitious people. I have been stoned and spat upon, hurled to the ground, had half-wild dogs set on me, and my horse frightened that he might throw me. I have been refused police help, or been called to the office to give an account of myself, all because I was a Protestant, or infidel, as they prefer to term it. At those times great patience was needed, for at the least sign of resistance on my part I should have been attacked by the whole village in one mass. The policeman on the street has looked expectantly on, eager to see me do this, and on one occasion he escorted me to the station for snatching a bottle from the hand of a boy who was in the act of throwing it at my head. Arriving there I was most severely reprimanded, although, fortunately, not imprisoned.

Women have crossed themselves and run from me in terror to seek the holy water bottle blessed by the father. Doors have been shut in my face, and angry voices bade me begone, at the instigation of this black-robed believer in the Virgin. Congregations of worshippers in the dark-aisled church have listened to a fabulous description of my mission and character, until the barber would not cut my hair or the butcher sell me his meat! Many a mother has hurriedly called her children in and precipitately shut the door, that my shadow in passing might not enter and pollute her home. Perhaps a senorita, more venturesome, with her black hair hanging in two long plaits behind each shoulder, has run to her iron-barred window to smile at me, and then penitently fallen before her patron saint imploring forgiveness, or hurried to confess her sin to the wily *padre*. If the confession was accompanied by a gift, she has been absolved by him; if she were poor, her tear-stained face, perhaps resembling that of the suffering Madonna over the confessional, has moved his heart to tenderness, for well he knows that

"Maidens, like moths, are ever caught by glare,
And Mammon wins his way where seraphs might despair."

The punishment imposed has only been that she repeat fifty or a hundred *Ave Marias* or *Paternosters*. Poor deluded creature! Her sin only consisted in permitting her black eyes to gaze on me as I passed down the street.

"These poor creatures often go to confession, not to be forgiven the wretched past, but to get a new license to commit sin. One woman, to whom we offered a tract, refused it, and, showing us an indulgence of three hundred days, said: 'These are the papers I like.'"

A young university man in the capital confessed that he had never read the New Testament and never would read it, because he knew it was against the Church of Rome. The mass of the people have not the slightest notion of goodness, as we count piety, and lying is not considered wrong. A native will often entreat the help of his favorite saint to commit a theft.

"To the Protestant the idea of religion without morals is inconceivable; but in South America Romanism divorces morals and religion. It is quite possible to break every command of the Decalogue and yet be a devoted, faithful Romanist." [Rev. J. H. La Fetra, in "Protestant Missions in South America"]

I can only describe Roman Catholicism on the South American continent as a species of heathenism. The Church, to gain proselytes, accepted the old gods of the Indians as saints, and we find idolatrous superstition and Catholic display blended together. The most ignorant are invariably the most pious. The more civilized the Criollo becomes, the less he believes in the Church, and the priest in return condemns him to eternal perdition.

"It is not necessary to detail the multitude of pagan superstitions with which the religion of South America is encumbered. It is enough to point out that it does not preach Christ crucified and risen again. It preaches Mary, whom it proclaims from the lips of thousands of lecherous priests to be of perpetual virginity. And it is by its deliberate falsehood and deceit, as well as by its misrepresentation, that the Roman Catholic Church in South America has not only not taught Christianity, but has directly fostered deception and untruth of character." [Missions in South America. Robert E. Speer.]

When I desired respectfully to enter a church with bared head and deferential mien, they have followed me to see that I did not steal the trinkets from the saints or desecrate the altar. If I have touched the font of holy water, instead of it purifying me, I have defiled it for their use; and when I have looked at the images of the saints the people have seen them frown at me. After my exit the priest would sprinkle holy water on the spots where I had stood, to drive away "the evil influence."

In those churches one may see an image, with inscription beneath, stating that those who kiss it receive an indulgence for sin and a promise of heaven. When preaching in Parana I inadvertently dropped a word in disparagement of the worship of the Virgin, when, quick as thought, a man dashed towards me with gleaming steel. The Criollo's knife never errs, and one sharp lunge too well completes his task; but an old Paraguayan friend then with me sprang upon him and dashed the knife to the ground, thus leaving my heart's blood warm within me, and not on the pavement. I admired my antagonist for the strength of his convictions--true loyalty he displayed for his goddess, who, however, does not, I am sure, teach her devotees to assassinate those who prefer to put their faith rather in her Divine Son. Had I been killed the priest would on no account have buried me, and would most willingly have absolved the assassin and kept him from the "arm of justice." That arm in those places is very short indeed, for I have myself met dozens of murderers rejoicing in their freedom. Hell is only for Protestants.

On the door of my lodging I found one morning a written paper, well pasted on, which read:

MUERA! VIVA LA VIRGEN CON TODOS LOS SANTOS!

"Die! Live the Virgin and all the Saints!" That paper I took from the door and keep as a souvenir of fanaticism.

The Bible is an utterly unknown book, except to the priests, who forbid its entrance to the houses. It, however, could do little good or harm, for the masses of the people are utterly unlettered. All Protestant literature stolen into the town is invariably gathered and burned by the priest, who would not hesitate also to burn the bringer if he could without fear of some after-enquiry into the matter.

Rome is to-day just what she always was. Her own claim and motto is: **Semper idem** (Always the same). But for this age of enlightenment her inquisitorial fires would still burn. "Rome's contention is, not that she does not persecute, but only that she does not persecute **saints**. She punishes heretics--a very different thing. In the Rhemish New Testament there is a note on the words, 'drunken with the blood of saints,' which runs as follows: 'Protestants foolishly expound this of Rome **because heretics are there put to death**. But **their** blood is not called **the blood of saints**, any more than the blood of thieves or man-killers, or other malefactors; and for the shedding of it no commonwealth shall give account.'"

During my residence in Argentina a Jesuit priest in Cordoba publicly stated that if he had his way he would burn to death every Protestant in the country.

The following statements are from authorized documents, laws and decrees of the Papacy:

"The papacy teaches all her adherents that it is a sacred duty to exterminate heresy.

"Urban II. issued a decree that the murder of heretics was excusable. 'We do not count them murderers who, burning with the zeal of their Catholic mother against the excommunicate, may happen to have slain some of them.'" ["Romanism and Reformation."]

In Argentine life the almanac plays an important part; in that each day is dedicated to the commemoration of some saint, and the child born must of necessity be named after the saint on whose day he or she arrives into the world. The first question is, "What name does it bring?" The baby may have chosen to come at a time when the calendar shows an undesirable name, still the parents grumble not, for a saint is a saint, and whatever names they bear must be good. The child is, therefore, christened "Caraciollo," or "John Baptist," when, instead of growing up to be a forerunner of Christ, he or she may, with more likelihood, be a forerunner of the devil. Whatever name a child brings, however, has Mary tacked on to it.

All names serve equally well for male or female children, as a concluding "o" or "a" serves to distinguish the sex. Many men bear the name of Joseph Mary. Numbers, also, both male and female, have been baptized by the name of "Jesus," "Saviour," or "Redeemer." If I were asked the old question, "What's in a name?" I should answer, "Very little," for in South America the most insolent thief will often boast in the appellation of **Don Justice**, and the lowest girl in the village may be **Senorita Celestial**. **Don Jesus** may be found incarcerated for riotous conduct, and I have known **Don Saviour** throw his unfortunate wife and children down a well; **Don Destroyer** would have been a more appropriate name for him. **Mrs. Angel** her husband sometimes finds not such an angel after all, when she puts poison into his mate cup, a not infrequent occurrence. Let none be deceived in thinking that the appellation is any index to a man's character.

Dark, needy people--Rome's true children!

The school-books read: Which is the greatest country? *Ans.*, Spain. Who is the greatest man? *Ans.*, The Pope. Why? Because he is infallible.

It is his wish, and the priest's duty, to keep them in this darkness. Yet,--One came from God, "a light to lighten the Gentiles," and He said, "I am the Light of the world." Some day they may hear of Him and themselves see the Light.

Already the day is breaking, and superstition must prepare to hide itself. The uneducated native no longer pursues the railway train at thundering pace to lasso it because the priest raved against its being built. He even in some cases doubts if it is "an invention of hell," as he was taught.

The educated native, Alberdi, a publicist and an advocate of freedom, in the discussion over religious rights of foreigners in the Argentine, wrote: "Spanish America reduced to Catholicism, with the exclusion of any other cult, represents a solitary and silent convent of monks. The dilemma is fatal,--either Catholics and unpopulated, or populated and prosperous and tolerant in the matter of religion."

CHAPTER IV.
TEE PRAIRIE AND ITS INHABITANTS.

The Pampas, or prairie lands of the Argentine, stretch to the south and west of Buenos Ayres, and cover some 800,000 square miles. On this vast level plain, watered by sluggish streams or shallow lakes, boundless as the ocean, seemingly limitless in extent, there is an exhilarating air and a rich herbage on which browse countless herds of cattle, horses, and flocks of sheep. The grass grows tall, and miles upon miles of rich scarlet, white, or yellow flowers mingle with or overtop it. Beds of thistles, in which the cattle completely hide themselves, stretch away for leagues and leagues, and present an almost unbroken sheet of purple flowers. So vast are these thistle- beds that a day's ride through them only leaves the traveller with the same purple forest stretching away to the horizon. The florist would be enchanted to see whole tracts of land covered by the **Verbena Melindres**, which appears, even long before you reach it, to be of a bright scarlet. There are also acres and acres of the many- flowered camomile and numberless other plants; while large tracts of low-lying land are covered with coarse pampa grass, affording shelter for numberless deer, and many varieties of ducks, cranes, flamingoes, swans and turkeys. Wood there is none, with the exception of a solitary tree here and there at great distances, generally marking the site of some cattle establishment OP **estancia**. An **ombu**, or cluster of blue gums, is certain to be planted there.

On this prairie, man, notwithstanding the fact that he is the "lord of creation," is decidedly in the minority. Millions of four-footed animals roam the plains, but he may be counted by hundreds. Let us turn to him, however, in his isolated home, for the **Gaucho** has been described as one of the most interesting races on the face of the earth. A descendant of the old conquerors, who, leaving their fair ones in the Spanish peninsula, took unto them as wives the unclothed women of the new world, he inherits the color and habits of the one with the vices and dignity of the other. Living the wild, free life of the Indian, and retaining the language of Spain; the finest horseman of the world, and perhaps the worst assassin; the most open-handed and hospitable, yet the accomplished purloiner of his neighbor's cattle; imitating the Spaniard in the beautifully-chased silver trappings of his horse, and the untutored Indian in his miserable adobe hovel; spending his whole wealth in heavy gold or silver bell-shaped stirrups, bridle, or spurs (the rowel of the latter sometimes having a diameter of six inches), and leaving his home destitute of the veriest necessities of life--such is the Gaucho. A horn or shell from the river's bed makes his spoon, gourds provide him with his plates and dishes; but his knife, with gold or silver handle and sheath, is almost a little fortune in itself. Content in his dwelling to sit on a bullock's skull, on horseback his saddle must be mounted in silver. His own beard and hair he seldom trims, but his horse's mane and tail must be assiduously tended. The baked-mud floor of his abode is littered with filth and dirt, while he raves at a speck of mud on his embroidered silk saddle-cloth.

The Gaucho is a strange contradiction. He has blushed at my good but plain-looking saddle, yet courteously asked me to take a skull seat. He may possess five hundred horses, but you search his kitchen in vain for a plate. If you please him he will present you with his best horse, waving away your thanks. If you displease him, his long knife will just as readily find its way to your heart, for he kills his enemies with as little compunction as he kills the ostrich. "The Gaucho, with his proud and dissolute air, is the most unique of all South American characters. He is courageous and cruel, active and tireless. Never more at ease than when on the wildest horse; on the ground, out of his element. His politeness is excessive, his nature fierce." The children do not, like ours, play with toys, but delight the parents' hearts by teasing a cat or dog. These they will stick with a thorn or pointed bone to hear them yell, or, later on, lasso and half choke them. "They will put out their eyes, and such like childish games, innocent little darlings that they are." Cold-blooded torture is their delight, and they will cheer at the sight of blood.

To describe the dress of this descendant of Adam I feel myself incapable. A shirt and a big slouch hat seem to be the only articles of attire like ours. Coat, trousers or shoes he does not wear. Instead of the first mentioned, he uses the *poncho*, a long, broad blanket, with a slit in the centre to admit his head. For trousers he wears very wide white drawers, richly embroidered with broad needlework and stiffly starched. Over these he puts a black ***chiripa***, which really I cannot describe other than as similar to the napkins the mother provides for her child. Below this black and white leg covering come the long boots, made from one piece of seamless hide. These boots are nothing more than the skin from the hind legs of an animal--generally a full-grown horse. The bend of the horse's leg makes the boot's heel. Naturally the toes protrude, and this is not sewn up, for the Gaucho never puts more than his big toe in the stirrup, which, like the bit in his horse's mouth, must be of solid silver. A dandy will beautifully scallop these rawhide boots around the tops and toes, and keep them soft with an occasional application of grease. No heel is ever attached. Around the man's waist, holding up his drawers and chiripa, is wound a long colored belt, with tasseled ends left hanging over his boot, down the right side; and over that he invariably wears a broad skin belt, clasped at the front with silver and adorned all around with gold or silver coins. In this the long knife is carried.

What shall I say of the domestic life of these people? Unfortunately, marriage is practically unknown among them. The father gives his son a few cattle, and the young man, after building himself a house, conducts thither his chosen one. Unhappily, constancy in either man or woman is a rare virtue.

Of the superstitious side of the Gancho race I might speak much. In the saints the female especially implicitly believes. These, her deities, are all-powerful, and to them she appeals for the satisfaction of her every desire. Saint Clementina's help is sought by the girl when her lover betrays her. Another saint will aid her in poisoning him. If the wife thinks her husband long in bringing the evening meal, she has informed me, a word with Saint Anthony is sufficient, and she hears the sound of his horse's hoofs. Saint Anthony seems to be useful on many occasions of distress. One evening I called at a ***rancho*** made of dry thistle-stalks bound together with hide and thatched with reeds, Finding the inmates very hospitable, I stayed there two or three hours to rest. Coming out of the house again, I found to my dismay that during our animated gossip my horse had broken loose and left me. Now the loss of a horse is too trivial a matter to interest Anthony the saint, but a horse having saddle and bridle attached to him makes it quite a different matter, for these often cost ten times the price of the horse. One of the saint's especial duties is to find a lost saddled horse, if the owner or interested one only promises to burn a candle in his honor. The night was very dark, and no sign of the animal was to be seen. Mine host laid his ear to the ground and listened, then, leaping on his horse, he galloped into the darkness, from whence he brought my lost animal. I did not learn until afterwards that Mrs. Jesus, for such was the woman's name, had sought the help of Saint Anthony on my behalf. I am sure she lost her previous good opinion of me when I thanked her husband but did not offer a special colored candle to her saint.

Among these strange people I commenced a school, and had the joy of teaching numbers of them to read the Spanish Bible. Boys and girls came long distances on horseback, and, although some of them had perhaps never seen a book before, I found them exceedingly quick to learn. In four or five months the older ones were able to read any ordinary chapter. In arithmetic they were inconceivably dull, and after three months' tuition some of them could not count ten.

I have said the saints are greatly honored among these people. My Christmas cards generally found their way to adorn their altars. Every house has its favorite, and some of these are regarded as especially clever in curing sickness. It being a very unhealthful, low-lying district where my school was, I contracted malarial fever, and went to bed very sick. Every day some of the children would come to enquire after me, but Celestino, one of the larger boys, came one morning with a very special message from his mother. This communication was to the effect that they did not wish the school- teacher to die, he being "rather a nice kind of a man and well liked." Because of this she would be pleased to let me have her favorite saint. This image I could stand at the head of my bed, and its very presence would cure me. When I refused this offer and smiled at its absurdity, the boy thought me very strange. To be so wise in some respects, and yet so ignorant as to refuse such a chance, was to him incomprehensible. The saints, I found, are there often lent out to friends that they may exercise their healing powers, or rented out to strangers at so much a day, When they are not thus on duty, but in a quiet corner of the hut, they get lonely. The woman will then go for a visit, taking her saint with her, either in her arms or tied to the saddle. This image she will place with the saint her host owns, and ***they will talk together and teach one another***. A saint is supposed to know only its own particular work, although one named Santa Rita is said to be a worker of impossibilities. Some of them are only very rudely carved images, dressed in tawdry finery. I have sometimes thought that a Parisian doll of modern make, able to open and close its eyes, etc., would in their esteem be even competent to raise the dead! [Writing of Spanish American Romanism, Everybody's Magazine says: "To the student of human nature, which means the study of evil as well as good, this religious body is of absorbing interest. One would look to find these enthusiasts righteous and virtuous in their daily life; but, apart from the annual week of penance, their religion influences them not at all, and on the whole the members of the Brotherhood constitute a desperate class, dangerous to society."]

In cases of sickness very simple remedies are used, and not a few utterly non-sensical. To cure pains in the stomach they tie around them the skin of the ***comadreka***, a small, vile-smelling animal. This they told me was a sovereign remedy. If the sufferer be a babe, a cross made on its stomach is sufficient to perfectly cure it. I have seen seven pieces of the root of the white lily, which there grows wild, tied around the neck of an infant in order that its teeth might come with greater promptitude and less pain. A string of dog's teeth serves the same purpose. To cure a bad wound, the priest will be called in that he may write around the sore some Latin prayer backwards. Headache is easily cured by tying around the head the cast-off skin of a snake. Two puppies are killed and bound one on each side of a broken limb. If a charm is worn around the neck no poison can be harmful. For a sore throat it is sufficient to expectorate in the fire three times, making a cross. Lockjaw is effectually stopped by tying around the sufferer's jaws the strings from a virgin's skirt; and they say also that powdered excrement of a dog, taken in a glass of water, cures the smallpox patient,

As Mrs. Jesus sent her boy to my school, so Mrs. Flower sent her girl. The latter was perhaps the most deluded woman I have met. Her every act was bad in itself or characterized by superstitious devotion. She was one of the Church's favorite worshippers, and while I was in the neighborhood she sold her cows and horses and presented the priest at the nearest town with a large and expensive silver cross--the emblem of suffering purity. Near her lived a person for whom she had an especial aversion, but that enemy she got rid of in surely the strangest of ways, which she described to me. Catching a snake, and holding it so that its poison might not reach her, she passed a threaded needle through both its eyes. When this was done she let it go again, alive, and, carefully guarding the needle, approached the person from behind and made a cross with the thread. The undesired one disappeared, having probably heard of the enchantment, and being equally superstitious, or--the charm worked!

Mrs. Flower was a most repulsive-looking creature. Her skin was exactly the color of an old copper coin. She did not resemble any *flower* I have seen in either hemisphere. Far was she from being a rose, but she certainly possessed the thorn. Her love for the saints was most marked, and I have known her promise St. Roque that she would walk six miles carrying his image if he would only grant her a certain prayer. This petition he granted, and off she trudged with her divine (?) load. Those acquainted with dwellers on the prairie know that this was indeed a great task, horses being so cheap and riding so universal. Mrs. Flower was unaccustomed to walk even the shortest distance. I myself can bear witness to the fact that even strong men find it hard to walk a mile after spending years in equestrian travel. The native tells you that God formed your legs so that you might be able to sit on a horse rather than to walk with them. A favorite expression with them is, "I was born on horseback."

Stone not being found on the pampas, these people generally build their houses of square sods, with a roof of plaited grasses-- sometimes I have observed these beautifully woven together. Two or more holes, according to the size of the house, are left to serve for door and window. Wood cannot be obtained, glass has not been introduced, so the holes are left as open spaces, across which, when the pampa wind blows, a hide is stretched. No hole is left in the roof for the smoke of the fire to escape, for this to the native is no inconvenience whatever. When I have been compelled to fly with racking cough and splitting head, he has calmly asked the reason. Never could I bear the blinding smoke that issues from his fire of sheep or cow dung burning on the earthen floor, though he heeds it not as, sitting on a bullock's skull, he ravenously eats his evening meal.

If entertaining a stranger, he will press uncut joint after joint of his *asado* upon him. This asado is meat roasted over the fire on a spit; if beef, with the skin and hair still attached. Meat cooked in this way is a real delicacy. A favorite dish with them (I held a different opinion) is a half-formed calf, taken before its proper time of birth. The meat is often dipped in the ashes in lieu of salt. I have said the Gaucho has no chair. I might add that neither has he a table, for with his fingers and knife he eats the meat off the fire. Forks he is without, and a horn or shell spoon conveys the soup to his mouth direct from the copper pan. So universal is the use of the shell for this service that the native does not speak of it as *caracol*, the real word for shell, but calls it *cuchara del agua*, or water spoon. Of knives he possesses more than enough, and heavy, long, sharp-pointed ones they are. When his hunger is appeased the knife goes, not to the kitchen, but to his belt, where, when not in his hand, you may always see it. With that weapon he kills a sheep, cuts off the head of a serpent--seemingly, however, not doing it much harm, for it still wriggles--sticks his horse when in anger, and, alas, as I have said, sometimes stabs his fellow-man. Being so far isolated from the coast, he is necessarily entirely uneducated. The forward march of the outer world concerns him not; indeed he imagines that his native prairie stretches away to the end of the world. He will gaze with wonder on your watch, for his only mode of ascertaining the time is by the shadow the sun casts. As that luminary rises and sets, so he sleeps and wakes. His only bed is the sheepskin, which when riding he fastens over his saddle, and the latter article forms his pillow. His coverlet is the firmament of heaven, the Southern Cross and other constellations, unseen by dwellers in the Northern Hemisphere, seeming to keep watch over him; or in the colder season his poncho, which I have already described. Around his couch flit the fireflies, resembling so many stars of earth with their strangely radiant lights. The brightness of one, when held near the face of my watch, made light enough to enable me to ascertain the hour, even on the darkest night.

The Gaucho with his horse is at home anywhere. When on a journey he will stop for the evening meal beside the dry bones of some dead animal. With these and grass he will make a fire and cook the meat he carries hanging behind him on the saddle. I have known an animal killed and the meat cooked with its own bones, but this is not usual. Dry bones burn better, and thistle-stalks better still. He will then lie down on mother earth with the horse-cloth under him and the saddle for a pillow. When travelling with these men I have known them, without any comment, stretch themselves on the ground, even though the rain was falling, and soon be in dreamland. After having passed a wretched night myself, I have asked them, "How did you sleep?" *"Muy Bien, Senor"* (Very good, sir), has been the invariable answer. They would often growl much, however, over the wet saddle- cloths, for these soon cause a horse's back to become sore.

Here and there, but sometimes at long distances apart, there is a ***pulperia*** on the road. This is always designated by having a white flag flying on the end of a long bamboo. At these places cheap spirits of wine and very bad rum can be bought, along with tobacco, hard ship-biscuits (very often full of maggots, as I know only too well), and a few other more necessary things. I have observed in some of these wayside inns counters made of turf, built in blocks as bricks would be. Here the natives stop to drink long and deep, and stew their meagre brains in bad spirits. These draughts result in quarrels and sometimes in murder.

The Gaucho, like the Indian, cannot drink liquor without becoming maddened by it. He will then do things which in his sober moments he would not dream of. I was acquainted with a man who owned a horse of which he was very fond This animal bore him one evening to a pulperia some miles distant, and was left tied outside while he imbibed his fill inside. Coming out at length beastly intoxicated, he mounted his horse and proceeded homeward. Arriving at a fork in the path, the faithful horse took the one leading home, but the rider, thinking in his stupor that the other way was the right one, turned the horse's head. As the poor creature wanted to get home and have the saddle taken off, it turned again. This affront was too much for the Gaucho, who is a man of volcanic passions, so drawing his knife, he stabbed it in the neck, and they dropped to the ground together. When he realized that he had killed his favorite horse he cried like a child. I passed this dead animal several times afterwards and saw the vultures clean its bones. It served me as a witness to the results of ungoverned passion.

The Gaucho does not, and would not under any consideration, ride a mare; consequently, for work she is practically valueless. Strain, who rode across the pampas, says: "In a single year ten million hides were exported." For one or two dollars each the buyer may purchase any number; indeed, of such little worth are the mares that they are very often killed for their hide, or to serve as food for swine. At one estancia I visited I was informed that one was killed each day for pig feed. The mare can be driven long distances, even a hundred miles a day, for several successive days, The Argentine army must surely be the most mobile of any in the world, for its soldiers, when on the march, get nothing but mare's flesh and the custom gives them great facility of movement. The horse has, more or less, its standard value, and costs four or five times the price of the mare.

Sometimes it happens that the native finds a colt which is positively untamable. On the cheek of such an animal the Gaucho will burn a cross and then allow it to go free, like the scape-goat mentioned in the book of Leviticus.

The native horse is rather small, but very wiry and wild. I was once compelled, through sickness, to make a journey of ninety-seven miles, being in the saddle for seventeen consecutive hours, and yet my poor horse was unable to get one mouthful of food on the journey, and the saddle was not taken off his back for a moment. He was very wild, yet one evening between five and eight o'clock, he bore me safely a distance of thirty-six miles, and returned the same distance with me on the following morning. He had not eaten or drunk anything during the night, for the locusts had devoured all pasturage and no rain had fallen for a space of five months.

The horse is not indigenous to America, although Darwin tells us that South America had a native horse, which lived and disappeared ages ago. Spanish history informs us that they were first landed in Buenos Ayres in 1537. We are further told that the Indians flew away in terror at the sight of a man on horseback, which they took to be one animal of a strange, two-headed shape. When the colony was for a time deserted these horses were suffered to run wild. Those animals so multiplied and spread over such a vast area that they were found, forty-three years later, even down to the Straits of Magellan, a distance of eleven hundred miles. With good pasture and a limitless expanse to roam over, they soon turned from the dozens to thousands, and may now be counted by millions. The Patagonian "foot" Indians quickly turned into "horse" Indians, for on those wide prairie lands a man without a horse is almost comparable to a man without legs. In former years, thousands of wild horses roamed over these extensive plains, but the struggle of mankind in the battle of life turned men's attention to them, and they were captured and branded by whomsoever had the power and cared to take the trouble. In the more isolated districts, there may still be found numbers which are born and die without ever feeling the touch of saddle or bridle. Far away from the crowded busses and perpetually moving hansoms of the city, they feel not the driver's whip nor the strain of the wagon, as, with tail trailing on the ground and head erect, they gallop in freedom of life. Happy they!

In all directions on the prairie ostriches are found. The natives catch them with *boliadoras*, an old Indian weapon, which is simply three round stones, incased in bags of hide, tied together by twisted ropes, also of hide. When the hunters have, by galloping from different directions, baffled the bird in his flight, they thunder down upon him, and, throwing the *boliadoras* round his legs, where they entangle, effectually stop his flight. I have seen this weapon thrown a distance of about eighty yards.

The ostrich is a bird with wonderful digestive powers, which I often have envied him; he eats grass or pebbles, insects or bones, as suits his varying fancy. If you drop your knife or any other article, he will stop to examine it, being most inquisitive, and, if possible, he will swallow it. The flesh of the ostrich is dry and tough, and its feathers are not to be compared in beauty with those of the African specimen. Generally a very harmless bird, he is truly formidable during breeding time. If one of the eggs is so much as touched he will break the whole number to shivers. Woe to the man whom he savagely attacks at such times; one kick of his great foot, with its sharp claws, is sufficient to open the body of man or horse. The Gaucho uses the skin from the neck of this bird as a tobacco pouch, and the eggs are considered a great delicacy. One is equal to about sixteen hen's eggs.

As all creation has its enemy, the ostrich finds his in the *iguana*, or lizard-- an unsightly, scaly, long-tailed species of land crocodile. This animal, when full-grown, attains the length of five feet, and is of a dark green color. He, when he can procure them, feeds on the ostrich eggs, which I believe must be a very strengthening diet. The lizard, after fattening himself upon them during the six hotter months of the year, is enabled to retire to the recesses of his cave, where he tranquilly sleeps through the remaining six. The shell of the ostrich's egg is about the thickness of an antique china cup, but the iguana finds no difficulty in breaking it open with a slash of his tail This wily animal is more astute than the bird, which lays its eggs in the open spaces, for the lizard, with her claws, digs a hole in the ground, in which hers are dropped to the number of dozens. The lizard does not provide shells for her eggs, but only covers them with a thick, soft skin, and they, buried in the soil, eventually hatch themselves.

When the Gaucho cannot obtain a better meal, the tail of the lizard is not considered such a despicable dish by him, for he is no epicure. When he has nothing he is also contented. His philosophy is: *"Nunca tenga hambre cuando no hay que comer"* (Never be hungry when no food is to be had).

The estancia, or catile ranch, is a feature of the Argentine prairie. Some of these establishments are very large, even up to one hundred square miles in extent. On them hundreds of thousands of cattle, sheep and horses are herded. "It is not improbable that there are more cattle in the pampas and llanos of South America than in all the rest of the world." [Dr. Hartwig in "Argentina," 1910] An estancia is almost invariably called by the name of some saint, as are the different fields belonging to it. "Holy Mary field" and "Saint Joseph field" are common names. Notwithstanding the fact that there may be thousands of cows on a ranch, the visitor may be unable to get a drop of milk to drink. "Cows are not made to milk, but to eat," they say. Life on these establishments is rough and the fare generally very coarse. Even among the wealthy people I have visited you may sit down to dinner with nothing but meat put before you, without a bite of bread or any vegetables. All drink water out of an earthenware pitcher of peculiar shape, which is the centrepiece of the table.

Around the ranches of the people are many mice, which must be of a ferocious nature, for if one is caught in a trap it will be found next morning half, if not almost wholly, eaten by its own comrades. Well is it called "the cannibal mouse."

In times of drought the heat of the sun dries up all vegetation. The least spark of fire then suffices to create a mighty blaze, especially if accompanied by the *pampero* wind, which blows with irresistible force in its sweep over hundreds of miles of level ground. The fire, gathering strength as it goes, drives all before it, or wraps everything in its devouring flames. Casting a lurid light in the heavens, towards which rise volumes of smoke, it attracts the attention of the native, who lifts his starting eyes towards heaven in a speechless prayer to the Holy Virgin. Madly leaping on his fleetest horse, without saddle, and often without bridle, he wildly gallops down the wind, as the roaring, crackling fire gains upon him. In this mad race for life, men, horses, ostriches, deer, bullocks, etc., join, striving to excel each other in speed. Strange to say, the horse the native rides, cheered on by the touch of his master, is often the first to gain the lake or river, where, beneath its waters at least, refuge may be found. In their wild stampede, vast herds of cattle trample and fall on one another and are drowned. A more complete destruction could not overtake the unfortunate traveller than to be caught by this remorseless foe, for not even his ashes could be found by mourning friends. The ground thus burnt retains its heat for days. I have had occasion to cross blackened wastes a week after this most destructive force in nature had done its work, and my horse has frequently reared in the air at the touch of the hot soil on his hoofs.

The Gaucho has a strange method of fighting these fires. Several mares are killed and opened, and they, by means of lassos, are dragged over the burning grass.

The immensity of the pampas is so great that one may travel many miles without sighting a single tree or human habitation. The weary traveller finds his only shade from the sun's pitiless rays under the broad brim of his sombrero. At times, with ears forward and extended nostrils, the horse gazes intently at the rippling blue waters of the *mirage*, that most tantalizingly deceptive phenomenon of nature. May it never be the lot of my reader to be misled by the illusive mirage as I have been. How could I mistake vapor for clear, gurgling water? Yet, how many times was I here deceived! Visions of great lakes and broad rivers rose up before me, lapping emerald green shores, where I could cool my parched tongue and lave in their crystal depths; yet to-day those waters are as far off as ever, and exist only in my hopes of Paradise. Not until I stand by the "River of Life" shall I behold the reality.

The inhabitant of these treeless, trackless solitudes, which, with their waving grass, remind one of the bosom of the ocean, develops a keen sight Where the stranger, after intently gazing, descries nothing, he will not only inform him that animals are in sight, but will, moreover, tell him what they are. I am blest with a very clear vision, but even when, after standing on my horse's back, I have made out nothing, the Gaucho could tell me that over there was a drove of cattle, a herd of deer, a troop of horses, or a house.

It is estimated that there are two hundred and forty millions of acres of wheat land in the Argentine, and of late years the prairie has developed into one of the largest wheat-producing countries in the world, and yet only one per cent, of its cultivable area is so far occupied.

The Gaucho is no farmer, and all his land is given up to cattle grazing, so *chacras* are worked generally by foreign settlers. The province of Entre Rios has been settled largely by Swiss and Italian farmers from the Piedmont Hills. Baron Hirsch has also planted a colony of Russian Jews there, and provided them with farm implements. Wheat, corn, and linseed are the principal crops, but sweet potatoes, tobacco, and fruit trees do well in this virgin ground, fertilized by the dead animals of centuries. The soil is rich, and two or three crops can often be harvested in a year.

No other part of the world has in recent years suffered from such a plague of locusts as the agricultural districts of Argentina. They come from the north in clouds that sometimes darken the sun. Some of the swarms have been estimated to be sixty miles long and from twelve to fifteen miles wide. Fields which in the morning stand high with waving corn, are by evening only comparable to ploughed or burnt lands. Even the roots are eaten up.

In 1907 the Argentine Government organized a bureau for the destruction of locusts, and in 1908 $4,500,000 was placed by Congress at the disposal of this commission. An organized service, embracing thousands of men, is in readiness at any moment to send a force to any place where danger is reported. Railway trains have been repeatedly stopped, and literally many tons of them have had to be taken off the track. A fine of $100 is imposed upon any settler failing to report the presence of locust swarms or hopper eggs on his land. Various means are adopted by the landowner to save what he can from the voracious insects. Men, women and children mount their horses and drive flocks of sheep to and fro over the ground to kill them. A squatter with whom I stayed got his laborers to gallop a troop of mares furiously around his garden to keep them from settling there. All, however, seemed useless. About midsummer the locust lays its eggs under an inch or two of soil. Each female will drop from thirty to fifty eggs, all at the same time, in a mass resembling a head of wheat. As many as 50,000 eggs have been counted in a space less than three and a half feet square.

During my sojourn in Entre Rios, the province where this insect seems to come in greatest numbers, a law was passed that every man over the age of fourteen years, whether native or foreigner, rich or poor, was compelled to dig out and carry to Government depots, four pounds weight of locusts' eggs. It was supposed that this energetic measure would lessen their numbers. Many tons were collected and burnt, but, I assure the reader, no appreciable difference whatever was made in their legions. The young *jumpers* came, eating all before them, and their numbers seemed infinite. Men dug trenches, kindled fires, and burned millions of them. Ditches two yards wide and deep and two hundred feet long were completely filled up by these living waves. But all efforts were unavailing--the earth remained covered. A Waldensian acquaintance suffered for several years from this fearful plague. Some seasons he was not even able to get back so much as the seed he planted. If the locusts passed him, it so happened that the ***pampero*** wind blew with such terrific force that we have looked in vain even for the straw. The latter was actually torn up by the roots and whirled away, none knew whither. At other times large hailstones, for which the country is noted, have destroyed everything, or tens of thousands of green paroquets have done their destructive work. When a five-months' drought was parching everything, I have heard him reverently pray that God would spare him wheat sufficient to feed his family. This food God gave him, and he thankfully invited me to share it. I rejoice in being able to say that he afterwards became rich, and had his favorite saying, ***"Dios no me olvidae"*** (God will not forget me), abundantly verified.

Notwithstanding natural drawbacks, which every country has, Argentina can claim to have gone forward as no other country has during the last ten years. There are many estates worth more than a million dollars. Dr. W. A. Hirot, in "Argentina," says: "Argentina has more live stock than any other country of the world. Ten million hides have been exported in one year, and it is not improbable that there are more cattle in South America than there are in all the rest of the world combined." Belgium has 220 people occupying the space one person has in Argentina, so who can prophesy as to its future?

PART II.
BOLIVIA

Have you gazed on naked grandeur where there's nothing
else to gaze on,
Set pieces and drop curtain scenes galore,
Big mountains heaved to heaven, which the blinding sunsets
blazon,
Black canyons where the rapids rip and roar?

--Robert W. Service.

BOLIVIA

Bolivia, having no sea-coast, has been termed the Hermit Republic of South America. Its territory is over 600,000 square miles in extent, and within its bounds Nature displays almost every possible panorama, and all climates. There are burning plains, the home of the emu, armadillos, and ants; sandy deserts, where the wind drifts the sand like snow, piling it up in ever-shifting hills about thirty feet in height. Bolivia, shut in geographically and politically, is a world in itself--a world of variety, in scenery, climate, products and people. Its capital city, La Paz, has a population of 70,000, but the vast interior is almost uninhabited. In the number of inhabitants to the square mile, Bolivia ranks the lowest of all the nations of the earth.

Perhaps no country of the world has been, and is, so rich in precious metals as

Bolivia. "The mines of Potosi alone have furnished the world over $1,500,000,000 worth of silver since the Spaniards first took possession of them." ["Protestant Missions in South America."]

Bolivia can lay claim to the most wonderful body of water in the world--Lake Titicaca. This lake, nearly two and a half miles high in the air, is literally in the clouds. "Its lonely waters have no outlet to the sea, but are guarded on their southern shores by gigantic ruins of a prehistoric empire--palaces, temples, and fortresses--silent, mysterious monuments of a long-lost golden age." Some of the largest and most remarkable ruins of the world are found on the shores of Lake Titicaca, and as this was the centre of the great Incan Dynasty, that remarkable people have also left wonderful remains, to build which stones thirty-eight feet long, eighteen feet wide, and six feet thick, were quarried, carried and elevated. The Temple of the Sun. the most sacred edifice of the Incas, was one of the richest buildings the sun has ever shone upon, and it was itself a mine of wealth. From this one temple, Pizarro, the Spanish conqueror, took 24,000 pounds of gold and 82,000 pounds of silver. "Ninety million dollars' worth of precious metals was torn from Inca temples alone." The old monarch of the country, Atahuallpa, gave Pizarro twenty-two million dollars in gold to buy back his country and his liberty from the Spaniards, but their first act on receiving the vast ransom was to march him after a crucifix at the head of a procession, and, because he refused to become a Roman Catholic, put him to death. Perhaps never in the world's history was there a baser act of perfidy, but this was urged by the soldier-priest of the conquerors, Father Valverde, who himself signed the King's death- warrant. This priest was afterwards made Bishop of Atahuallpa's capital.

Surely no country of the world has had a darker or a sadder history than this land of the Incas. The Spaniards arrived when the "Children of the Sun" were at the height of their prosperity. "The affair of reducing the country was committed to the hands of irresponsible individuals, soldiers of fortune, desperate adventurers who entered on conquest as a game which they had to play in the most unscrupulous manner, with little care but to win it. The lands, and the persons as well, of the conquered races were parcelled out and appropriated by the victors as the legitimate spoils of victory. Every day outrages were perpetrated, at the contemplation of which humanity shudders. They suffered the provident arrangements of the Incas to fall into decay. The poor Indian, without food, now wandered half-starved and naked over the plateau. Even those who aided the Spaniards fared no better, and many an Inca noble roamed a mendicant over the fields where he once held rule; and if driven, perchance, by his necessities to purloin something from the superfluity of his conquerors, he expiated it by a miserable death." [Prescott's "Conquest of Peru."]

Charles Kingsley says there were "cruelties and miseries unexampled in the history of Christendom, or perhaps on earth, save in the conquests of Sennacherib and Zinghis-Khan." Millions perished at the forced labor of the mines, The Incan Empire had, it is calculated, a population of twenty millions at the arrival of the Spaniards, In two centuries the population fell to four millions.

When the groans of these beasts of burden reached the ears of the good (?) Queen Isabel of Spain, she enacted a law that throughout her new dominions no Indian, man or woman, should be compelled to carry more than three hundred pounds' weight at one load! Is it cause for wonder that the poor, down-trodden natives, seeing the flaunting flag of Spain, with its stripe of yellow between stripes of red, should regard it as representing a river of gold between two rivers of blood?

"Not infrequently," said a reliable witness, "I have seen the Spaniards, long after the Conquest, amuse themselves by hunting down the natives with blood hounds, for mere sport, or in order to train their dogs to the game. The most unbounded scope was given to licentiousness. The young maiden was torn remorselessly from the arms of her family to gratify the passion of her brutal conqueror. The sacred houses of the Virgins of the Sun were broken open and violated, and the cavalier swelled his harem with a troop of Indian girls, making it seem that the crescent would have been a more fitting emblem for his banner than the immaculate cross."

With the inexorable conqueror came the more inexorable priest. "Attendance at Roman Catholic worship was made compulsory. Men and women with small children were compelled to journey as much as thirty-six miles to attend mass. Absentees were punished, therefore the Indian feared to disobey." [Neely, "Spanish America."]

As is well known, the ancient inhabitants worshipped the sun and the moon. The Spanish priest, in order to gain proselytes with greater facility, did not forbid this worship, but placed the crucifix between the two. Where the Inca suns and moons were of solid gold and silver, they were soon replaced by painted wooden ones. The crucifix, with sun and moon images on each side, is common all over Bolivia to-day.

Now, four hundred years later, see the Indian under priestly rule. The following is taken from an official report of the Governor of Chimborazo: "The religious festivals that the Indians celebrate--not of their own will, but by the inexorable will of the priest--are, through the manner in which they are kept, worse than those described to us of the times of Paganism, and of monstrous consequences to morality and the national welfare ... they may be reckoned as a barbarous mixture of idolatry and superstition, sustained by infamous avarice. The Indian who is chosen to make a feast either has to use up in it his little savings, leaving his family submerged in misery, or he has to rob in order to invest the products of his crime in paying the fees to the priest and for church ceremonies. These are simply brutal orgies that last many days, with a numerous attendance, and in which all manner of crimes and vices have free license."

"For the idols of the aborigines were substituted the images of the Virgin Mary and the Roman saints. The Indians gave up their old idols, but they went on with their image-worship. Image-worship is idolatry, whether in India, Africa, or anywhere else, and the worship of Roman images is essentially idolatry as much as the worship of any other kind of images. Romanism substituted for one set of idols another set. So the Indians who were idolaters continued to be idolaters, only the new idols had other names and, possibly, were a little better-looking." [Neely, "South America."]

What has Romanism done for the Indians of Bolivia in its four hundred years of rule? Compare the people of that peaceful, law-keeping dynasty which the Spaniards found with the Bolivian Indian of to-day! Now the traveller can report: "The Indians are killing the whites wherever they find them, and practising great cruelties, having bored holes in the heads of their victims and sucked the brains out while they were yet alive. Sixteen whites are said to have been killed in this way! These same Indians are those who have been Christianized by the Roman priests for the past three centuries, but such cruelties as they have been practising show that as yet not a ray of Christ's love has entered their darkened minds." How can the priest teach what he is himself ignorant of?

Where the Indian has been civilized, as well as Romanized, Mr. Milne, of the American Bible Society, could write:

"Since the Spanish conquest the progress of the Indians has been in the line of deterioration and moral degradation. They are oppressed by the Romish clergy, who can never drain contributions enough out of them, and who make the children render service to pay for masses for deceased parents and relatives. Tears came to our eyes as Mr. Penzotti and I watched them practising their heathen rites in the streets of La Paz, the chief city of Bolivia. They differ from the other Indians in that they are domesticated, but *they know no more of the Gospel than they did under the rule of the Incas.*"

What is to be the future of these natives? Shall they disappear from the stage of the world's history like so many other aborigines, victims of civilization, or will a hand yet be stretched out to help them? Civilization, after all, is not entirely made up of greed and lust, but in it there is righteousness and truth. May the day soon dawn when some of the latter may be extended to them ere they take the long, dark trail after their fathers, and have hurled the last malediction at their cursed white oppressors!

> "We suffer yet a little space
> Until we pass away,
> The relics of an ancient race
> That ne'er has had its day."

For four hundred years Bolivia has thus been held in chains by Romish priest-craft. Since its Incan rulers were massacred, its civilization has been of the lowest. Buildings, irrigation dams, etc., were suffered to fall into disrepair, and the country went back to pre-Incan days.

The first Christian missionaries to enter the country were imprisoned and murdered. Now "the morning light is breaking." A law has been passed granting liberty of worship.

Bolivia, with its vast natural riches, must come to the forefront, and already strides are being taken forward. She can export over five million dollars' worth of rubber in one year, and is now spending more than fifty million dollars on railways. So Bolivia is a country of the past and the future.

CHAPTER V.
JOURNEY TO "THE UNEXPLORED LAKE."

Since the days when Pizarro's adventurers discovered the hitherto un-dreamed-of splendor of the Inca Dynasty, Bolivia has been a land of sur-prises and romantic discovery. Strange to say, even yet much of the eastern portion of this great republic remains practically unexplored. The following account of exploration in those regions, left for men of the twentieth century, may not, I am persuaded, be without interest to the general reader. Bolivia has for many years been seriously handicapped through having no adequate water outlet to the sea, and the immense resources of wealth she undoubtedly possesses have, for this reason, been suffered to go, in a measure, unworked. Now, however, in the onward progress of nations, Bolivia has stepped forward. In the year 1900, the Government of that country despatched an expedition to locate and explore Lake Gaiba, a large sheet of water said to exist in the far interior of Bolivia and Brazil, on the line divid-ing the two republics. The expedition staff consisted of Captain Bolland, an English-man; M. Barbiere, a Frenchman; Dr. Perez, Bolivian; M. Gerard D'Avezsac, French artist and hunter, and the writer of these pages. The crew of ten men was made up of Paraguayans and Argentines, white men and colored, one Bolivian, one Italian, and one Brazilian. Strange to relate, there was no Scotchman, even the ship's engi-neer being French. Perhaps the missing Scotch engineer was on his way to the Pole, in order to be found sitting there on its discovery by----(?)

The object of this costly journey was to ascend the rivers La Plata, Paraguay and Alto Paraguay, and see if it were possible to establish a port and town in Bo-livian territory on the shores of the lake. After some months of untiring energy and perseverance, there was discovered for Bolivia a fine port, with depth of water for any ordinary river steamer, which will now be known to the world as **Puerto**

Quijarro. A direct fluvial route, therefore, exists between the Atlantic and this far inland point.

The expedition left Buenos Ayres, the capital of the Argentine Republic. Sailing up the western bank of the River of Silver, we entered the Parana River, and after an uneventful voyage of six days, passed the mouth of the River of Gold, and turned into the Paraguay.

Three hundred miles up the Higher Parana, a mighty stream flowing from the northeast, which we here left to our right, are the Falls of Yguasu. These falls have been seen by few white men. The land on each side of the river is infested by the Bugres Indians, a tribe of cannibals, of excessively ferocious nature. The Falls of Big Water must be the largest in the world--and the writer is well acquainted with Niagara.

The river, over two and a half miles wide, containing almost as much water as all the rivers of Europe together, rushes between perpendicular cliffs. With a current of forty miles an hour, and a volume of water that cannot be less than a million tons a minute, the mighty torrent rushes with indescribable fury against a rocky island, which separates it into two branches, so that the total width is about two miles and a half. The Brazilian arm of the river forms a tremendous horseshoe here, and plunges with a deafening roar into the abyss two hundred and thirteen feet below. The Argentine branch spreads out in a sort of amphitheatre form, and finishes with one grand leap into the jagged rocks, more than two hundred and twenty- nine feet below, making the very earth vibrate, while spray, rising in columns, is visible several miles distant.

"Below the island the two arms unite and flow on into the Parana River. From the Brazilian bank the spectator, at a height of two hundred and eighty feet, gazes out over two and a half miles of some of the wildest and most fantastic water scenery he can ever hope to see. Waters stream, seethe, leap, bound, froth and foam, 'throwing the sweat of their agony high in the air, and, writhing, twisting, screaming and moaning, bear off to the Parana.' Under the blue vault of the sky, this sea of foam, of pearls, of iridescent dust, bathes the great background in a shower of beauty that all the more adds to the riot of tropical hues already there. When a high wind is blowing, the roar of the cataract can be heard nearly twenty miles away. A rough estimate of the horse-power represented by the falls is fourteen million."

Proceeding up the Paraguay River, we arrived at Asuncion, the capital of Paraguay, and anchored in a beautiful bay of the river, opposite the city. As many necessary preparations had still to be made, the expedition was detained in Asuncion for fifteen days, after which we boarded the S.S. *Leda*, for the second stage of our journey.

Steaming up the Alto Paraguay, we passed the orange groves of that sunny land on the right bank of the river, and on the left saw the encampments of the Tobas Indians, The dwellings of these people are only a few branches of trees stuck in the ground. Further on, we saw the Chamococos Indians, a fine muscular race of men and women, who cover their bronze-colored bodies with the oil of the alligator, and think a covering half the size of a pocket-handkerchief quite sufficient to hide their nakedness. As we stayed to take in wood, I tried to photograph some of these, our brothers and sisters, but the camera was nothing but an object of dread to them. One old woman, with her long, black, oily hair streaming in the breeze, almost withered me with her flashing eyes and barbarous language, until I blushed as does a schoolboy when caught in the act of stealing apples. Nevertheless, I got her photo.

The Pilcomayo, which empties its waters into the Paraguay, is one of the most mysterious of rivers. Rising in Bolivia, its course can be traced down for some considerable distance, when it loses itself in the arid wastes, or, as some maintain, flows underground. Its source and mouth are known, but for many miles of its passage it is invisible. Numerous attempts to solve its secrets have been made. They have almost invariably ended disastrously. The Spanish traveller, Ibarete, set out with high hopes to travel along its banks, but he and seventeen men perished in the attempt. Two half- famished, prematurely-old, broken men were all that returned from the unknown wilds. The Pilcomayo, which has proved itself the river of death to so many brave men, remains to this day unexplored. The Indians inhabiting these regions are savage in the extreme, and the French explorer, Creveaux, found them inhuman enough to leave him and most of his party to die of hunger. The Tobas and the Angaitaes tribes are personally known to me, and I speak from experience when I say that more cruel men I have never met. The Argentine Government, after twenty years of warfare with them, was compelled, in 1900, to withdraw the troops from their outposts and leave the savages in undisputed possession. If the following was the type of civilization offered them, then they are better left to themselves: "Two hundred Indians who have been made prisoners are ***compelled to be baptized***. The ceremony takes place in the presence of the Governor and officials of the district, and a great crowd of spectators. The Indians kneel between two rows of soldiers, an officer with drawn sword compels each in turn to open his mouth, into which a second officer throws a handful of salt, amid general laughter at the wry faces of the Indians. Then a Franciscan padre comes with a pail of water and besprinkles the prisoners. They are then commanded to rise, and each receives a piece of paper inscribed with his new name, a scapulary, and--a glass of rum" [Report of British and Foreign Bible Society, 1900.] What countries these for missionary enterprise!

After sailing for eighteen days up the river, we transhipped into a smaller steamer going to Bolivia. Sailing up the bay, you pass, on the south shore, a small Brazilian customs house, which consists of a square roof of zinc, without walls, supported on four posts, standing about two meters from the ground. A Brazilian, clothed only in his black skin, came down the house ladder and stared at us as we passed. The compliment was returned, although we had become somewhat accustomed to that style of dress--or undress. A little farther up the bay, a white stone shone out in the sunlight, marking the Bolivian boundary, and giving the name of Piedra Blanca to the village. This landmark is shaded by a giant tamarind tree, and numerous barrel trees, or ***palo boracho***, grow in the vicinity. In my many wanderings in tropical America, I have seen numerous strange trees, but these are extraordinarily so. The trunk comes out of the ground with a small circumference, then gradually widens out to the proportions of an enormous barrel, and at the top closes up to the two-foot circumference again. Two branches, like giant arms spread themselves out in a most weird-looking manner on the top of all. About five leaves grow on each bough, and, instinctively, you consider them the fingers of the arms.

It was only three leagues to the Bolivian town of Piedra Blanca, but the "Bahia do Marengo" took three hours to steam the short distance, for five times we had to stop on the way, owing to the bearings becoming heated. These the Brazilian engineer cooled with pails of water.

In the beautiful Bay of Caceres, much of which was grown over with lotus and Victoria Regia, we finally anchored. This Bolivian village is about eighteen days' sail up the river from Montevideo on the seacoast.

Chartering the "General Pando," a steamer of 25 h.p. and 70 ft. long, we there completed our preparations, and finally steamed away up the Alto Paraguay, proudly flying the Bolivian flag of red, yellow, and green. As a correct plan of the river had to be drawn, the steamer only travelled by day, when we were able to admire the grandeur of the scenery, which daily grew wilder as the mountains vied with each other in lifting their rugged peaks toward heaven. From time to time we passed one of the numerous islands the Paraguay is noted for. These are clothed with such luxuriant vegetation that nothing less than an army of men with axes could penetrate them. The land is one great, wild, untidy, luxuriant hot-house, "built by nature for herself." The puma, jaguar and wildcat are here at home, besides the anaconda and boa constrictor, which grow to enormous lengths. The Yaci Reta, or Island of the Moon, is the ideal haunt of the jaguar, and as we passed it a pair of those royal beasts were playing on the shore like two enormous cats. As they caught sight of us, one leapt into the mangrove swamp, out of sight, and the other took a plunge into the river, only to rise a few yards distant and receive an explosive bullet in his head. The mangrove tree, with its twisting limbs and bright green foliage, grows in the warm water and fotid mud of tropical countries. It is a type of death, for pestilence hangs round it like a cloud. At early morning this cloud is a very visible one. The peculiarity of the tree is that its hanging branches themselves take root, and, nourished by such putrid exhalations, it quickly spreads.

There were also many floating islands of fantastic shape, on which birds rested in graceful pose. We saw the ***garza blanca***, the aigrets of which are esteemed by royalty and commoner alike, along with other birds new and strange. To several on board who had looked for years on nothing but the flat Argentine pampas, this change of scenery was most exhilarating, and when one morning the sun rose behind the "Golden Mountains," and illuminated peak after peak, the effect was glorious. So startlingly grand were some of the colors that our artist more than once said he dare not paint them, as the world would think that his coloring was not true to nature.

Many were the strange sights we saw on the shore. Once we were amused at the ludicrous spectacle of a large bird of the stork family, which had built its nest in a tree almost overhanging the river. The nest was a collection of reeds and feathers, having two holes in the bottom, through which the legs of the bird were hanging. The feet, suspended quite a yard below the nest, made one wonder how the bird could rise from its sitting position.

Every sight the traveller sees, however, is not so amusing. As darkness creeps over earth and sky, and the pale moonbeams shed a fitful light, it is most pathetic to see on the shore the dead trunk and limbs of a tree, in the branches of which has been constructed a rude platform, on which some dark-minded Indian has reverently lifted the dead body of his comrade. The night wind, stirring the dry bones and whistling through the empty skull, makes weird music!

The banks of the stream had gradually come nearer and nearer to us, and the great river, stretching one hundred and fifty miles in width where it pours its volume of millions of tons of water into the sea at Montevideo, was here a silver ribbon, not half a mile across.

Far be it from me to convey the idea that life in those latitudes is Eden. The mosquitos and other insects almost drive one mad. The country may truly be called a naturalists' paradise, for butterflies, beetles, and creeping things are multitudinous, but the climate, with its damp, sickly heat, is wholly unsuited to the Anglo-Saxon. Day after day the sun in all his remorseless strength blazes upon the earth, is if desirous of setting the whole world on fire. The thermometer in the shade registered 110, 112 and 114 degrees Fahrenheit, and on one or two memorable days 118 degrees. The heat in our little saloon at times rose as high as 130 degrees, and the perspiration poured down in streams on our almost naked bodies. We seemed to be running right into the brazen sun itself.

One morning the man on the look-out descried deer on the starboard bow, and arms were quickly brought out, ready for use. Our French hunter was just taking aim when it struck me that the deer moved in a strange way. I immediately asked him to desist. Those dark forms in the long grass seemed, to my somewhat trained eyes, naked Indians, and as we drew nearer to them so it proved, and the man was thankful he had withheld his fire.

After steaming for some distance up the river several dug-outs, filled with Guatos Indians, paddled alongside us. An early traveller in those head-waters wrotes of these: "Some of the smaller tribes were but a little removed from the wild brutes of their own jungles. The lowest in the scale, perhaps, were the Guatos, who dwell to the north of the Rio Apa. This tribe consisted of less than one hundred persons, and they were as unapproachable as wild beasts. No other person, Indian or foreigner, could ever come near but they would fly and hide in impenetrable jungles. They had no written language of their own, and lived like unreasoning animals, without laws or religion."

The Guato Indian seems now to be a tame and inoffensive creature, but well able to strike a bargain in the sale of his dug-out canoes, home-made guitars and other curios. In the wrobbling canoe they are very dexterous, as also in the use of their long bows and arrows; the latter have points of sharpened bone. When hungry, they hunt or fish. When thirsty, they drink from the river; and if they wish clothing, wild cotton grows in abundance.

These Indians, living, as they do, along the banks of the river and streams, have recently been frequently visited by the white man on his passage along those natural highways. It is, therefore superfluous for me to add that they are now correspondingly demoralized. It is a most humiliating fact that just in proportion as the paleface advances into lands hitherto given up to the Indian so those races sink. This degeneration showed itself strikingly among the Guatos in their inordinate desire for *cachaca*, or "firewater." Although extremely cautious and wary in their exchanges to us, refusing to barter a bow and arrows for a shirt, yet, for a bottle of cachaca, they would gladly have given even one of their canoes. These *ketchiveyos*, twenty or twenty-five feet long by about twenty inches wide, they hollow from the trunk of the cedar, or *lapacho* tree. This is done with great labor and skill; yet, as I have said, they were boisterously eager to exchange this week's work for that which they knew would lead them to fight and kill one another.

As a mark of special favor, the chief invited me to their little village, a few miles distant. Stepping into one of their canoes--a large, very narrow boat, made of one tree-trunk hollowed out by fire-- I was quickly paddled by three naked Indians up a narrow creek, which was almost covered with lotus. The savages, standing in the canoe, worked the paddles with a grace and elegance which the civilized man would fail to acquire, and the narrow craft shot through the water at great speed. The chief sat in silence at the stern. I occupied a palm-fibre mat spread for me amidships. The very few words of Portuguese my companions spoke or understood rendered conversation difficult, so the stillness was broken only by the gentle splash of the paddles. On each side the dense forest seemed absolutely impenetrable, but we at last arrived at an opening. As we drew ashore I noticed that an Indian path led directly inland.

Leaving our dug-out moored with a fibre rope to a large mangrove tree, we started to thread our way through the forest, and finally reached a clearing. Here we came upon a crowd of almost naked and extremely dejected-looking women. Many of these, catching sight of me, sped into the jungle like frightened deer. The chief's wife, however, at a word from him, received me kindly, and after accepting a brass necklace with evident pleasure, showed herself very affable. Poor lost Guatos! Their dejected countenances, miserable grass huts, alive with vermin, and their extreme poverty, were most touching. Inhabiting, as they do, one of the hottest and dampest places on the earth's surface, where mosquitos are numberless, the wonder is that they exist at all. Truly, man is a strange being, who can adapt himself to equatorial heat or polar frigidity. The Guatos' chief business in life seemed to consist in sitting on fibre mats spread on the ground, and driving away the bloodthirsty mosquitos from their bare backs. For this they use a fan of their own manufacture, made from wild cotton, which there seems to abound. Writing of mosquitos, let me say these Indian specimens were a terror to us all. What numbers we killed! I could write this account in their blood. It was *my* blood, though--before they got it! Men who hunt the tiger in cool bravery boiled with indignation before these awful pests, which stabbed and stung with marvellous persistency, and disturbed the solitude of nature with their incessant humming. I write the word *incessant* advisedly, for I learned that there are several kinds of mosquitos. Some work by day and others by night. Naturalists tell us that only the female mosquito bites. Did they take a particular liking to us because we were all males?

Some of the Indians paint their naked bodies in squares, generally with red and black pigment. Their huts were in some cases large, but very poorly constructed. When any members of the tribe are taken sick they are supposed to be "possessed" by a stronger evil power, and the sickness is "starved out." When the malady flies away the life generally accompanies it. The dead are buried under the earth inside the huts, and in some of the dwellings graves are quite numerous. This custom of interior burial has probably been adopted because the wild animals of the forest would otherwise eat the corpse. Horrible to relate, their own half-wild dogs sometimes devour the dead, though an older member of the tribe is generally left home to mount guard.

Seeing by the numerous gourds scattered around that they were drinking *chicha*, I solicited some, being anxious to taste the beverage which had been used so many centuries before by the old Incas. The wife of the chief immediately tore off a branch of the feather palm growing beside her, and, certainly within a minute, made a basket, into which she placed a small gourd. Going to the other side of the clearing, she commenced, with the agility of a monkey, to ascend a long sapling which had been laid in a slanting position against a tall palm tree. The long, graceful leaves of this cabbage palm had been torn open, and the heart thus left to ferment. From the hollow cabbage the woman filled the gourd, and lowered it to me by a fibre rope. The liquid I found to be thick and milky, and the taste not unlike cider.

Prescott tells us that Atahuallpa, the Peruvian monarch, came to see the conqueror, Pizarro, "quaffing chicha from golden goblets borne by his attendants." [Este Embajador traia servicio de Senor, i cinco o seis Vasos de Oro fino, con que bebia, i con ellos daba a beber a los Espanoles de la chicha que traia."--Xerez.] Golden goblets did not mean much to King Atahuallpa, however, for his palace of five hundred different apartments is said to have been tiled with beaten gold.

In these Guato Indians I observed a marked difference to any others I had visited, in that they permitted the hair to grow on their faces. The chief was of quite patriarchal aspect, with full beard and mild, intelligent-looking eyes. The savages inhabiting the Chaco consider this custom extremely "dirty."

Before leaving these people I procured some of their bows and arrows, and also several cleverly woven palm mats and cotton fans.

Some liquor our cook gave away had been taken out by the braves to their women in another encampment. These spirits had so inflamed the otherwise retiring, modest females that they, with the men, returned to the steamer, clamoring for more. All the stores, along with some liquors we carried, were under my care, and I kept them securely locked up, but in my absence at the Indian camp the store-room had been broken open, and our men and the Indians--men and women--had drunk long and deep. A scene like Bedlam, or Dante's "Inferno," was taking place when I returned. Willing as they were to listen to my counsel and admit that I was certainly a great white teacher, with superior wisdom, on this love for liquor and its debasing consequences they would hear no words. The women and girls, like the men, would clamor for the raw alcohol, and gulp it down in long draughts. When ardent spirits are more sought after by women and girls than are beads and looking-glasses it surely shows a terribly depraved taste. Even the chattering monkeys in the trees overhead would spurn the poison and eagerly clutch the bright trinket. Perhaps the looking-glasses I gave the poor females would, after the orgies were over, serve to show them that their beauty was not increased by this beastly carousal, and thus be a means of blessing. It may be asked, Can the savage be possessed of pride and of self-esteem? I unhesitatingly answer yes, as I have had abundant opportunity of seeing. They will strut with peacock pride when wearing a specially gaudy-colored headdress, although that may be their only article of attire.

Having on board far more salt than we ourselves needed, I was enabled to generously distribute much of that invaluable commodity among them. That also, working in a different way, might be a means of restoring them to a normal soundness of mind after we left.

Poor lost creatures! For this draught of the white man's poison, far more terrible to them than the deadly nightshade of their forests, more dangerous than the venom of the loathsome serpent gliding across their path, they are willing to sell body or soul. Soul, did I say? They have never heard of that. To them, so far as I could ascertain, a future life is unknown. The explorer has penetrated some little way into their dark forests in search of rubber, or anything else which it would pay to exploit, but the missionary of the Cross has never sought to illumine their darker minds. They live their little day and go out into the unknown unconscious of the fact that One called Jesus, who was the Incarnate God, died to redeem them. As a traveller, I have often wondered why men should be willing to pay me hundreds of dollars to explore those regions for ultimate worldly gain, and none should ever offer to employ me in proclaiming the greatest wonder of all the ages--the story of Calvary--for eternal gain. After all, are the Indians more blind to the future than we are? Yet, strange to say, we profess to believe in the teachings of that One who inculcated the practice of laying up treasure in heaven, while they have not even heard His name. For love of gain men have been willing to accompany me through the most deadly fever-breeding morass, or to brave the poisoned arrows of the lynx-eyed Indian, but few have ever offered to go and tell of Him whom they profess to serve.

The suffocating atmosphere quite precluded the idea of writing, for a pen, dipped in ink, would dry before reaching the paper, and the latter be saturated with perspiration in a few seconds; so these observations were penned later. So far as I could ascertain, the Romish Church has never touched the Guatos, and, notwithstanding all I have said about them, I unhesitatingly affirm that it is better so. Geo. R. Witte, missionary to Brazil, says: "With one exception, all the priests with whom I came in contact (when on a journey through Northern Brazil) were immoral, drunken, and ignorant. The tribes who have come under priestly care are decidedly inferior in morals, industry, and order to the tribes who refuse to have anything to do with the whites. The Charentes and Apinages have been, for years, under the care of Catholic friars--this is the way I found them: both men and women walk about naked."

"We heard not one contradiction of the general testimony that the people who were not under the influence of the Roman Catholic Church as it is in S. America were better morally than those who were." [Robert E. Speer, "Missions in South America."]

In Christendom organs peal out the anthems of Divine love, and well- dressed worshippers chant in harmonious unison, "Lord, incline our hearts to keep Thy law." That law says: "Thou shalt love thy neighbor as thyself." To the question: "Who is my neighbor?" the Divine voice answers: "A certain man." May he not be one of these neglected Indians?

CHAPTER VI.
ARRIVAL AT THE LAKE.

"It sleeps among a hundred hills
Where no man ever trod,
And only Nature's music fills
The silences of God."

After going about two thousand three hundred miles up this serpentine river, we discovered the entrance to the lake. Many had been the conjectures and counsels of would-be advisers when we started. Some said that there was no entrance to the lake from the river; others, that there was not sufficient depth of water for the steamer to pass through. On our port bow rose frowning rocks of forbidding aspect. Drawing nearer, we noticed, with mingled feelings of curiosity and wonder, that the face of these rocks was rudely carved by unmistakably Indian art. There were portrayed a rising sun, tigers' feet, birds' feet, etc. Why were they thus carved? Are those rocks the everlasting recorders of some old history--some deed of Indian daring in days of old? What these hieroglyphics signify we may never know; the workman is gone, and his stone hammer is buried with him. To twentieth century civilization his carving tells nothing. No Indians inhabit the shores of the lake now, perhaps because of this "writing on the wall."

With the leadsman in his place we slowly and cautiously entered the unexplored lake, and thus for the first time in the world's history its waters were ploughed by a steamer's keel.

Soon after our arrival the different guards were told off for the silent watches. Night shut in upon the lake, and all nature slept. The only lights on shore were those of the fire-flies as they danced through the myrtle boughs. The stars in the heavens twinkled above us. Now and again an alligator thrust his huge, ugly nose out of the water and yawned, thus disturbing for the moment its placid surface, which the pale moon illuminated with an ethereal light; otherwise stillness reigned, or, rather, a calm mysterious peace which was deep and profound. Somehow, the feeling crept upon us that we had become detached from the world, though yet we lived. Afterwards, when the tigers [Jaguars are invariably called tigers in South America.] on shore had scented our presence, sleep was often broken by angry roars coming from the beach, near which we lay at anchor; but before dawn our noisy visitors always departed, leaving only their footprints. Early next morning, while the green moon was still shining (the color of this heavenly orb perplexed us, it was a pure bottle green), each one arose to his work. This was no pleasure excursion, and duties, many and arduous, lay before the explorers. The hunter sallied forth with his gun, and returned laden with pheasant and mountain hen, and over his shoulder a fine duck, which, unfortunately, however, had already begun to smell--the heat was so intense. In his wanderings he had come upon a huge tapir, half eaten by a tiger, and saw footprints of that lord of the forest in all directions.

Let me here say, that to our hunter we were indebted for many a good dish, and when not after game he lured from the depths of the lake many a fine perch or turbot. Fishing is an art in which I am not very skilled, but one evening I borrowed his line. After a few moments' waiting I had a "bite," and commenced to haul in my catch, which struggled, kicked, and pulled until I shouted for help. My fish was one of our Paraguayan sailors, who for sport had slipped down into the water on the other side of the steamer, and, diving to my cord, had grasped it with both hands. Not every fisher catches a man!

Lake Gaiba is a stretch of water ten miles long, with a narrow mouth opening into the River Paraguay. The lake is surrounded by mountains, clad in luxuriant verdure on the Bolivian side, and standing out in bare, rugged lines on the Brazilian side. The boundary of the two countries cuts the water into two unequal halves. The most prominent of the mountains are now marked upon the exhaustive chart drawn out. Their christening has been a tardy one, for who can tell what ages have passed since they first came into being? Looking at Mount Ray, the highest of these peaks, at sunset, the eye is startled by the strange hues and rich tints there reflected. Frequently we asked ourselves: "Is that the sun's radiance, or are those rocks the fabled 'Cliffs of Opal' men have searched for in vain?" We often sat in a wonder of delight gazing at the scene, until the sun sank out of sight, taking the "opal cliffs" with it, and leaving us only with the dream.

On the shores of the lake the beach is covered with golden sand and studded with innumerable little stones, clear as crystal, which scintillate with all the colors of the rainbow. Among these pebbles I found several arrowheads of jasper. In other parts the primeval forest creeps down to the very margin, and the tree-roots bathe in the warm waters. Looking across the quivering heat-haze, the eye rests upon palms of many varieties, and giant trees covered with orchids and parasites, the sight of which would completely intoxicate the horticulturist. Butterflies, gorgeous in all the colors of the rainbow, flit from flower to flower; and monkeys, with curiously human faces, stare at the stranger from the tree-tops. White cotton trees, tamarinds, and strangely shaped fruits grow everywhere, and round about all are entwined festoons of trailing creepers, or the loveliest of **scarlet** mistletoe, in which humming-birds build their nests. Blue macaws, parrots, and a thousand other birds fly to and fro, and the black fire-bird darts across the sky, making lightning with every flutter of his wings, which, underneath, are painted a bright, vivid red. Serpents of all colors and sizes creep silently in the undergrowth, or hang from the branches of the trees, their emerald eyes ever on the alert; and the broad-winged eagle soars above all, conscious of his majesty.

Here and there the coast is broken by silent streams flowing into the lake from the unexplored regions beyond. These **riachos** are covered with lotus leaves and flowers, and also the Victoria Regia in all its gorgeous beauty. Papyrusa, reeds and aquatic plants of all descriptions grow on the banks of the streams, making a home for the white stork or whiter **garza**. Looking into the clear warm waters you see little golden and red fishes, and on the bed of the stream shells of pearl.

On the south side of the Gaiba, at the foot of the mountains, the beach slopes gently down, and is covered with golden sand, in which crystals sparkle as though set in fine gold by some cunning workman. A Workman, yes--but not of earth, for nature is here untouched, unspoilt as yet by man, and the traveller can look right away from it to its Creator.

During our stay in these regions the courses of several of the larger streams were traced for some distance. On the Brazilian side there was a river up which we steamed. Not being acquainted with the channel, we had the misfortune to stick for two days on a tosca reef, which extended a distance of sixty-five feet. [The finding of tosca at this point confirms the extent inland of the ancient Pampean sea.--Colonel Church, in "Proceedings of the Royal Geographical Society," January, 1902.] During this time, a curious phenomenon presented itself to our notice. In one day we clearly saw the river flow for six hours to the north-west, and for another six hours to the south-east. This, of course, proved to us that the river's course depends on the wind.

On the bank, right in front of where we lay, was a gnarled old tree, which seemed to be the home, or parliament house, of all the paroquets in the neighborhood. Scores of them kept up an incessant chatter the whole time. In the tree were two or three hanging nests, looking like large sacks suspended from the boughs. Ten or twenty birds lay in the same nest, and you might find in them, at the one time, eggs just laid, birds recently hatched, and others ready to fly. Sitting and rearing go on concurrently. I procured a tame pair of this lovely breed of paroquets from the Guatos. Their prevailing color was emerald green, while the wings and tail were made up of tints of orange, scarlet, and blue, and around the back of the bird was a golden sheen rarely found even in equatorial specimens. Whether the bird is known to ornithologists or not I cannot tell. One night our camp was pitched near an ant-hill, inhabited by innumerable millions of those insects. None of us slept well, for, although our hammocks were slung, as we thought, away from them, they troubled us much. What was my horror next morning when the sun, instead of lighting up the rainbow tints of my birds, showed only a black moving mass of ants! My parrots had literally been eaten alive by them!

But I am wandering on and the ship is still aground on the reef! After much hauling and pulling and breaking of cables, she at last was got off into deep water. We had not proceeded far, however, when another shock made the vessel quiver. Were we aground again? No, the steamer had simply pushed a lazy alligator out of its way, and he resented the insult by a diabolical scowl at us.

Continuing on our way, we entered another body of hitherto unexplored water, a fairy spot, covered with floating islands of lotus, anchored with aquatic cables and surrounded by palm groves. On the shallow, pebbly shore might be seen, here and there, scarlet flamingoes. These beautiful birds stood on one leg, knee deep, dreaming of their enchanted home. Truly it is a perfect paradise, but it is almost as inaccessible as the Paradise which we all seek. What long-lost civilizations have ruled these now deserted solitudes? Penetrate into the dark, dank forest, as I have done, and ask the question. The only answer is the howling of the monkeys and the screaming of the cockatoos. You may start when you distinctly hear a bell tolling, but it is no call to worship in some stately old Inca temple with its golden sun and silver moon as deities. It is the wonderful bell-bird, which can make itself heard three miles away, but it is found only where man is not. Ruins of the old Incan and older pre-Incan civilizations are come across, covered now with dense jungle, but their builders have disappeared. To have left behind them until this day ruins which rank with the pyramids for extent, and Karnak for grandeur, proves their intelligence.

The peculiar rasping noise you now hear in the undergrowth has nothing to do with busy civilization--'tis only the rattlesnake drawing his slimy length among the dead leaves or tangled reeds. No, all that is past, and this is an old new world indeed, and romance must not rob you of self possession, for the rattle means that in the encounter either he dies--or you.

Meanwhile the work on shore progressed. Paths were cut in different directions and the wonders of nature laid bare. The ring of the axe and the sound of falling trees marked the commencement of civilization in those far-off regions. Ever and anon a loud report rang out from the woods, for it might almost be said that the men worked with the axe in one hand and a rifle in the other. Once they started a giant tapir taking his afternoon snooze. The beast lazily got up and made off, but not before he had turned his piercing eyes on the intruders, as though wondering what new animals they were. Surely this was his first sight of the "lords of creation," and probably his last, for a bullet quickly whizzed after him. Another day the men shot a puma searching for its prey, and numerous were the birds, beasts and reptiles that fell before our arms. The very venomous *jaracucu*, a snake eight to twelve feet long, having a double row of teeth in each jaw, is quite common here.

The forests are full of birds and beasts in infinite variety, as also of those creatures which seem neither bird nor beast. There are large black howling monkeys, and little black-faced ones with prehensile tails, by means of which they swing in mid-air or jump from tree to tree in sheer lightness of heart. There is also the sloth, which, as its name implies, is painfully deliberate in its motions. Were I a Scotchman I should say that "I dinna think that in a' nature there is a mair curiouser cratur." Sidney Smith's summary of this strange animal is that it moves suspended, rests suspended, sleeps suspended, and passes its whole life in suspense. This latter state may also aptly describe the condition of the traveller in those regions; for man, brave though he may be, does not relish a *vis-a-vis* with the enormous anaconda, also to be seen there at most inconvenient times. I was able to procure the skins of two of these giant serpents.

The leader of the "forest gang," a Paraguayan, wore round his neck a cotton scapular bought from the priest before he started on the expedition. This was supposed to save him from all dangers, seen and unseen. Poor man, he was a good Roman Catholic, and often counted his beads, but he was an inveterate liar and thief.

Taking into consideration the wild country, and the adventurous mission which had brought us together, our men were not at all a bad class. One of them, however, a black Brazilian, used to boast at times that *he had killed his father while he slept.* In the quiet of the evening hour he would relate the story with unnatural gusto.

We generally slept on the deck of the steamer, each under a thin netting, while the millions of mosquitos buzzed outside--and inside when they could steal a march. Mosquitos? Why *"mosquitos a la Paris"* was one of the items on our menu one day. The course was not altogether an imaginary one either. Having the good fortune to possess candles, I used sometimes to read under my gauzy canopy. This would soon become so black with insects of all descriptions as to shut out from my sight the outside world.

After carefully surveying the Bolivian shore, we fixed upon a site for the future port and town. [The latitude of Port Quijarro is 17 47' 35", and the longitude, west of Greenwich, 57 44' 38". Height above the sea, 558 feet.] Planting a hugh palm in the ground, with a long bamboo nailed to the crown, we then solemnly unfurled the Bolivian flag. This had been made expressly for the expedition by the hands of Senora Quijarro, wife of the Bolivian minister residing in Buenos Ayres. As the sun for the first time shone upon the brilliant colors of the flag, nature's stillness was broken by a good old English hurrah, while the hunter and several others discharged their arms in the air, until the parrots and monkeys in the neighborhood must have wondered (or is wondering only reserved for civilized man?) what new thing had come to pass. There we, a small company of men in nature's solitudes, each signed his name to the *Act of Foundation* of a town, which in all probability will mean a new era for Bolivia. We fully demonstrated the fact that Puerto Quijarro will be an ideal port, through which the whole commerce of south-eastern Bolivia can to advantage pass.

Next day the Secretary drew out four copies of this *Act*. One was for His Excellency General Pando, President of the Bolivian Republic; another for the Mayor of Holy Cross, the nearest Bolivian town, 350 miles distant; a third for Senor Quijarro; while the fourth was enclosed in a stone bottle and buried at the foot of the flagstaff, there to await the erection of the first building. Thus a commencement has been made; the lake and shores are now explored. The work has been thoroughly done, and the sweat of the brow was not stinted, for the birds of the air hovered around the theodolite, even on the top of the highest adjacent mountain. [The opening of the country must, from its geographical situation, be productive of political consequences of the first magnitude to South America.-- Report of the Royal Geographical Society, January, 1902.]

At last, this work over and an exhaustive chart of the lake drawn up, tools and tents collected, specimens of soil, stones, iron, etc., packed and labelled, we prepared for departure.

The weather had been exceptionally warm and we had all suffered much from the sun's vertical rays, but towards the end of our stay the heat was sweltering-- killing! The sun was not confined to one spot in the heavens, as in more temperate climes; here he filled all the sky, and he scorched us pitilessly! Only at early morning, when the eastern sky blushed with warm gold and rose tints, or at even, when the great liquid ball of fire dropped behind the distant violet- colored hills, could you locate him. Does the Indian worship this awful majesty out of fear, as the Chinaman worships the devil?

Next morning dawned still and portentous. Not a zephyr breeze stirred the leaves of the trees. The sweltering heat turned to a suffocating one. As the morning dragged on we found it more and more difficult to breathe; there seemed to be nothing to inflate our lungs. By afternoon we stared helplessly at each other and gasped as we lay simmering on the deck. Were we to be asphyxiated there after all? I had known as many as two hundred a day to die in one South American city from this cause. Surely mortal men never went through such awful, airless heat as this and lived. We had been permitted to discover the lake, and if the world heard of our death, would that flippant remark be used again, as with previous explorers, "To make omelettes eggs must be broken"?

However, we were not to **melt**. Towards evening the barometer, which had been falling all day, went lower and lower. All creation was still. Not a sound broke the awful quiet; only in our ears there seemed to be an unnatural singing which was painful, and we closed our eyes in weariness, for the sun seemed to have blistered the very eyeballs. When we mustered up sufficient energy to turn our aching eyes to the heavens, we saw black storm-clouds piling themselves one above another, and hope, which "springs eternal in the human breast," saw in them our hope, our salvation.

The fall of the barometer, and the howling of the monkeys on shore also, warned us of the approaching tempest, so we prepared for emergencies by securing the vessel fore and aft under the lee of a rugged **sierra** before the storm broke--and break it did in all its might.

Suddenly the wind swept down upon us with irresistible fury, and we breathed--we lived again. So terrific was the sweep that giant trees, which had braved a century's storms, fell to the earth with a crash. The hurricane was truly fearful. Soon the waters of the lake were lashed into foam. Great drops of rain fell in blinding torrents, and every fresh roll of thunder seemed to make the mountains tremble, while the lightning cleft asunder giant trees at one mighty stroke.

In the old legends of the Inca, read on the "Quipus," we find that Pachacamac and Viracocha, the highest gods, placed in the heavens "Nusta," a royal princess, armed with a pitcher of water, which she was to pour over the earth whenever it was needed. When the rain was accompanied by thunder, lightning, and wind, the Indians believed that the maiden's royal brother was teasing her, and trying to wrest the pitcher from her hand. Nusta must indeed have been fearfully teased that night, for the lightning of her eyes shot athwart the heavens and the sky was rent in flame.

Often in those latitudes no rain falls for long months, but when once the clouds open the earth is deluged! Weeks pass, and the zephyr breezes scarcely move the leaves of the trees, but in those days of calm the wind stores up his forces for a mighty storm. On this dark, fearful night he blew his fiercest blasts. The wild beast was affrighted from his lair and rushed down with a moan, or the mountain eagle screamed out a wail, indistinctly heard through the moaning sounds. During the whole night, which was black as wickedness, the wind howled in mournful cadence, or went sobbing along the sand. As the hours wore on we seemed to hear, in every shriek of the blast, the strange tongue of some long-departed Indian brave, wailing for his happy hunting-grounds, now invaded by the paleface. Coats and rugs, that had not for many months been unpacked, were brought out, only in some cases to be blown from us, for the wind seemed to try his hardest to impede our departure. The rain soaked us through and through. Mists rose from the earth, and mists came down from above. Next morning the whole face of nature was changed.

After the violence of the tempest abated we cast off the ropes and turned the prow of our little vessel civilizationward. When we entered the lake the great golden sun gave us a warm welcome, now, at our farewell, he refused to shine. The rainy season had commenced, but, fortunately for us, after the work of exploration was done. This weather continued--day after day clouds and rain. Down the rugged, time-worn face of the mountains foaming streams rushed and poured, and this was our last view--a good-bye of copious tears! Thus we saw the lake in sunshine and storm, in light and darkness. It had been our aim and ambition to reach it, and we rejoiced in its discovery. Remembering that "we were the first who ever burst into that silent sea," we seemed to form part of it, and its varying moods only endeared it to us the more. In mining parlance, we had staked out our claims there, for--

"O'er no sweeter lake shall morning break,
Or noon cloud sail;
No fairer face than this shall take
The sunset's golden veil."

CHAPTER VII.
PIEDRA BLANCA.

In due time we again reached Piedra Blanca, and, notwithstanding our ragged, thorn-torn garments, felt we were once more joined on to the world.

The bubonic plague had broken out farther down the country, steamboats were at a standstill, so we had to wait a passage down the river. Piedra Blanca is an interesting little spot. One evening a tired mule brought in the postman from the next town, Holy Joseph. He had been eight days on the journey. Another evening a string of dusty mules arrived, bringing loads of rubber and cocoa. They had been five months on the way.

When the Chiquitana women go down to the bay for water, with their pitchers poised on their heads, the sight is very picturesque. Sometimes a little boy will step into one of the giant, traylike leaves of the Victoria Regia, which, thus transformed into a fairy boat, he will paddle about the quiet bay.

The village is built on the edge of the virgin forest, where the red man, with his stone hatchet, wanders in wild freedom. It contains, perhaps, a hundred inhabitants, chiefly civilized Chiquitanos Indians. There is here a customs house, and a regular trade in rubber, which is brought in from the interior on mule-back, a journey which often takes from three to four months.

One evening during our stay two men were forcibly brought into the village, having been caught in the act of killing a cow which they had stolen. These men were immediately thrown into the prison, a small, dark, palm-built hut. Next morning, ere the sun arose, their feet were thrust into the stocks, and a man armed with a long hide whip thrashed them until the blood flowed in streamlets down their bare backs! What struck us as being delicately thoughtful was that while the whipping proceeded another official tried his best to drown their piercing shrieks by blowing an old trumpet at its highest pitch!

The women, although boasting only one loose white garment, walk with the air and grace of queens, or as though pure Inca blood ran in their veins. Their only adornment is a necklace of red corals and a few inches of red or blue ribbon entwined in their long raven-black hair, which hangs down to the waist in two plaits. Their houses are palm-walled, with a roof of palm-leaves, through which the rain pours and the sun shines. Their chairs are logs of wood, and their beds are string hammocks. Their wants are few, as there are no electric- lighted store windows to tempt them. Let us leave them in their primitive simplicity. Their little, delicately-shaped feet are prettier without shoes and stockings, and their plaited hair without Parisian hats and European tinsel. They neither read nor write, and therefore cannot discuss politics. Women's rights they have never heard of. Their bright-eyed, naked little children play in the mud or dust round the house, and the sun turns their already bronze-colored bodies into a darker tint; but the Chiquitana woman has never seen a white baby, and knows nothing of its beauty, so is more than satisfied with her own. The Indian child does not suffer from teething, for all have a small wooden image tied round the neck, and the little one, because of this, is supposed to be saved from all baby ailments! Their husbands and sons leave them for months while they go into the interior for rubber or cocoa, and when one comes back, riding on his bullock or mule, he is affectionately but silently received. The Chiquitano seldom speaks, and in this respect he is utterly unlike the Brazilian. The women differ from our mothers and sisters and wives, for they (the Chiquitanas) have nothing to say. After all, ours are best, and a headache is often preferable to companioning with the dumb. I unhesitatingly say, give me the music, even if I have to suffer the consequences.

The waiting-time was employed by our hunter in his favorite sport. One day he shot a huge alligator which was disporting itself in the water some five hundred yards from the shore. Taking a strong rope, we went out in an Indian dug-out to tow it to land. As my friend was the more dexterous in the use of the paddle, he managed the canoe, and I, with much difficulty, fixed the rope by a noose to the monster's tail. When the towing, however, commenced, the beast seemed to regain his life. He dived and struggled for freedom until the water was lashed into foam. He thrust his mighty head out of the water and opened his jaws as though warning us he could crush the frail dug-out with one snap. Being anxious to obtain his hide, and momentarily expecting his death, for he was mortally wounded, I held on to the rope with grim persistency. He dived under the boat and lifted it high, but as his ugly nose came out on the other side the canoe regained its position in the water. He then commenced to tow us, but, refusing to obey the helm, took us to all points of the compass. After an exciting cruise the alligator gave a deep dive and the rope broke, giving him his liberty again. On leaving us he gave what Waterton describes as "a long-suppressed, shuddering sigh, so loud and so peculiar that it can be heard a mile." The bullet had entered the alligator's head, but next morning we saw he was still alive and able to "paddle his own canoe." The reader may be surprised to learn that these repulsive reptiles lay an egg with a pure white shell, fair to look upon, and that the egg is no larger than a hen's.

One day I was called to see a dead man for whom a kind of wake was being held. He was lying in state in a grass-built hovel, and raised up from the mud floor on two packing-cases of suspiciously British origin. His hard Indian face was softened in death, but the observant eye could trace a stoical resignation in the features. Several men and women were sitting around the corpse counting their beads and drinking native spirits, with a dim, hazy belief that that was the right thing to do. They had given up their own heathen customs, and, being civilized, must, of course, be Roman Catholics. They were "reduced," as Holy Mother Church calls it, long ago, and, of course, believe that civilization and Roman Catholicism are synonymous terms. Poor souls! How they stared and wondered when they that morning heard for the first time the story of Jesus, who tasted death for us that we might live. To those in the home lands this is an old story, but do they who preach it or listen to it realize that to millions it is still the newest thing under the sun?

Next day the man was quietly carried away to the little forest clearing reserved for the departed, where a few wooden crosses lift their heads among the tangled growth. Some of these crosses have four rudely carved letters on them, which you decipher as I. N. R. I. The Indian cannot tell you their meaning, but he knows they have something to do with his new religion.

As far as I could ascertain, the departed had no relatives. One after another had been taken from him, and now he had gone, for "when he is forsaken, withered and shaken, what can an old man do but die?"--it is the end of all flesh. Poor man!

Had he been able to retain even a spark of life until Holy Week, he might then have been saved from purgatory. Rome teaches that on two days in the year--Holy Thursday and Corpus Christi--the gates of heaven are unguarded, because, they say, *God is dead*. All people who die on those days go straight to heaven, however bad they may have been! At no other time is that gate open, and every soul must pass through the torments of purgatory.

A missionary in Oruru wrote: "The Thursday and Friday of so-called Holy Week, when Christ's image lay in a coffin and was carried through the streets, *God being dead*, was the time for robberies, and some one came to steal from us, but only got about fifty dollars' worth of building material. Holy Week terminates with the 'Saturday of Glory,' when spirits are drunk till there is not a dram left in the drink-shops, which frequently bear such names as 'The Saviour of the World,' 'The Grace of God,' 'The Fountain of Our Lady,' etc. The poor deluded Romanists have a holiday on that day over the tragic end of Judas. A life-size representation of the betrayer is suspended high in the air in front of the cafes. At ten a.m. the church bells begin to ring, and this is the signal for lighting the fuse. Then, with a flash and a bang, every vestige of the effigy has disappeared! At night, if the town is large enough to afford a theatre, the crowds wend their way thither. This place of very questionable amusement will often bear the high-sounding name, *Theatre of the Holy Ghost!*"

There is no church or priest in the village of Piedra Blanca. Down on the beach there is a church bell, which the visitor concludes is a start in that direction, but he is told that it is destined for the town of Santa Cruz de la Sierra, three hundred miles inland. The bell was a present to the church by some pious devotee, but the money donated did not provide for its removal inland. This cost the priests refuse to pay, and the Chiquitanos equally refuse to transport it free. There is no resident priest to make them, so there it stays. In the meantime the bell is slung up on three poles. It was solemnly beaten with a stick on Christmas Eve to commemorate the time when the "Mother of Heaven" gave birth to her child Jesus. In one of the principal houses of the village the scene was most vividly reproduced. A small arbor was screened off by palm leaves, in which were hung little colored candles. Angels of paper were suspended from the roof, that they might appear to be bending over the Virgin, which was a highly-colored fashion-plate cut from a Parisian journal that somehow had found its way there. The child Jesus appeared to be a Mellin's Food-fed infant. Round this fairy scene the youth and beauty of the place danced and drank liberal potations of chicha, the Bolivian spirits, until far on into morning, when all retired to their hammocks to dream of their goddess and her lovely babe.

After this paper Virgin the next most prominent object of worship I saw in Piedra Blanca was a saint with a dress of vegetable fibre, long hair that had once adorned a horse's tail, and eyes of pieces of clamshell.

Poor, dark Bolivia! It would be almost an impossible thing to exaggerate the low state of religion there. A communication from Sucre reads: "The owners of images of Jesus as a child have been getting masses said for their figures. A band of music is employed, and from the church to the house a procession is formed. A scene of intoxication follows, which only ends when a good number lie drunk before the image--the greater the number the greater the honor to the image?" The peddler of chicha carries around a large stone jar, about a yard in depth. The payment for every drink sold is dropped into the jar of liquor, so the last customers get the most "tasty" decoction.

Naturally the masses like a religion of license, and are as eager as the priests to uphold it. Read a tale of the persecution of a nineteenth century missionary there. Mr. Payne in graphic language tells the story:

"Excommunication was issued. To attend a meeting was special sin, and only pardoned by going on the knees to the bishop. Sermons against us were preached in all the churches. I was accused before the Criminal Court. It was said I carried with me the 'special presence' of the devil, and had blasphemed the Blessed Virgin, and everyone passing should say: 'Maria, Joseph.' One day a crowd collected, and sacristans mixed with the multitude, urging them on to 'vengeance on the Protestants.' About two p.m. we heard the roar of furious thousands, and like a river let loose they rushed down on our house. Paving-stones were quickly torn up, and before the police arrived windows and doors were smashed, and about a thousand voices were crying for blood. We cried to the Lord, not expecting to live much longer. The Chief of Police and his men were swept away before the mob, and now the door burst in before the huge stones and force used. There were two parties, one for murder and one for robbery. I was beaten and dragged about, while the cry went up, 'Death to the Protestant!' The fire was blazing outside, as they had lots of kerosene, and with all the forms, chairs, texts, clothes and books the street was a veritable bonfire. Everything they could lay hands on was taken. At this moment the cry arose that the soldiers were coming, and a cavalry regiment charged down the street, carrying fear into the hearts of the people. A second charge cleared the street, and several soldiers rode into the *patio* slashing with their swords."

In this riot the missionary had goods to the value of one thousand dollars burnt, and was himself hauled before the magistrates and, after a lengthy trial, condemned to *die* for heresy!

Baronius, a Roman Catholic writer, says: "The ministry of Peter is twofold--to feed and to kill; for the Lord said, 'Feed My sheep,' and he also heard a voice from heaven saying, 'Kill and eat.'" Bellarmine argues for the necessity of *burning* heretics. He says: "Experience teaches that there is no other remedy, for the Church has proceeded by slow steps, and tried all remedies. First, she only excommunicated. Then she added a fine of money, and afterwards exile. Lastly she was compelled to come to the punishment of death. If you threaten a fine of money, they neither fear God nor regard men, knowing that fools will not be wanting to believe in them, and by whom they may be sustained. If you shut them in prison, or send them into exile, they corrupt those near to them with their words, and those at a distance with their books. Therefore, the only remedy is to send them betimes into their own place."

As this mediaeval sentence against Mr. Payne could hardly be carried out in the nineteenth century, he was liberated, but had to leave the country. He settled in another part of the Republic. In a letter from him now before me as I write he says: "The priests are circulating all manner of lies, telling the people that we keep images of the Virgin in order to scourge them every night. At Colquechaca we were threatened with burning, as it was rumored that our object was to do away with the Roman Catholic religion, which would mean a falling off in the opportunities for drunkenness." So we see he is still persecuted.

The Rev. A. G. Baker, of the Canadian Baptist Mission, wrote: "The Bishop of La Paz has sent a letter to the Minister of Public Worship of which the following is the substance: 'It is necessary for me to call attention to the Protestant meetings being held in this city, which cause scandal and alarm throughout the whole district, and which are contrary to the law of Bolivia. Moreover, it is indispensable that we prevent the sad results which must follow such teachings, so contrary to the true religion. On the other hand, if this is not stopped, ***we shall see a repetition of the scenes that recently took place in Cochabamba.***" [Referring to the sacking and burning of Mr. Payne's possessions previously referred to.]

Bolivia was one of the last of the Republics to hold out against "liberty of worship," but in 1907 this was at last declared. Great efforts were made that this law should not be passed.

In my lectures on this continent I have invariably stated that in South America the priest is the real ruler of the country. I append a recent despatch from Washington, which is an account of a massacre of revolutionary soldiers, under most revolting circumstances, committed at the instigation of the ecclesiastical authorities: "The Department of State has been informed by the United States Minister at La Paz, Bolivia, that Col. Pando sent 120 men to Ayopaya. On arriving at the town of Mohoza, the commander demanded a loan of two hundred dollars from the priest of the town, and one hundred dollars from the mayor. These demands being refused, the priest and the mayor were imprisoned. Meanwhile, however, the priest had despatched couriers to the Indian village, asking that the natives attack Pando's men. A large crowd of Indians came, and, in spite of all measures taken to pacify them, the arms of the soldiers were taken away, the men subjected to revolting treatment, and finally locked inside the church for the night. In the morning the priest, after celebrating the so-called 'mass of agony,' allowed the Indians to take out the unfortunate victims, two by two, and 103 were deliberately murdered, each pair by different tortures. Seventeen escaped death by having departed the day previous on another mission."

After Gen. Pando was elected President of the Republic of Bolivia, priestly rule remained as strong as ever. To enter on and retain his office he must perforce submit to Church authority. When in his employ, however, I openly declared myself a Protestant missionary; and, because of exploration work, was made a Bolivian citizen.

In 1897 it was my great joy to preach the gospel in Ensenada. Many and attentive were the listeners as for the first time in their lives they were told of the Man of Calvary who died that they might live. With exclamations of wonder they sometimes said: "What fortunate people we are to have heard such words!" Four men and five women were born again. Ensenada, built on a malarial swamp, was reeking with miasma, and the houses were raised on posts about a yard above the slime. I was in consequence stricken with malarial fever. One day a man who had attended the meetings came into my room, and, kneeling down, asked the Lord not to let me suffer, but to take me quickly. After long weeks of illness, God, however, raised me up again, and the meetings were resumed, when the reason of the priest's non- interference was made known to me. He had been away on a long vacation, and, on his return, hearing of my services, he ordered the church bells rung furiously. On my making enquiries why the bells clanged so, I was informed that a special service was called in the church. At that service a special text was certainly taken, for I was the text. During the course of the sermon, the preacher in his fervid eloquence even forbade the people to look at me. After that my residence in the town was most difficult. The barber would not cut my hair, nor would the butcher sell me his meat, and I have gone into stores with the money ostentatiously showing in my hand only to hear the word, "Afuera!" (Get out!) When I appeared on the street I was pelted with stones by the men, while the women ran away from me with covered faces! It was now a sin to look at me!

I reopened the little hall, however, for public services. It had been badly used and was splashed with mud and filth. The first night men came to the meetings in crowds just to disturb, and one of these shot at me, but the bullet only pierced the wall behind. A policeman marched in and bade me accompany him to the police station, and on the way thither I was severely hurt by missiles which were thrown at me. An official there severely reprimanded me for thus disturbing the quiet town, and I was ushered in before the judge. That dignified gentleman questioned me as to the object of my meetings. Respectfully answering, I said: "To tell the people how they can be saved from sin." Then, as briefly as possible, I unfolded my mission. The man's countenance changed. Surely my words were to him an idle tale--he knew them not. After cautioning me not to repeat the offence, he gave me my liberty, but requested me to leave the town. Rev. F. Penzotti, of the B. & F. B. Society, was imprisoned in a dungeon for eight long months, so I was grateful for deliverance.

An acquaintance who was eye-witness to the scene, though himself not a Christian, tells the following sad story:

"Away near the foot of the great Andes, nestling quietly in a fertile valley, shut away, one would think, from all the world beyond, lay the village of E---. The inhabitants were a quiet, home-loving people, who took life as they found it, and as long as they had food for their mouths and clothes for their backs, cared little for anything else. One matter, however, had for some little time been troubling them, viz., the confession of their sins to a priest. After due consideration, it was decided to ask Father A., living some seventeen leagues distant, to state the lowest sum for which he would come to receive their confessions. 'One hundred dollars,' he replied, 'is the lowest I can accept, and as soon as you send it I will come.'

"After a great effort, for they were very poor, forty dollars was raised amongst them, and word was sent to Father A. that they could not possibly collect any more. Would he take pity on them and accept that sum? 'What! only forty dollars in the whole of E---,' was his reply, 'and you dare to offer me that! No! I will not come, and, furthermore, from this day I pronounce a curse on your village, and every living person and thing there. Your children will all sicken and die, your cattle all become covered with disease, and you will know no comfort nor happiness henceforth. I, Father A., have said it, and it will come to pass.'

"Where was the quiet, peaceful scene of a few weeks before? Gone, and in its place all terror and confusion. These ignorant people, believing the words of the priest, gathered together their belongings and fled. As I saw those poor, simple people leaving the homes which had sheltered them for years, as well as their ancestors before them, and with feverish haste hurrying down the valley--every few minutes looking back, with intense sorrow and regret stamped on their faces-- I thought surely these people need some one to tell them of Jesus, for, little as I know about Him, I am convinced that He does not wish them to be treated thus."

The priest is satisfied with nothing less than the most complete submission of the mind and body of his flock. A woman must often give her last money for masses, and a man toil for months on the well- stocked land of the divine father to save his soul. If he fail to do this, or any other sentence the priest may impose, he is condemned to eternal perdition.

Mr. Patrick, of the R. B. M. U., has described to me how, soon after he landed in Trujilla, he attended service at a Jesuit church. He had introduced some gospels into the city, and a special sermon was preached against the Bible. During the service the priest produced one of the gospels, and, holding it by the covers, solemnly put the leaves into the burning candle by his side, and then stamped on the ashes on the pulpit floor. The same priest, however, Ricardo Gonzales by name, thought it no wrong to have seventeen children to various mothers, and his daughters were leaders in society. "Men love darkness rather than light because their deeds are evil." In Trujilla, right opposite my friend's house, there lived, at the same time, a highly respected priest, who had, with his own hands, lit the fire that burnt alive a young woman who had embraced Christianity through missionary preaching. Bear in mind, reader, I am not writing of the dark ages, but of what occurred just outside Trujilla during my residence in the country. Even in 1910, Missionary Chapman writes of a convert having his feet put in the stocks for daring to distribute God's Word. [I never saw greater darkness excepting in Central Africa. I visited 70 of the largest cathedrals, and, after diligent enquiry, found only one Bible, and that a Protestant Bible about to be burned--Dr. Robert E. Speer, in "Missionary Review of the World," August, 1911.]

Up to four years ago, the statute was in force that "Every one who directly or through any act conspires to establish in Bolivia any other religion than that which the republic professes, namely, that of the Roman Catholic Apostolic Church, is a traitor, and shall suffer the penalty of death."

After a week's stay in Piedra Blanca, during which I had ample time for such comparisons as these I have penned, quarantine lifted, and the expedition staff separated. I departed on horseback to inspect a tract of land on another frontier of Bolivia 1,300 miles distant.

PART III.
PARAGUAY

"I need not follow the beaten path;
I do not hunt for any path;
I will go where there is no path,
And leave a trail."

PARAGUAY

Paraguay, though one of the most isolated republics of South America, is one of the oldest. A hundred years before the "Mayflower" sailed from old Plymouth there was a permanent settlement of Spaniards near the present capital. The country has 98,000 square miles of territory, but a population of only 800,000. Paraguay may almost be called an Indian republic, for the traveller hears nothing but the soft Guarani language spoken all over the country. It is in this republic that the yerba mate grows. That is the chief article of commerce, for at least fifteen millions of South Americans drink this tea, already frequently referred to. Thousands of tons of the best oranges are grown, and its orange groves are world-famed.

The old capital, founded in 1537, was built without regularity of plan, but the present city, owing to the despotic sway of Francia, is most symmetrical. That South American Nero issued orders for all houses that were out of his lines to be demolished by their owners. "One poor man applied to know what remuneration he was to have, and the dictator's answer was: 'A lodgment gratis in the public prison.'

Another asked where he was to go, and the answer was, 'To a state dungeon.' Both culprits were forthwith lodged in their respective new residences, and their houses were levelled to the ground."

"Such was the terror inspired by the man that the news that he was out would clear the streets. A white Paraguayan dared not utter his name. During his lifetime he was 'El Supremo,' and after he was dead for generations he was referred to simply as 'El Difunto.'" [Robertson's "Reign of Terror."]

Paraguay, of all countries, has been most under the teaching of the Jesuit priest, and the people in consequence are found to be the most superstitious. Being an inland republic, its nearest point a thousand miles from the sea-coast, it has been held in undisputed possession.

Here was waged between 1862 and 1870 what history describes as the most annihilating war since Carthage fell. The little republic, standing out for five and a half years against five other republics, fought with true Indian bravery and recklessness, until for every man in the country there could be numbered nine women (some authorities say eleven); and this notwithstanding the fact that the women in thousands carried arms and fought side by side with the men. The dictator Lopez, who had with such determination of purpose held out so long, was finally killed, and his last words, "Muero con la patria" (I die with the country) were truly prophetic, for the country has never risen since.

Travellers agree in affirming that of all South Americans the Paraguayans are the most mild-mannered and lethargic; yet when these people are once aroused they fight with tigerish pertinacity. The pages of history may be searched in vain for examples of warfare waged at such odds; but the result is invariably the same, the weaker nation, whether right or wrong, goes under. Although the national mottoes vary with the different flags, yet the Chilian is the most universally followed in South America, as elsewhere: "Por la razon o la fuerza" (By right or by might). The Paraguayans contended heroically for what they considered their rights, and such bloody battles were fought that at Curupaita alone 5,000 dead and dying were left on the field! Added to the carnage of battle was disease on every hand. The worst epidemic of smallpox ever known in the annals of history was when the Brazilians lost 43,000 men, while this war was being waged against Paraguay. One hundred thousand bodies were left unburied, and on them the wild animals and vultures gorged themselves. The saying now is a household word, that the jaguar of those lands is the most to be dreaded, through having tasted so much human blood.

"Lopez, the cause of all this sacrifice and misery, has gone to his final account, his soul stained with the blood of seven hundred thousand of his people, the victims of his ambition and cruelty." Towns which flourished before the outbreak of hostilities were sacked by the emboldened Indians from the Chaco and wiped off the map, San Salvador (Holy Saviour) being a striking example. I visited the ruins of this town, where formerly dwelt about 8,000 souls. Now the streets are grass-grown, and the forest is creeping around church and barracks, threatening to bury them. I rode my horse through the high portal of the cannon-battered church, while the stillness of the scene reminded me of a city of the dead. City of the dead, truly--men and women and children who have passed on! My horse nibbled the grass growing among the broken tiles of the floor, while I, in imagination, listened to the "passing bell" in the tower above me, and under whose shade I sought repose. A traveller, describing this site, says: "It is a place of which the atmosphere is one great mass of malaria, and the heat suffocating--where the surrounding country is an uninterrupted marsh--where venomous insects and reptiles abound." San Salvador as a busy mart has ceased to exist, and the nearest approach to "the human form divine," found occasionally within its walls, is the howling monkey. Such are the consequences of war! During the last ten years Paraguay has been slowly recovering from the terrible effects of this war, but a republic composed mostly of women is severely handicapped. [Would the suffragettes disagree with the writer here?]

Paraguay is a poor land; the value of its paper currency, like that of most South American countries, fluctuates almost daily. In 1899 the dollar was worth only twelve cents, and for five gold dollars I have received in exchange as many as forty-six of theirs. Yet there is a great future for Paraguay. It has been called the Paradise of South America, and although the writer has visited sixteen different countries of the world, he thinks of Paraguay with tender longing. It is perhaps the richest land on earth naturally, and produces so much mate that one year's production would make a cup of tea for every man, woman and child on the globe. Oranges and bananas can be bought at six cents a hundred, two millions of cattle fatten on its rich pasture lands; but, of all the countries the writer has travelled in, Mexico comes first as a land of beggars, and poor Paraguay comes second.

CHAPTER VIII.
ASUNCION.

Being in England in 1900 for change and rest, I was introduced to an eccentric old gentleman of miserly tendencies, but possessed of $5,000,000. Hearing of my wanderings in South America, he told me that he owned a tract of land thirteen miles square in Paraguay, and would like to know something of its value. The outcome of this visit was that I was commissioned by him to go to that country and explore his possession, so I proceeded once more to my old field of labor. Arriving at the mouth of the River Plate, after five weeks of sea- tossing, I was, with the rest, looking forward to our arrival in Buenos Ayres, when a steam tug came puffing alongside, and we were informed that as the ship had touched at the infected port of Bahia, all passengers must be fumigated, and that we must submit to three weeks' quarantine on Flores Island. The Port doctor has sent a whole ship-load to the island for so trifling a cause as that a sailor had a broken collar-bone, so we knew that for us there was nothing but submission. Disembarking from the ocean steamer on to lighters, we gave a last look at the coveted land, "so near and yet so far," and were towed away to three small islands in the centre of the river, about fifty miles distant. One island is set apart as a burial ground, one is for infected patients, and the other, at which we were landed, is for suspects. On that desert island, with no other land in sight than the sister isles, we were given time to chew the cud of bitter reflection. They gave us little else to chew! The food served up to us consisted of strings of dried beef, called *charqui*, which was brought from the mainland in dirty canvas bags. This was often supplemented by boiled seaweed. Being accustomed to self- preservation, I was able to augment this diet with fish caught while sitting on the barren rocks of our sea-girt prison. Prison it certainly was, for sentries, armed with Remingtons, herded us like sheep.

The three weeks' detention came to an end, as everything earthly does, and then an open barge, towed by a steam-launch, conveyed us to Montevideo. Quite a fresh breeze was blowing, and during our eleven hours' journey we were repeatedly drenched with spray. Delicate ladies lay down in the bottom of the boat in the throes of seasickness, and were literally washed to and fro, and saturated, as they said, to the heart. We landed, however, and I took passage up to Asuncion in the "Olympo."

The "Olympo" is a palatial steamer, fitted up like the best Atlantic liners with every luxury and convenience. On the ship there were perhaps one hundred cabin passengers, and in the steerage were six hundred Russian emigrants bound for Corrientes, three days' sail north. Two of these women were very sick, so the chief steward, to whom I was known, hurried me to them, and I was thankful to be able to help the poor females.

The majestic river is broad, and in some parts so thickly studded with islands that it appears more like a chain of lakes than a flowing stream. As we proceeded up the river the weather grew warmer, and the native clothing of sheepskins the Russians had used was cast aside. The men, rough and bearded, soon had only their under garments on, and the women wore simply that three-quarter length loose garment well known to all females, yet they sweltered in the unaccustomed heat.

At midnight of the third day we landed them at Corrientes, and the women, in their white (?) garments, with their babies and ikons, and bundles--and husbands-- trod on terra firma for the first time in seven weeks.

After about twelve days' sail we came to Bella Vista, at which point the river is eighteen miles wide. Sixteen days after leaving the mouth of the river, we sighted the red-tiled roofs of the houses at Asuncion, the capital of Paraguay, built on the bank of the river, which is there only a mile wide, but thirty feet deep. The river boats land their passengers at a rickety wooden wharf, and Indians carry the baggage on their heads into the dingy customs house. After this has been inspected by the cigarette-smoking officials, the dark- skinned porters are clamorously eager to again bend themselves under the burden and take your trunks to an hotel, where you follow, walking over the exceedingly rough cobbled streets. There is not a cab for hire in the whole city. The two or three hotels are fifth- rate, but charge only about thirty cents a day.

Asuncion is a city of some 30,000 inhabitants Owing to its isolated position, a thousand miles from the sea-coast, it is perhaps the most backward of all the South American capitals. Although under Spanish rule for three hundred years, the natives still retain the old Indian language and the Guarani idiom is spoken by all.

The city is lit up at night with small lamps burning oil, and these lights shed fitful gleams here and there. The oil burned bears the high-sounding trade-mark, "Light of the World," and that is the only "light of the world" the native knows of. The lamps are of so little use that females never dream of going out at night without carrying with them a little tin farol, with a tallow dip burning inside.

I have said the street lamps give little light. I must make exception of one week of the year, when there is great improvement. That week they are carefully cleaned and trimmed, for it is given up as a feast to the Virgin, and the lights are to shed radiance on gaudy little images of that august lady which are inside of each lamp. The Pal, or father priest, sees that these images are properly honored by the people. He is here as elsewhere, the moving spirit.

San Bias is the patron saint of the country, It is said he won for the Paraguayans a great victory in an early war. St. Cristobel receives much homage also because he helped the Virgin Mary to carry the infant Jesus across a river on the way to Egypt.

Asuncion was for many years the recluse headquarters of the Jesuits, so of all enslaved Spanish-Americans probably the Guaranis are the worst. During Lent they will inflict stripes on their bodies, or almost starve themselves to death; and their abject humility to the Pai is sad to witness. On special church celebrations large processions will walk the streets, headed by the priests, chanting in Latin. The people sometimes fall over one another in their eager endeavors to kiss the priest's garments, They prostrate themselves, count their beads, confess their sins, and seek the coveted blessing of this demi-god, "who shuts the kingdom of heaven, and keeps the key in his own pocket."

A noticeable feature of the place is that all the inhabitants go barefooted. Ladies (?) will pass you with their stiffly-starched white dresses, and raven-black hair neatly done up with colored ribbons, but with feet innocent of shoes. Soldiers and policemen tramp the streets, but neither are provided with footwear, and their clothes are often in tatters. The Jesuits taught the Indians to *make* shoes, but they alone *wore* them, exporting the surplus. Shoes are not for common people, and when one of them dares to cover his feet he is considered presumptuous. Hats they never wear, but they have the beautiful custom of weaving flowers in their hair. When flowers are not worn the head is covered by a white sheet called the ***tupoi***, and in some cases this garment is richly embroidered. These females are devoted Romanists, as will be seen from the following description of a feast held to St. John:

"Dona Juana's first care was to decorate with uncommon splendor a large image of St. John, which, in a costly crystal box, she preserved as the chief ornament of her principal drawing-room. He was painted anew and re-gilded. He had a black velvet robe purchased for him, and trimmed with deep gold lace. Hovering over him was a cherub. Every friend of Dona Juana had lent some part of her jewellery for the decoration of the holy man. Rings sparkled on his fingers; collars hung around his neck; a tiara graced his venerable brow. The lacings of his sandals were studded with pearls; a precious girdle bound his slender waist, and six large wax candles were lighted up at the shrine. There, embosomed in fragrant evergreens--the orange, the lime, the acacia--stood the favorite saint, destined to receive the first homage of every guest that should arrive. These all solemnly took off their hats to the image."

Such religious mummery as this is painful to witness, and to see the saint borne round in procession, with men carrying candles, and white-clad girls with large birds' wings fastened to their shoulders, dispels the idea of its being Christianity at all.

The people are gentle and mild-spoken. White-robed women lead strings of donkeys along the streets, bearing huge panniers full of vegetables, among which frequently play the women's babies. The panniers are about a yard deep, and may often be seen full to the brim with live fowls pinioned by the legs. Other women go around with large wicker trays on their heads, selling ***chipa***, the native bread, made from Indian corn, or ***mandioca*** root, the staple food of the country. Wheat is not grown in Paraguay, and any flour used is imported. These daughters of Eve often wear nothing more than a robe- de-chambre, and invariably smoke cigars six or eight inches long. Their figure is erect and stately, and the laughing eyes full of mischief and merriment; but they fade into old age at forty. Until then they seem proud as children of their brass jewellery and red coral beads. The Paraguayans are the happiest race of people I have met; care seems undreamed of by them.

In the post-office of the capital I have sometimes been unable to procure stamps, and "Dypore" (We have none) has been the civil answer of the clerk. When they *had* stamps they were not provided with mucilage, but a brush and pot of paste were handed the buyer. If you ask for a one cent stamp the clerk will cut a two cent stamp and give you a half. They have, however, stamps the tenth part of a cent in value, and a bank note in circulation whose face value is less than a cent. There are only four numerals in the Guarani language: 1, *petei*; 2,moncoi; 3,bohapy; 4,irundu. It is not possible to express five or six. No wonder, therefore, that when I bought five 40-cent stamps, I found the clerk was unable to count the sum, and I had to come to the rescue and tell him it was $2.00. At least eighty per cent. of the people are unable to read. When they do, it is of course in Spanish, A young man to whom I gave the Gospel of John carefully looked at it, and then, turning to me, said: "Is this a history of that wonderful lawyer we have been hearing about?" To those interested in the dissemination of Scriptures, let me state that no single Gospel has as yet been translated into Guarani.

A tentative edition of the "Sermon on the Mount" has recently been issued by the British and Foreign Bible Society, a copy of which I had the honor to be the first to present to the head executive.

Gentle simplicity is the chief characteristic of the people. If the traveller relates the most ordinary events that pass in the outside world, they will join in the exclamation of surprise-"Ba-eh-pico! Ba-eh-pico!"

Information that tends to their lowering is not always accepted thus, however, for a colonel in the army, when told that Asuncion could be put into a large city graveyard, hastily got up from the dinner table and went away in wounded pride and incredulity. The one who is supposed to "know a little" likes to keep his position, and the Spanish proverb is exemplified: *"En tierra de los ciegos, el tuerto es rey"* (In the blind country the one-eyed are kings). The native is most guileless and ignorant, as can well be understood when his language is an unwritten one.

Paraguay is essentially a land of fruit, 200 oranges may be bought for the equivalent of six cents. Small mountains of oranges may always be seen piled up on the banks ready to be shipped down the river. Women are employed to load the vessels with this fruit, which they carry in baskets on their heads. Everything is carried on their heads, even to a glass bottle. My laundress, Cunacarai [The Guarani idiom can boast of but few words, and Mr., Mrs. and Miss are simply rendered "carai" (man), "cuna-carai" (woman) and "cunatai" (young woman); "mita cuna" is girl, "mita cuimbai" is boy, and "mita mishi"--baby.] Jesus, although an old woman, could bear almost incredible weights on her hard skull.

As the climate is hot, a favorite occupation for men and women is to sit half-submerged in the river, smoking vigorously "The Paraguayans are an amphibious race, neither wholly seamen nor wholly landsmen, but partaking of both." All sleep in cotton hammocks,--beds are almost unknown. The hammocks are slung on the verandah of the house in the hotter season and all sleep outside, taking off their garments with real *sang froid*. In the cooler season the visitor is invited to hang his hammock along with the rest inside the house, and in the early morning naked little children bring mate to each one. If the family is wealthy this will be served in a heavy silver cup and *bombilla*, or sucking tube, of the same metal. After this drink and a bite of *chipa*, a strangely shaped, thin-necked bottle, made of sun-baked clay, is brought, and from it water is poured on the hands. The towels are spotlessly white and of the finest texture. They are hand-made, and are so delicately woven and embroidered that I found it difficult to accustom myself to use them. The beautifully fine lace called *nanduti* (literally spider's web) is also here made by the Indian women, who have long been civilized. Some of the handkerchiefs they make are worth $50 each in the fashionable cities of America and Europe. A month's work may easily be expended on such a dainty fabric.

The women seem exceptionally fond of pets. Monkeys and birds are common in a house, and the housewife will show you her parrot and say, "In this bird dwells the spirit of my departed mother." An enemy, somehow, has always turned into an alligator--a reptile much loathed by them.

In even the poorest houses there is a shrine and a "Saint." These deities can answer all prayers if they choose to. Sometimes, however, they are not "in the humor," and at one house the saint had refused, so he was laid flat on the floor, face downwards. The woman swore that until he answered her petition she would not lift him up again. He laid thus all night; whether longer or not I do not know.

Having heard much concerning the *moralite* of the people, I asked the maid at a respectable private house where I was staying: "Have you a father?" "No, sir," she answered, "we Paraguayans are not accustomed to have a father." Children of five or six, when asked about that parent, will often answer, "Father died in the war." The war ended thirty-nine years ago, but they have been taught to say this by the mother.

As in Argentina the first word the stranger learns is **manana** (to- morrow), so here the first is **dy-qui** (I don't know). Whatever question you ask the Guarani, he will almost invariably answer, "Dy- qui." Ask him his age, he answers "Dy-qui" To your question: "Are you twenty or one hundred and twenty?" he will reply "Dy-qui." Through the long rule of the Jesuits the natives stopped thinking; they had it all done for them. "At the same time that they enslaved them, they tortured them into the profession of the religion they had imported; and as they had seen that in the old land the love of this world and the deceitfulness of riches were ever in the way of conversion to the true faith, they piously relieved the Indians of these snares of the soul, even going so far in the discharge of this painful duty as to relieve them of life at the same time, if necessary to get their possessions into their own hands," [Robertson's "Letters on Paraguay."]

"The stories of their hardness, and perfidy, and immorality beggar description. The children of the priests have become so numerous that the shame is no longer considered." [Service.]

As the Mahometans have their Mecca, so the Paraguayans have Caacupe; and the image of the Virgin in that village is the great wonder- worker. Prayers are directed to her that she will raise the sick, etc., and promises are made her if she will do this. One morning I had business with a storekeeper, and went to his office. "Is the carai in?" I asked. "No," I was answered, "he has gone to Caacupe to pay a promise." That promise was to burn so many candles before the Virgin, and further adorn her bejewelled robes. She had, as he believed, healed him of a sickness.

The village of Caacupe is about forty miles from Asuncion. "The Bishop of Paraguay formally inaugurated the worship of the Virgin of Caacupe, sending forth an episcopal letter accrediting the practice, and promising indulgences to the pilgrims who should visit the shrine. Thus the worship became legal and orthodox. Multitudes of people visit her, carrying offerings of valuable jewels. There are several **well-authenticated** cases of persons, whose offerings were of inferior quality, being overtaken with some terrible calamity." [Washburn's "History of Paraguay."]

Funds must be secured somehow, for the present Bishop's sons, to whom I was introduced as among the aristocrats of the capital, certainly need a large income from the lavish manner I noticed them "treat" all and sundry in the hotel. "It is admitted by all, that in South America the church is decadent and corrupt. The immorality of the priests is taken for granted. Priests' sons and daughters, of course not born in wedlock, abound everywhere, and no stigma attaches to them or to their fathers and mothers." ["The Continent of Opportunity." Dr. Clark.] Hon. S. H. Blake, in the *Neglected Continent*, writes: "I was especially struck by the statement of a Roman Catholic--a Consular agent with a large amount of information as to the land and its inhabitants. He stopped me in speaking of the priests by saying, 'I know all that. You cannot exaggerate their immorality. Everybody knows it--but the Latin race is a degenerate race. Nothing can be done with it. The Roman Church has had four centuries of trial and has made a failure of it.'"

When a person is dying, the Pai is hurriedly sent for. To this call he will readily respond. A procession will be formed, and, preceded by a boy ringing a bell, the *Host*, or, to use an everyday expression, *God*, will be carried from the church down the street to the sick one. All passers-by must kneel as this goes along, and the police will arrest you if you do not at least take off your hat. "Liberty of conscience is a most diabolical thing, to be stamped out at any cost," is the maxim of Rome, and the Guarani has learned his lesson well. "In Inquisition Square men were burned for daring to think, therefore men stopped thinking when death was the penalty."

Wakes for the dead are always held, and in the case of a child the little one lies in state adorned with gilded wings and tinselled finery. All in the neighborhood are invited to the dance which takes place that evening around the corpse. At a funeral the Pai walks first, followed by a crowd of men, women and children bearing candles, some of which are four and five feet long. The dead are carried through the streets in a very shallow coffin, and the head is much elevated. An old woman generally walks by the side, bearing the coffin lid on her head. The dead are always buried respectfully, for an old law reads: "No person shall ride in the dead cart except the corpse that is carried, and, therefore, nobody shall get up and ride behind. It is against Christian piety to bury people with irreverent actions, or drag them in hides, or throw them into the grave without consideration, or in a position contrary to the practice of the Church."

All Saints Day is a special time for releasing departed ones out of purgatory. Hundreds of people visit the cemeteries then, and pay the waiting priests so much a prayer, If that "liberator of souls" sings the prayer the price is doubled, but it is considered doubly efficacious.

A good feature of Romanism in Paraguay is that the people have been taught something of Christ, but there seems to be an utter want of reverence toward His person, for one may see a red flag on the public streets announcing that there are the "Auction Rooms of the child God." In his "Letters on Paraguay," Robertson relates the following graphic account of the celebration of His death: "I found great preparations making at the cathedral for the sermon of 'the agony on the cross.' A wooden figure of our Saviour crucified was affixed against the wall, opposite the pulpit; a large bier was placed in the centre of the cathedral, and the great altar at the eastern extremity was hung with black; while around were disposed lighted candles and other insignia of a great funeral. When the sermon commenced, the cathedral was crowded to suffocation, a great proportion of the audience being females. The discourse was interrupted alternately by the low moans and sobbings of the congregation. These became more audible as the preacher warmed with his discourse, which was partly addressed to his auditory and partly to the figure before him; and when at length he exclaimed, 'Behold! Behold! He gives up the ghost!' the head of the figure was slowly depressed by a spring towards the breast, and one simultaneous shriek--loud, piercing, almost appalling--was uttered by the whole congregation. The women now all struggled for a superiority in giving unbounded vent to apparently the most distracting grief. Some raved like maniacs, others beat their breasts and tore their hair. Exclamations, cries, sobs and shrieks mingled, and united in forming one mighty tide of clamor, uproar, noise and confusion. In the midst of the raging tempest could be heard, ever and anon, the stentorian voice of the preacher, reproaching in terms of indignation and wrath the apathy of his hearers! 'Can you, oh, insensate crowd!' he would cry, 'Can you sit in silence?'--but here his voice was drowned in an overwhelming cry of loudest woe, from every part of the church; and for five minutes all further effort to make himself heard was unavailing. This singular scene continued for nearly half an hour; then, by degrees, the vehement grief of the congregation abated, and when I left the cathedral it had subsided once more into low sobs and silent tears.

"I now took my way, with many others, to the Church of San Francisco, where, in an open space in front of the church, I found that the duty of the day had advanced to the funeral service, which was about being celebrated. There a scaffolding was erected, and the crucifixion exactly represented by wooden figures, not only of our Lord, but of the two thieves. A pulpit was erected in front of the scaffold; and the whole square was covered by the devout inhabitants of the city. The same kind of scene was being enacted here as at the cathedral, with the difference, however, of the circumstantial funeral in place of the death. The orator's discourse when I arrived was only here and there interrupted by a suppressed moan, or a struggling sigh, to be heard in the crowd. But when he commenced giving directions for the taking down of the body from the cross, the impatience of grief began to manifest itself on all sides, 'Mount up,' he cried, 'ye holy ministers, mount up, and prepare for the sad duty which ye have to perform!' Here six or eight persons, covered from head to foot with ample black cloaks, ascended the scaffold. Now the groans of the people became more audible; and when at length directions were given to strike out the first nail, the cathedral scene of confusion, which I have just described, began, and all the rest of the preacher's oratory was dumb show. The body was at length deposited in the coffin, and the groaning and shrieking of the assembled multitude ceased. A solemn funeral ceremony took place: every respectable person received a great wax taper to carry in the procession: the coffin after being carried all round was deposited in the church: the people dispersed; and the great day of Passion Week was brought to a close."

CHAPTER IX.
EXPEDITION TO THE SUN-WORSHIPPERS.

[An account of this expedition was requested by and sent to the Royal Geographical Society of London, Eng.]

I took passage on the "Urano," a steamer of 1,500 tons, for Concepcion, 200 miles north of Asuncion.

On the second day of our journey the people on board celebrated a church feast, and the pilot, in his anxiety to do it well, got helplessly drunk. The result was that during that night I was thrown out of the top berth I occupied by a terrific thud. The steamer had run on the sandbank of an uninhabited island, and there she stuck fast--immovable. We were landed on the shore, and there had further time for reflection on the mutability of things. In the white sand there were distinct footprints of a large jaguar and cub, probably come to prey on the lazy alligators that were lying on the beach; and I caught sight of a large spotted serpent, which glided into the low jungle where the tiger also doubtless was in hiding.

After three days' detention here, a Brazilian packet took us off. On stepping aboard, I saw what I thought to be two black pigs lying on the deck. I assure the reader that it was some seconds before I discovered that one was not a pig, but a man!

At sunset it is the custom on these river boats for all to have a bath. The females go to one side of the ship, and the males to the other; buckets are lowered, and in turn they throw water over each other. After supper, in the stillness of the evening, dancing is the order, and bare feet keep time to the twang of the guitar.

We occasionally caught sight of savages on the west bank of the river, and the captain informed me that he had once brought up a bag of beans to give them. The beans had been ***poisoned***, in order that the miserable creatures might be ***swept off*** *the earth!*

We landed at Concepcion, and I walked ashore. I found the only British subject living there was a university graduate, but--a prodigal son Owing to his habit of constant drinking, the authorities of the town compelled him to work. As I passed up the street I saw him mending a road of the "far country" There I procured five horses, a stock of beads, knives, etc, for barter, and made ready for my land journey into the far interior. The storekeeper, hearing of my plans, strongly urged me not to attempt the journey, and soon all the village talked. Vague rumors of the unknown savages of the interior had been heard, and it was said the expedition could only end in disaster, especially as I was not even going to get the blessing of the Pai before starting. I was fortunate, however, in securing the companionship of an excellent man who bore the suggestive name of "Old Stabbed Arm"; and Dona Dolores (Mrs. Sorrows), true to her name, whom I engaged to make me about twenty pounds of chipa, said she would intercede with her saint for me. Loading the pack-horse with chipa, beads, looking-glasses, knives, etc., Old Stabbed Arm and I mounted our horses, and, each taking a spare one by the halter, drove the pack-saddle mare in front, leaving the tenderhearted Mrs. Sorrows weeping behind. The roads are simply paths through deep red sand, into which the horses sank up to their knees; and they are so uneven that one side is frequently two feet higher than the other, so we could travel only very slowly. From time to time we had to push our way into the dense forest on either side, in order to give space for a string of bullock carts to go past. These vehicles are eighteen or twenty feet long, but have only two wheels. They are drawn by ten or twelve oxen, which are urged on by goads fastened to a bamboo, twenty feet long, suspended from the roof of the cart, which is thatched with reeds. The goads are artistically trimmed with feathers of parrots and macaws, or with bright ribbons. These are of all colors, but those around the sharp nail at the end are further painted with red blood every time the goad is used.

The carts, rolling and straining like ships in foul weather, can be heard a mile off, owing to the humming screech of the wheels, which are never greased, but on the contrary have powdered charcoal put in them to *increase* the noise. Without this music (?) the bullocks do not work so well. How the poor animals could manage to draw the load was often a mystery to me, Sections of the road were partly destroyed by landslides and heavy rains, but down the slippery banks of rivers, through the beds of torrents or up the steep inclines they somehow managed to haul the unwieldy vehicle. Strings of loaded donkeys or mules, with jingling bells, also crawled past, and I noticed with a smile that even the animals in this idolatrous land cannot get on without the Virgin, for they have tiny statuettes of her standing between their ears to keep them from danger. Near the town the rivers and streams are bridged over with tree trunks placed longitudinally, and the crevices are filled in with boughs and sods. Some of them are so unsafe and have such gaping holes that I frequently dismounted and led my horse over.

The tropical scenery was superb. Thousands of orange trees growing by the roadside, filled with luscious fruit on the lower branches, and on the top with the incomparable orange blossoms, afforded delight to the eye, and notwithstanding the heat, kept us cool, for as we rode we could pluck and eat. Tree ferns twenty and thirty feet high waved their feathery fronds in the gentle breeze, and wild pine-apples growing at our feet loaded the air with fragrance.

There was the graceful pepper tree, luxuriant hanging lichens, or bamboos forty feet high, which riveted the attention and made one think what a beautiful world God has made. Many of the shrubs and plants afford dyes of the richest hues, Azara found four hundred new species of the feathered tribe in the gorgeous woods and coppices of Paraguay, and all, with the melancholy *caw, caw* of the toucans overhead, spoke of a tropical land. Parrots chattered in the trees, and sometimes a serpent glided across the red sand road. Unfortunately, flies were so numerous and so tormenting that, even with the help of a green branch, we could not keep off the swarms, and around the horses' eyes were dozens of them. Several menacing hornets also troubled us. They are there so fierce that they can easily sting a man or a horse to death!

As night fell we came to an open glade, and there beside a clear, gurgling brook staked out our horses and camped for the night. Building a large fire of brushwood, we ate our supper, and then lay down on our saddlecloths, the firmament of God with its galaxy of stars as our covering overhead.

By next evening we reached the village of Pegwaomi. On the way we had passed a house here and there, and had seen children ten or twelve years of age sucking sticks of sugar-cane, but content with no other clothing than their rosary, or an image of the Virgin round their necks, like those the mules wear. Pegwaomi,

I saw, was quite a village, its pretty houses nestling among orange and lime trees, with luscious bananas in the background. There was no Pai in Pegwaomi, so I was able to hold a service in an open shed, with a roof but no walls. The chief man of the village gave me permission to use this novel building, and twenty-three people came to hear the stranger speak. After the service a poor woman was very desirous of confessing her sins to me, and she thought I was a strange preacher when I told her of One in heaven to whom she should confess.

"Paraguay, from its first settlement, never departed from 'the age of faith' Neither doubt nor free-thinking in regard to spiritual affairs ever perplexed the people, but in all religious matters they accepted the words of the fathers as the unquestionable truth. Unfortunately, the priests were, with scarcely an exception, lazy and profligate; yet the people were so superstitious and credulous that they feared to disobey them, or reserve anything which they might be required to confess." [Washburn's "History of Paraguay."]

In the front gardens of many of the rustic houses I noticed a wooden cross draped with broad white lace. The dead are always interred in the family garden, and these marked the site of the graves. When the people can afford it, a priest is brought to perform the sad rite of burial, but the Paraguayan Pai is proverbially drunken and lazy. Once after a church feast, which was largely given up to drinking, the priest fell over on the floor in a state of intoxication. "While he thus lay drunk, a boy crawled through the door to ask his blessing, whereupon the priest swore horribly and waved him off, 'Not to-day, not to-day those farces! I am drunk, very drunk!'" Such an one has been described by Pollock: "He was a man who stole the livery of the court of heaven to serve the devil in; in holy guise transacted villainies that ordinary mortals durst not meddle with."

Lest it might be thought that I am strongly prejudiced, I give this extract from a responsible historian of that unhappy land: "The simple-minded and superstitious Paraguayans reverenced a Pai, or father, as the immediate representative of God. They blindly and implicitly followed the instructions given to them, and did whatever was required at his hands. Many of the licentious brotherhood took advantage of this superstitious confidence placed in them by the people to an extent which, in a moral country, would not only shock every feeling of our nature to relate, but would, in the individual instances, appear to be incredible, and, in the aggregate, be counted as slanderous on humanity."

During my stay in Pagwaomi, a dance was held on the sward outside one of the houses, and the national whirl, the **sarandiy**, gave pleasure to all. The females wove flowers in their hair, and made garlands of them to adorn their waists. Others had caught fire-flies, which nestled in the wavy tresses and lit up the semi-darkness with a soft light, like so many green stars. Love whisperings, in the musical Guarani, were heard by willing ears, and eyelight was thus added to starlight. As the dancers flitted here and there in their white garments, or came out from the shade of the orange trees, they looked ethereal, like the inhabitants of another world one sees at times in romantic dreams, for this village is surely a hundred years behind the moon.

From this scene of innocent happiness I was taken to more than one sick-bed, for it soon became known that I carried medicines.

Will the reader accompany me? Enter then--a windowless mud hut See, lying on sheepskins and burning with fever, a young woman-almost a girl-wailing "Che raciy!>" (I am sick!) Notice the intense eagerness of her eyes as she gazes into mine when I commence to minister to her. Watch her submit to my necessarily painful treatment with child-like faith. Then, before we quietly steal out again, listen to her low-breathed "Acuerame" (Already I feel better).

In a larger house, a hundred yards away, an earthenware lamp, with cotton wick dipping in raw castor oil, sheds fitful gleams on a dying woman. The trail of sin is only too evident, even in thoughtless Pegwaomi. The tinselled saints are on the altar at the foot of the bed, and on the woman's breast, tightly clutched, is a crucifix, but Mrs. Encarnacion has never heard of the Incarnate One whom she is soon to meet. Perhaps, if Christians are awake by that time, her grandchildren may hear the "story."

In that rustic cottage, half covered with jasmine, and shaded by a royal palm, a child lies very sick. Listen to its low, weak moaning as we cross the threshold. The mother has procured a piece of tape, the length of which, she says, is the exact measure of the head of Saint Blas. This she has repeatedly put around her babe's head as an unfailing cure. Somehow the charm does not work and the woman is sorely perplexed. While we helplessly look on the infant dies! Outside, the moon soared high, throwing a silver veil over the grim pathos of it all; but in the breast of the writer was a surging dissatisfaction and--anger, at his fellow--Christians in the homeland, who in their thoughtless selfishness will not reach out a helping hand to the perishing of other lands.

Would the ever-present Spirit, who wrote "Be ye angry" not understand? Would the Master of patience and forbearance, who Himself showed righteous anger, enter into it? Is the Great God, who sees these sheep left without a shepherd, Himself angry? Surely it is well to ask?

"Oh, heavy lies the weight of ill on many hearts, And comforters are needed sore of Christlike touch."

In this village I made inquiries for another servant and guide, and was directed to "Timoteo, the very man." Liking his looks, and being able to come to satisfactory terms, I engaged him as my second helper. Timoteo had a sister called Salvadora (Saviour). She pounded corn in a mortar with a hardwood pestle, and made me another baking of chipa, with which we further burdened the pack-horse, and away we started again, with affectionate farewells and tears, towards the unknown.

Next day we were joined by a traveller who was escaping to the interior. He plainly declared himself as a murderer, and told us he had shot one of the doctors in Asuncion. Through being well connected, he had, after three weeks' detention in prison, been liberated, as he boasted to us, con todo buen nombre y fama (with good name and report). The relatives of the murdered man, however, did not agree with this verdict, and sought his life. During the day we shot an iguana, and after a meal from its fat tail our new acquaintance, finding the pace too slow for his hasty flight, left us, and I was not sorry. We met a string of bullock carts, each drawn by six animals and having a spare one behind. The lumbering wagons were on their way from the Paraguayan mate fields, and had a load of over two thousand pounds each. Jolting over huge tree-trunks, or anon sinking in a swamp, followed by swarms of gad-flies, the patient animals wended their way.

Here and there one may see by the roadside a large wooden cross, with a rudely carved wooden rooster on the top, while below it are the nails, scourge, hammer, pincers and spear of gruesome crucifixion memory. At other places there are smaller shrines with a statuette of the Virgin inside, and candles invariably burning, provided by the generous wayfarers. It is interesting to note that the old Indians had, at the advent of the Spaniards, cairns of stones along their paths, and the pious

Indian would contribute a stone when he passed as an offering to Pachacamac, who would keep away the evil spirits. That custom is still kept up by the Christian (?) Paraguayan, with the difference that *now* it is given to the Virgin. My guide would get down from his horse when we arrived at these altars, and contribute a stone to the ever-growing heap. If a specially bright one is offered, he told me it was more gratifying to the goddess. Feeling that we were very likely to meet with many *evil spirits*, Timoteo carefully sought for bright stones. The people are *very* religious, yet with it all are terribly depraved! The truth is seldom spoken, and my guide was, unfortunately, no exception to the rule. As we left the haunts of men, and difficulties thickened, he would often entreat the help of Holy Mary, but in the same breath would lie and curse!

Sighting a miserable hut, we called to inquire for meat. The master of the house, I discovered, was a leper, and I further learned, on asking if I might water my horses, that the nearest water was three miles away. The man and wife and their large family certainly looked as though water was a luxury too costly to use on the skin. The leper was most hospitable, however; he killed a sheep for us, and we sat down to a feast of mutton. After this we pushed on to water the horses. By sunset we arrived at a cattle ranch near the river Ipane, and there we stayed for the night. At supper all dipped in the same stew-pan, and afterwards rinsed out the mouth with large draughts of water, which they squirted back on the brick floor of the dining- room. The men then smoked cigarettes of tobacco rolled in corn leaves, and the women smoked their six-inch-long cigars. Finding that two of the men understood Spanish, I read some simple parts of scripture to them by the light of a dripping grease lamp. They listened in silence, and wondered at the strange new story. The mosquitoes were so troublesome that a large platform, twenty feet high, had been erected, and after reading all the inmates of the house, with us, ascended the ladder leading to the top. There the mosquitoes did not disturb us, so we slept peacefully on our aerial roost between the fire-flies of the earth and the stars of heaven.

Next day we came to a solitary house, where I noticed strings of meat hung in the sun to dry. This is left, like so many stockings and handkerchiefs, hanging there until it is hard as wood; it will then keep for an indefinite time. There we got a good dinner of fresh beef, and about ten pounds of the dried meat (charqui) to take away with us. At this place I bought two more horses, and we each got a large bullock's horn in which to carry water, swinging from the saddle-tree. I was not sorry to leave this house, for, tearing up the offal around the building, I counted as many as sixty black vultures. Their king, a dirty white bird with crimson neck covered with gore and filth, had already gorged himself with all the blood he could get. "All his sooty subjects stand apart at a respectful distance, whetting their appetites and regaling their nostrils, but never dreaming of an approach to the carcass till their master has sunk into a state of repletion. When the kingly bird, by falling on his side, closing his eyes, and stretching on the ground his unclenched talons, gives notice to his surrounding and expectant subjects that their lord and master has gone to rest, up they hop to the carcass, which in a few minutes is stripped of everything eatable." Here we left the high-road, which is cut through to Punta Pona on the Brazilian frontier, and struck off to the west. Over the grassy plains we made good progress, and by evening were thirty miles farther on our journey. But when we had to cut the path before us through the forest, ten or twelve miles was a good day's work. When the growth was very dense, the morning and evening camps were perhaps only separated by a league. Anon we struggled through a swamp, or the horses stuck fast in a bog, and the ***carapatas*** feasted on our blood. "What are carapatas?" you ask. They are leeches, bugs, mosquitos, gad-flies, etc., all compounded into one venomous insect! These voracious green ticks, the size of a bug, are indeed a terrible scourge. They fasten on the body in scores, and when pulled away, either the piece of flesh comes with them or the head of the carapata is torn off. ***It was easy to pick a hundred of these bugs off the body at night***, but it was ***not*** easy to sleep after the ordeal! The poor horses, brushing through the branches on which the ticks wait for their prey, were sometimes ***half covered with them!***

As we continued our journey, a house was a rare sight, and soon we came to "the end of Christianity," as Timoteo said, and all civilization was left behind. The sandy road became a track, and then we could no longer follow the path, for there was none to follow. Timoteo had traversed those regions before in search of the mate plant, however, and with my compass I kept the general direction.

After about ten days' travel, during which time we had many reminders that the flesh-pots had been left behind, *"Che cane o"* (I am tired) was frequently heard. Game was exceedingly scarce, and it was possible to travel for days without sighting any animal or ostrich. We passed no houses, and saw no human beings. For two days we subsisted on hard Indian corn. Water was scarce, and for a week we were unable to wash. Jiggers got into our feet when sleeping on the ground, and these caused great pain and annoyance. Someone has described a jigger as "a cross between Satan and a woodtick." The little insects lay their eggs between the skin and flesh. When the young hatch out, they begin feeding on the blood, and quickly grow half an inch long and cause an intense itching. My feet were swollen so much that I could not get on my riding-boots, and, consequently, my lower limbs were more exposed than ever. If not soon cut out, the flesh around them begins to rot, and mortification sometimes ensues.

On some of the savannas we were able to kill deer and ostrich, but they generally were very scarce. Our fare was varied; sometimes we feaisted on parrot pie or vultures eggs; again we lay down on the hard, stony ground supperless. At such times I would be compelled to rise from time to time and tighten up my belt, until I must have resembled one of the ladies of fashion, so far as the waist was concerned. Again we came to marshy ground, filled with royal duck, teal, water-hens, snipe, etc, and forgot the pangs of past hunger. At such places we would fill our horns and drink the putrid water, or take off our shirts and wash them and our bodies. Mud had to serve for soap. Our washing, spread out on the reeds, would soon dry, and off we would start for another stage.

The unpeopled state of the country was a constant wonder to me; generations have disappeared without leaving a trace of their existence. Sometimes I stopped to admire the pure white water-lilies growing on stagnant black water, or the lovely Victoria Regia, the leaf of which is at times so large as to weigh ten pounds. The flowers have white petals, tinted with rose, and the centre is a deep violet. Their weight is between two and three pounds.

Wherever we camped we lit immense fires of brushwood, and generally slept peacefully, but with loaded rifle at arm's length.

A portion of land which I rode over while in that district must have been just a thin crust covering a mighty cave. The horses' footfalls made hollow sounds, and when the thin roof shook I half expected to be precipitated into unknown depths.

After many weeks of varied experiences we arrived at or near the land I was seeking. There, on the banks of a river, we struck camp, and from there I made short excursions in all directions in order to ascertain the approximate value of the old gentleman's estate. On the land we came upon an encampment of poor, half or wholly naked Caingwa Indians. By them we were kindly received, and found that, notwithstanding their extremely sunken condition and abject poverty, they seemed to have mandioca and bananas in abundance. In return for a few knives and beads, I was able to purchase quite a stock. Seeing that all the dishes, plates, and bottles they have grow in the form of gourds, they imagine all such things we use also grow. It was amusing to hear them ask for **seeds of the glass medicine bottles** I carried with me.

A drum, ingeniously made by stretching a serpent's skin over a large calabash, was monotonously beaten as our good-night lullaby when we stretched ourselves out on the grass.

The Caingwa men all had their lower lip pierced, and hanging down over the breast was a thin stick about ten inches long. Their faces were also painted in strange patterns.

Learning from their chief that the royal tribe to which they originally belonged lived away in the depths of the forest to the east, some moons distant, I became curious. After repeated enquiries I was told that a king ruled the people there, and that they daily worshipped the sun. Hearing of these sun-worshippers, I determined, if possible, to push on thither. The old chief himself offered to direct us if, in return, I would give him a shirt, a knife, and a number of white beads. The bargain was struck, and arrangements were made to start off at sunrise next day, My commission was not only to see the old gentleman's land, but to visit the surrounding Indians, with a view to missionary work being commenced among them.

The morning dawned clear and propitious, but the chief had decided not to go. On enquiring the reason for the change of mind, I discovered that his people had been telling him that I only wanted to get him into the forest in order to kill him, and that I would not give him the promised shirt and beads. I thought that it was much more likely for him to kill me than I him, and I set his mind at rest about the reward, for on the spot I gave him the coveted articles. On receipt of those luxuries his doubts of me fled, and I soon assured him that I had no intention whatever of taking his life. Towards noon we started off, and, winding our way through the Indian paths in single file, we again soon left behind us all signs of man, and saw nothing to mark that any had passed that way before.

That night, as we sat under a large silk-cotton tree silently eating supper off plates of palm leaves, the old chief suddenly threw down his meat, and, with a startled expression, said, "I hear spirits!" Never having heard such ethereal visitors myself, I smiled incredulously, whereupon the old savage glared at me, and, leaving his food upon the ground went away out of the firelight into the darkness. Afraid that he might take one of the horses and return to his people, I followed to soothe him, but his offended mood did not pass until, as he said, the *spirits* had gone.

On the third day scarcity of water began to be felt. We had been slowly ascending the rugged steeps of a mountain, and as the day wore on the thirst grew painful. That night both we and the horses had to be content with the dew-drops we sucked from the grass, and our dumb companions showed signs of great exhaustion. The Indian assured me that if we could push on we would, by next evening, come to a beautiful lake in the mountains: so, ere the sun rose next morning, we were in the saddle on our journey to the coveted water.

All that day we plodded along painfully, silently. Our lips were dried together, and our tongues swollen. Thirst hurts! The horses hung their heads and ears, and we were compelled to dismount and go afoot. The poor creatures were getting so thin that our weight seemed to crush them to the earth. The sun again set, darkness fell, and the lake was, for all I could see, a dream of the chief, our guide. At night, after repeating the sucking of the dew, we ate a little, drank the blood of an animal, and tried to sleep. The patient horses stood beside us with closed eyes and bowed heads, until the sight was more than I could bear. Fortunately, a very heavy dew fell, which greatly helped us, and two hours before sunrise next morning the loads were equally distributed on the backs of the seven horses and we started off once again through the mist for water! water! When the sun illuminated the heavens and lit up the rugged peaks of the strangely shaped mountains ahead of us, hope was revived. We sucked the fruit of the date palm, and in imagination bathed and wallowed in the water--beautiful water--we so soon expected to behold. The poor horses, however, not buoyed up with sweet hopes as we were, gave out, one after the other, and we were compelled to cruelly urge them on up the steep. With it all, I had to leave two of the weaker ones behind, purposing, if God should in kindness permit us to reach water, to return and save them.

That afternoon the Indian chief, who, though an old man, had shown wonderful fortitude and endurance, and still led the way, shouted: "Eyoape! Eyoape!" (Come! Come!) We were near the lake. With new- born strength I left all and ran, broke through the brushwood of the shore, jumped into the lake, and found--nothing but hard earth! The lake was dried up! I dug my heel into the ground to see if below the surface there might be soft mud, but failing to find even that, I dropped over with the world dancing in distorted visions before my eyes. More I cannot relate.

How long I lay there I never knew. The Indian, I learned later, exploring a deep gully at the other side, found a putrid pool of slime, full of poisonous frogs and alive with insects. Some of this liquid he brought to me in his hands, and, after putting it in my mouth, had the satisfaction of seeing me revive. I dimly remember that my next act was to crawl towards the water-hole he guided me to. In this I lay and drank. I suppose it soaked into my system as rain in the earth after a drought. That stagnant pool was our salvation. The horses were brought up, and we drank, and drank again. Not until our thirst was slaked did we fully realize how the water stank! When the men were sufficiently refreshed they returned for the abandoned horses, which were found still alive. Had they scented water somewhere and drank? At the foot of the mountains, on the other side, we later discovered much better water, and there we camped, our horses revelling in the abundant pasturage.

After this rest we continued our journey, and next day came to the edge of a virgin forest. Through that, the chief said, we must cut our way, for the royal tribe never came out, and were never visited. Close to the edge of the forest was a deep precipice, at the bottom of which we could discern a silvery streak of clear water. From there we must procure the precious fluid for ourselves and horses. Taking our kettle and horns, we sought the best point to descend, and after considerable difficulty, clinging to the branches of the overhanging trees and the dense under- growth, we reached the bottom. After slaking our thirst we ascended with filled horns and kettle to water the horses. As may be supposed, this was a tedious task, and the descent had to be made many times before the horses were satisfied. My hat served for watering pail.

Next morning the same process was repeated, and then the men, each with long *machetes* I had provided, set to work to cut a path through the forest, and Old Stabbed Arm went off in search of game. After a two hours' hunt, a fat ostrich fell before his rifle, and he returned to camp. We still had a little chipa, which had by this time become as hard as stone, but which I jealously guarded to use only in case of the greatest emergency. At times we had been very hungry, but my order was that it should not be touched.

Only the reader who has seen the virgin forest, with its interlacing *lianas*, thick as a man's leg--the thorns six inches long and sharp as needles--can form an idea of the task before us. As we penetrated farther and farther in the *selva*, the darkness became deeper and deeper. Giant trees reared their heads one hundred and fifty feet into the heavens, and beautiful palms, with slender trunks and delicate, feathery leaves, waved over us. The medicinal plants were represented by sarsaparilla and many others equally valuable. There was the cocoa palm, the date palm, and the cabbage palm, the latter of which furnished us good food, while the wine tree afforded an excellent and cooling drink. In parts all was covered with beautiful pendant air-flowers, gorgeous with all the colors of the rainbow. Monkeys chattered and parrots screamed, but otherwise there was a sombre stillness. The exhalations from the depth of rotting leaves and the decaying fallen wood rendered the steamy atmosphere most poisonous. Truly, the flora was magnificent, and the fauna, represented by the spotted jaguar, whose roar at times broke the awful quiet of the night, was equally grand.

As the chief, ignorant of hours and miles, could not tell me the extent of the forest, I determined to let him and Timoteo make their way through as best they could, crawling through the branches, to the Sun-Worshippers, and secure their help in cutting a way for the horses. After dividing the food I had, we separated. Timoteo and the Indian crept into the forest and were soon lost sight of, while Old Stabbed Arm and I, with the horses, retraced our steps, and reached the open land again. After an earnest conversation my companion shouldered his rifle and went off to hunt, and I was left with only the companionship of the grazing horses. I remained behind to water the animals, and protect our goods from any prowling savage who might chance to be in the neighborhood. My saddle-bed was spread under a large **burning bush**, or incense tree, and my self-imposed duty was to keep a fire burning in the open, that its smoke might be seen by day and its light by night.

Going exploring a little, I discovered a much better descent down the precipice, and water was more easily brought up. Indeed, I decided that, if a certain deep chasm were bridged over, it might be possible to get the horses themselves to descend by a winding way. With this object in view I felled saplings near the place, and in a few hours constructed a rough bridge, strong enough to bear a horse's weight. Whether the animals could smell the water flowing at the bottom, or were more agile than I had thought, I cannot tell, but they descended the almost perpendicular path most wonderfully, and soon were taking draughts of the precious liquid with great gusto. Leaving the horses to enjoy their drink, I ascended the stream for some distance, in order to discover, if possible, where the flow came from. Judge of my surprise when I found that the water ran out of a grotto, or cavern, in the face of the cliff-out of the unknown darkness into the sunlight! Walking up the bed of the stream, I entered the cave, and, striking a few matches, found it to be inhabited by hundreds of vampire bats, which were hanging from the sides and stalactites of the roof, like so many damp, black rags. On my entrance the unearthly creatures were disturbed, and many came flying in my face, so I made a quick exit. Several which I killed came floating down the stream with me; one that I measured proved to be twenty-two inches across the wings. My exploration had discovered the secret of the clots of blood we had been finding on the horses' necks every morning. The vampire-bats, in their nightly flights, had been sucking the life- blood of our poor, already starving animals! It is said these loathsome creatures--half beast, half bird--fan their victim to sleep while they drain out the red blood. Provided with palm torches, I again entered the cavern, but could not penetrate its depths; it seemed to go right into the bowels of the mountain. Exploring down stream was more successful, for large flamingoes and wild ducks and geese were found in plenty.

That night I carefully staked out the horses all around the camp-fire and lay down to think and sleep and dream. Old Stabbed Arm had not returned, and I was alone with nature. Several times I rose to see if the horses were securely tied, and to kill any bats I might find disturbing them. Rising in the grey dawn, I watered the horses, cooked a piece of ostrich meat, and started off on foot for a short distance to explore the country to the north, where I saw many indications that tapirs were numerous. My first sight of this peculiar animal of Paraguay I shall never forget. It resembles no other beast I have ever seen, but seems half elephant, with its muzzle like a short trunk. In size it is about six feet long and three and a half feet high. There were also ant-bears, peculiar animals, without teeth, but provided with a rough tongue to lick up the ants. The length of this animal is about four feet, but the thick tail is longer than the body. Whereas the tapir has a hog-like skin, the ant-bear has long, bristly hairs.

Returning to camp, judge of my surprise when I found it in possession of two savages of strange appearance. My first thought was that I had lost all, but, drawing nearer, I discovered that Timoteo and the chief were also there, squatting on the ground, devouring the remains of my breakfast. They had returned from the royal tribe, who had offered to cut a way from their side, and these two strangers were to assist us.

With this additional help we again penetrated the forest. The men cut with a will, and I drove the horses after them. Black, howling monkeys, with long beards and grave countenances, leapt among the trees. Red and blue macaws screeched overhead, and many a large serpent received its death-blow from our machetes. Sometimes we were fortunate enough to secure a bees' nest full of honey, or find luscious fruit. At times I stopped to admire a giant tree, eight or ten feet in diameter, or orchids of the most delicate hues, but the passage was hard and trying, and the stagnant air most difficult to breathe. The fallen tree-trunks, over which we had to step, or go around or under, were very numerous, and sometimes we landed in a bed, not of roses, but of thorns. Sloths and strange birds' nests hung from the trees, while the mosquitos and insects made life almost unendurable. We were covered with carapatas, bruised and torn, and almost eaten up alive with insects.

Under the spreading branches of one of the largest trees we came upon an abandoned Indian camp. This, I was told, had belonged to the "little men of the woods," hairy dwarfs, a few of whom inhabit the depths of the forest, and kill their game with blow-pipes. Of course we saw none of the poor creatures. Their scent is as keen as an animal's; they are agile as monkeys, and make off to hide in the hollow trunks of trees, or bury themselves in the decaying vegetation until danger is past. Poor pigmy! What place will he occupy in the life that is to be?

CHAPTER X.
WE REACH THE SUN-WORSHIPPERS.

After some days' journey we heard shouts, and knew that, like entombed miners, we were being dug out on the other side! The Caingwas soon met us, and I looked into their faces and gravely saluted. They stared at me in speechless astonishment, and I as curiously regarded them. Each man had his lower lip pierced and wore the **barbote** I have described, with the difference that these were made of gum.

With a clear path before us we now made better progress, and before long emerged from the living tomb, but the memory of it will ever remain a nightmare.

We found a crowd of excited Indians, young and old, awaiting us. Many of the females ran like frightened deer on catching sight of me, but an old man, whom I afterwards learned was the **High Priest** of the tribe, came and asked my business. Assuring him, through Timoteo, that my mission was peaceable, and that I had presents for them, he gave me permission to enter into the glade, where I was told **Nandeyara** ["Our Owner," the most beautiful word for God I have ever heard.] had placed them at the beginning of the world. Had I discovered the **Garden of Eden**, the place from which man had been wandering for 6,000 years? I was conducted by Rocanandiva (the high priest) down a steep path to the valley, where we came in view of several large peculiarly shaped houses, built of bamboo. Near these dwellings were perhaps a hundred men, women and children, remnants of a vanishing nation. Some had a mat around their loins, but many were naked. All the males had the **barbote** in the lip, and had exceptionally thick hair, matted with grease and mud. Most of them had a repellant look on their pigment-painted faces, and I could very distinctly see that I was not a welcome visitor. No, I had not reached

Eden! Only "beyond the clouds and beyond the tomb" would the bowers of Eden be discovered to me. Hearing domestic hens cackling around the houses, I bade Timoteo tell the priest that we were very hungry, and that if he killed two chickens for us I would give him a beautiful gift later on. The priest distinctly informed me, however, that I must give first, or no fowl would be killed. From that decision I tried to move him, urging that I was tired, the pack was hard to undo, and to-morrow, when I was rested, I would well repay them the kindness. My words were thrown away; not a bite should we eat until the promised knife was given. I was faint with hunger, but from the load on the packhorse I procured the knife, which I handed to my unwilling host with the promise of other gifts later. On receipt of this treasure he gave orders to the boys standing off at a distance to catch two chickens. The birds were knocked over by the stones thrown at them. Two women now came forward with clay pots on their heads and fire-sticks in their hands, and they superintended the cooking. Without cutting off either heads or legs, or pulling out the birds' feathers, the chickens were placed in the pots with water. Lying down near the fire, I, manlike, impatiently waited for supper. Perhaps a minute had dragged its weary length along when I picked up a stick from the ground and poked one of the fowls out of the water, which was not yet warm. Holding the bird in one hand, and pulling feathers out of my mouth with the other, I ate as my forefathers did ages ago. Years before this I had learned that a hungry man can eat what an epicure despises. After this feast I lay down on the ground behind one of the tepees, and, with my head resting on my most valued possessions, went to sleep.

Having promised to give the priest and his wife another present, I was awakened very early next morning. They had come for their gifts. Rising from my hard bed, I stretched myself and awoke my servant, under whose head were the looking-glasses. I presented one of these to the woman, who looked in it with satisfaction and evident pleasure. Whether she was pleased with her reflection or with the glass I cannot tell, but I feel sure it must have been the latter! A necklace to the daughter and a further gift to the old man gained their friendship, and food was brought to us. After partaking of this I was informed that the king desired to see me, and that I must proceed at once to his hut.

His majesty (?) lived on the other side of the river, close at hand. This water was of course unbridged, so, in order to cross, I was compelled to divest myself of my clothing and walk through it in nature's garb. The water came up to my breast, and once I thought the clothes I carried on my head would get wet. Dressing on the other side, I presented myself at the king's abode. There I was kindly received, being invited to take up my quarters with him and his royal family. The king was a tall man of somewhat commanding appearance, but, save for the loin cloth, he was naked, like the rest. The queen, a little woman, was as scantily dressed as her husband. She was very shy, and I noticed the rest of the inmates of the hut peeping through the crevices of the corn-stalk partition of an inner room. After placing around the shapely neck of the queen a specially fine necklace I had brought, and giving the king a large hunting-knife, I was regaled with roasted yams, and later on with a whole watermelon.

Timoteo, my servant, whose native language was Guarani, could understand most of the idiom of the Sun Worshippers, which we found to be similar to that spoken by the civilized inhabitants of the country. There must therefore have been some connection between the two peoples at one time. The questions, "Where have you come from?" "Why have you come?" were asked and answered, and I, in return, learned much of this strange tribe. Mate was served, but whereas in the outside world a rusty tin tube to suck it through is in possession of even the poorest, here they used only a reed. I was astonished to find the mate sweetened. Knowing that they could not possibly have any of the luxuries of civilization, I made enquiries regarding this, and was told that they used a herb which grew in the valley, to which they gave the name of **ca-ha he-he** (sweet herb). This plant, which is not unlike clover, is sweet as sugar, whether eaten green or in a dried state.

There was not a seat of any description in the hut, but the king said, "Eguapu" ("Sit down"), so I squatted on the earthen floor. A broom is not to be found in the kingdom, and the house had never been swept!

A curiosity I noticed was the calabash which the king carried attached to his belt. This relic was regarded with great reverence, and at first His Majesty declined to reveal its character; but after I had won his confidence by gifts of beads and mirrors, he became more communicative. One day, in a burst of pride, he told me that the gourd contained the ashes of his ancestors, who were the ancient kings. Though the Spaniards sought to carefully rout out and destroy all direct descendants of the royal family of the Incas, their historians tell us that some remote connections escaped. The Indians of Peru have legends to the effect that at the time of the Spanish invasion an Inca chieftain led an emigration of his people down the mountains. Humboldt, writing in the 18th century, said: "It is interesting to inquire whether any other princes of the family of Manco Capac have remained in the forests; and if there still exist any of the Incas of Peru in other places." Had I discovered some descendants of this vanished race? The Montreal *Journal*, commenting on my discovery, said: "The question is of extreme interest to the scientific enquirer, even if they are not what Mr. Ray thinks them."

The royal family consisted of the parents, a son and his wife, a daughter and her husband, and two younger girls. I was invited to sleep in the inner room, which the parents occupied, and the two married couples remained in the common room. All slept in fibre hammocks, made greasy and black by the smoke from the fire burning on the floor in the centre of the room. No chimney, window, door, or article of furniture graced the house.

"The court of the Incas rivalled that of Rome, Jerusalem, or any of the old Oriental countries, in riches and show, the palaces being decorated with a great profusion of gold, silver, fine cloth and precious stones." [Rev. Thomas Wood, LL.D., Lima, Peru, In "Protestant Missions in South America."]

An ancient Spanish writer who measured some of the stones of the Incan palace at Cuzco tells us there were stones so nicely adjusted that it was impossible to introduce even the blade of a knife between them, and that some of those stones were thirty-eight feet long, by eighteen feet broad, and six feet thick. What a descent for the "Children of the Sun"! "How are the mighty fallen!" Thoughts of the past and the mean present passed through my mind as I lay down in the dust of the earthen floor that first night of my stay with the king.

Owing to the thousands of fleas in the dust of the room it was hard for me to rest much, and that night a storm brewing made sleep almost impossible. As the thunder pealed forth all the Indians of the houses hastily got out of their hammocks and grasped gourd rattles and beautifully woven cotton banners. The rattles were shaken and the banners waved, while a droning chant was struck up by the high priest, and the louder the thunder rolled the louder their voices rose and the more lustily they shook the seeds in their calabashes. They were trying to appease the dread deity of Thunder, as did their Inca ancestors. The voice of the old priest led the worship, and for *four hours* there was no cessation of the monotonous song, except when he performed some mystic ceremony which I understood not.

Just as the old priest had awakened me the first morning to ask for his present, so the king came tapping me gently the second. In his hand he had a large sweet potato, and in my half-dreamy state I heard him saying, "Give me your coat. Eat a potato?" The change I thought was greatly to his advantage, but I was anxious to please him. I possessed two coats, while he was, as he said, a poor old man, and had no coat. The barter was concluded; I ate the potato, and he, with strange grimaces, donned a coat for the first time in his life. Think of this for an alleged descendant of the great Atahuallpa, whose robes and jewels were priceless!

I offered to give the queen a feminine garment of white cotton if she would wear it, but this I could not prevail upon her to do; it was "ugly." As a loin-cloth, she would use it, but put it on--no! In the latter savage style the shaped garment was thereafter worn. Women have *fashions* all over the globe.

The few inches of clothing worn by the Caingwa women are never washed, and the only attempt at cleansing the body I saw when among them was that of a woman who filled her mouth with water and squirted it back on her hands, which she then wiped on her loin-cloth!

Prescott, writing of the Incas, says: "They loved to indulge in the luxury of their baths, replenished by streams of crystal water which were conducted through subterraneous silver channels into basins of gold."

The shapely little mouth of the queen was spoilt by the habit she had of smoking a *heavy* pipe made of red clay. I was struck with the weight and shape of this, for it exactly resembled those made by the old cliff-dwellers, unknown centuries ago. One will weigh at least a quarter of a pound. For a mouth-piece they use a bird's quill. The tobacco they grow themselves.

Near the royal abode were the kitchen gardens. A tract of forest had been fired, and this clearing planted with bananas, mandioca, sweet potatoes, etc. The blackened trunks of the trees rose up like so many evil spirits above the green foliage. The garden implements used were of the most primitive description; a crooked stick served for hoe, and long, heavy, sharpened iron-wood clubs were used instead of the steel plough of civilization.

As I have already remarked, I found the people were sun-worshippers. Each morning, just as the rising sun lit up the eastern sky, young and old came out of their houses, the older ones carrying empty gourds with the dry seeds inside. At a signal from the high priest, a solemn droning chant was struck up, to the monotonous time kept by the numerous gourd rattles. As the sun rose higher and higher, the chanting grew louder and louder, and the echoes of *"He! he! he! ha! ha! ha! laima! laima!"* were repeated by the distant hills. When the altar of incense (described later) was illuminated by the sun-god, the chanting ceased.

After this solemn worship of the Orb of Day, the women, with quiet demeanor and in single file, went off to their work in the gardens. On returning, each carried a basket made of light canes, slung on the back and held up by plaited fibres forming a band which came across their foreheads. The baskets contained the day's vegetables. Meat was seldom eaten by them, but this was probably because of its scarcity, for when we killed an ostrich they clamored for a share. Reptiles of all kinds, and even caterpillars, are devoured by them when hungry.

The Caingwas are under the average height, but use the longest bows and arrows I have ever seen. Some I brought away measure nearly seven feet in length. The points are made of sharpened iron-wood, notched like the back of a fish-hook, and they are poisoned with serpent venom. Besides these weapons, it was certainly strange to find them living in the *stone age*, for in the hands of the older members of the tribe were to be seen stone axes. The handles of these primitive weapons are scraped into shape by flints, as probably our savage forefathers in Britain did theirs two thousand years ago.

Entering the low, narrow doorway of one of the bamboo frame houses, I saw that it was divided into ten-foot squares by corn-stalk partitions a yard high. These places, like so many stalls for horses, run down each side of the *hoga*. One family occupies a division, sleeping in net hammocks made of long, coarse grass. A "family man" usually has bands of human hair twisted around his legs below the knees, and also around the wrists. This hair is torn from his wife's head. Down the centre are numerous fires for cooking purposes, but the house was destitute of chimney. Wood is burned, and the place was at times so full of smoke that I could not distinguish one Indian from another. Fortunately, the walls of the house, as was also the roof, were in bad repair, and some of the smoke escaped through the chinks. Sixty people lived in the largest hoga, and I judged the number of the whole tribe to be about three hundred.

The doorways of all the houses faced towards the east, as did those of the Inca. In the principal one, where the high priest lived, a square altar of red clay was erected. I quickly noticed that on this elevation, which was about a yard high, there burned a very carefully tended fire of holy wood. Enquiring the meaning of this, I was informed that, very many moons ago, Nande-yara had come in person to visit the tribe, and when with them had lit the fire, which, he said, they must not under any circumstances suffer to die out. Ever since then the smoke of the incense had ascended to their "Owner" in his far-off dwelling.

How forcibly was I reminded of the scripture referring to the Jewish altar of long ago, "There the fire shall ever be burning upon the altar; it shall never go out." If I had not discovered Eden, I had at least found the altar and fire of Edenic origin.

Behind the altar, occupying the stall directly opposite the doorway, stood the tribal god. As the Caingwas are sun-worshippers, I was surprised to see this, but Rocanandivia, with grave demeanor, told me that when Nandeyara departed from them he left behind him his representative. In the chapter on Mariolatry, I have traced the natural tendency of man to sink from spiritual to image worship, and I found that the Caingwas, like all pagans, had reverted to a something they could see and feel. Remembering that they had never heard the second commandment, written by God because of this failing in man, we can excuse them, but what shall be said of the enlightened Romanists?

Being exceedingly anxious to procure their "Copy of God," I tried to bargain with the priest. I offered him one thing and another, but to all my proposals he turned a deaf ear, and finally, glaring at me, said that ***nothing*** would ever induce him to part with it. The people would never allow the image to be taken away, as the life of the tribe was bound up with it Seeing that he was not to be moved, I desisted, though a covetous look in his eye when I offered a beautiful colored rug in exchange gave me hope, Rocanandiva was, like most idolatrous priests, very fanatical. When he learned that I professed and taught a different religion, his jealousy was most marked, and he often told me to go from them, I was not wanted. Living with the king, however, saved me from ejection.

One day the priest, ever on the beg, was anxious to obtain some article from me, and I determined to give it only on one condition. Being anxious to tell the people the story of Jesus, I had repeatedly asked permission of him, but had been as often repulsed. They did not want *me*, or any new "words," he would reply. Turning to him now, I said, "Rocanandiva, if you will allow me to tell 'words' to the people you shall have the present." The priest turned on his heel and left me. Knowing his cupidity, I was not surprised when, later, he came to me and said that I could tell them *words*, and held out his hand for the gift.

After sun-worship next morning the king announced that I had something new to tell them. When all were seated on the ground in wondering silence, I began in simple language to tell "the old, old story." My address was somewhat similar to the following: "Many moons ago, Nandeyara, looking down from his abode, saw that all the men and women and children in the world were bad; that is, they had done wrong things, such as . . . Now God has a Son, and to Him He said, Look down and see. All are doing wicked things! He looked and saw. The Father said that for their sin they should have to die, but that Jesus, His Son, could come down and die in their place. The Son came, and lived on earth many moons; but was hated, and at last caught, and large pieces of iron (like the priest's knife) were put into His hands and feet, and He was fastened to a tree. After this a man came, and, with a very long knife, brought the blood out of the side of Jesus, and He died." Purposing to further explain my story, I was not pleased when the priest stopped me, and, stepping forth, told the people that my account was not true. He then in eloquent tones related to them what he called the *real story*, to which I listened in amazed wonder.

"Many moons ago," he began, "we were dying of hunger! One day the Sun, our god, changed into a man, and he walked down *that* road." (Here he pointed to the east.) "The chief met him. 'All your people are dying of hunger,' said god. 'Yes, they are,' the chief replied. 'Will you die instead of all the people?' Nandeyara said. 'Yes, I will,' the chief answered. He immediately dropped down dead, and god came to the village where we all are now. 'Your chief is lying dead up the road,' he said, 'go and bury him, and after three days are passed visit the grave, when you will find a plant growing out of his mouth; that will be corn, and it will save you!'" Then, turning to me, the priest said: "This we did, and behold us alive! That is the story!" A strange legend, surely, and yet the reader will be struck with the grains of truth intermingled--life, resulting from the sacrificial death of another; the substitution of the one for the many; the life-giving seed germinating after ***three days' burial***, reminding one of John 12:24: "Except a corn of wheat fall into the ground and die, it abideth alone; but if it die, it bringeth forth much fruit." Strange that so many aboriginal people have legends so near the truth.

Some days later the chiefs son and I were alone, and I saw that something troubled him. He tried to tell me, but I was somewhat ignorant of his language, so, after looking in all directions to see that we were really alone, he led the way into a dark corner of the hoga, where we were. There, from under a pile of garden baskets, calabashes, etc., he brought out a peculiarly-shaped gourd, full of some red, powdery substance. This, with trembling haste, he put into my hand, and seemed greatly relieved when I had it securely. Going then to the corner where I kept my goods, he took up a box of matches and made signs for me to exchange, which I did. When Timoteo returned I learned that the young man was custodian of the devil--the only and original one--and that he had palmed him off on me for a box of matches! How the superstition of the visible presence of the devil originated I have no idea, but there might be some meaning in the man's earnest desire to exchange it for matches, or lights, the emblem of their fire or sun-worship. Was this simple deal fallen man's feeble effort to rid himself of the ***Usurper*** and get back the ***Father***, for it is very significant that the Caingwa word, ***ta-ta*** (light), signifies also father. Do they need light, or are they sufficiently illumined for time and eternity? Will the reader reverently stand with me, in imagination, beside an Indian grave? A girl has died through snake poisoning. A shallow grave has been dug for her remains. Into this hole her body has been dropped, uncoffined, in a sitting position. Beside the body is placed some food and a few paltry trinkets, and the people stand around with that disconsolate look which is only seen upon the faces of those who know not the Father. As they thus linger, the witch-doctor asks, "Is the dog killed?" Someone replies, "Yes, the dog is killed." "Is the head cut off?" is then asked. "Yes, the head is off," is the reply. "Put it in the grave, then," says the medicine man; and then the dog's head is dropped at the girl's feet.

Why do they do this? you ask. Question their ***wise man***, and he will say: "A dog is a very clever animal. He can always find his way. A girl gets lost when alone. For that reason we place a dog's head with her, that it may guide her in the spirit life." I ask again, "Do they need missionaries?"

My stay with the sun-worshippers, though interesting, was painful. Excepting when we cooked our own food, I almost starved. Their habits are extremely filthy, indeed more loathsome and disgusting than I dare relate.

My horses were by now refreshed with their rest, and appeared able for the return journey, so I determined to start back to civilization. The priest heard of my decision with unfeigned joy, but the king and queen were sorrowful. These pressed me to return again some time, but said I must bring with me a *boca* (gun) like my own for the king, with some more strings of white beads for the queen's wrists.

While saddling our horses in the grey dawn, the wily priest came to me with a bundle, and, quietly drawing me aside, said that Nandeyara was inside, and in exchange for the bright rug I could take him away. The exchange was made, and I tied their god, along with bows and arrows, etc., on the back of a horse, and we said farewell. I had strict orders to cover up the idol from the eyes of the people until we got away. Even when miles distant, I kept looking back, fearing that the duped Indians were following in enraged numbers. Of course, the priest would give out that I had *stolen* the image.

Ah, Rocanandiva, you are not the first who has been willing to sell his god for worldly gain! The hand of Judas burned with "thirty pieces of silver," the earthly value of the Divine One. Pilate, for personal profit, said: "Let Him be crucified." And millions to-day sell Him for "a mess of pottage."

The same horse bore away the *devil* and *god*, so perhaps without the one there would be no need of the other.

So prolific is the vegetation that during our few weeks' stay with the Indians the creeping thorns and briars had almost covered up the path we had cut through the forest, and it was again necessary to use our machetes. The larger growth, however, being down, this was not difficult, and we entered its sombre stillness once more. What strange creatures people its tangled recesses we knew not.

"For beasts and birds have seen and heard
That which man knoweth not."

I hurried through with little wish to penetrate its secret. Mere existence was hard enough in its steaming semi-darkness. Our clothes were now almost torn to shreds (I had sought to mend mine with horse- hair thread, with poor results), and we duly emerged into daylight on the other side, ragged, torn and dirty.

Our journey back to civilization was similar to the outward way. We selected a slightly different route, but left the old chief safe and well with his people.

One night our horses were startled by a bounding jaguar, and were so terrified that they broke away and scattered in all directions. Searching for them detained us a whole day, but fortunately we were able to round them all up again. Two were found in a wood of strangely-shaped bushes, whose large, tough leaves rustled like parchment.

One afternoon a heavy rain came on, and we stopped to construct a shelter of green branches, into which we crept. The downpour became so heavy that it dripped through our hastily-constructed arbor, and we were soon soaking wet. Owing to the dampness of the fuel, it was only after much patient work that we were able to light a fire and dry our clothes. There we remained for three days, Timoteo sighing for Pegwaomi, and the wind sighing still louder, to our discomfort. Everything we had was saturated. Sleeping on the soaking ground, the poisonous tarantula spiders crept over us. These loathsome creatures, second only to the serpent, are frequently so large as to spread their thick, hairy legs over a six-inch diameter.

The storm passed, and we started off towards the river Ipane, which was now considerably swollen. Three times on the expedition we had halted to build rough bridges over chasms or mountain streams with perpendicular banks, but this was broad and had to be crossed through the water. As I rode the largest and strongest horse, it was my place to venture first into the rushing stream. The animal bravely stemmed the current, as did the rest, but Old Stabbed Arm, riding a weaker horse, nearly lost his life. The animal was washed down by the strong current, and but for the man's previous long experience in swimming rivers he would never have reached the bank. The pony also somehow struggled through to the side, landing half-drowned, and Old Stabbed Arm received a few hearty pats on the back. The load on the mare was further soaked, but most of our possessions had been ruined long ago. My cartridges I had slung around my neck, and I held the photographic plates in my teeth, while the left hand carried my gun, so these were preserved. To my care on that occasion the reader is indebted for some of the illustrations in this volume. Nandeyara got another wash, but he had been wet before, and never complained!

On the farther side of the river was a deserted house, and we could distinctly trace the heavy footprints of a tapir leading up the path and through the open door-way. We entered with caution. Was the beast in then? No. He had gone out by a back way, probably made by himself, through the wattled wall. We could see the place was frequented very often by wild pigs, which had left hundreds of footprints in the three-inch depth of dust on the floor. There we lit a fire to again dry our clothes, and prepared to pass the night, expecting a visit from the hogs. Had they appeared when we were ready for them, the visit would not have been unwelcome. Food was hard to procure, and animals did not come very often to be shot. Had they found us asleep, however, the waking would have been terrible indeed, for they will eat human flesh just as ravenously as roots. After spreading our saddle-cloths on the dust and filth, Old Stabbed Arm and I were chatting about the Caingwas and their dirty habits, when Timoteo, heaving a sigh of relief, said: "Thank God, we are clean at last!" He was satisfied with the pigpen as he recalled the ***hoga*** of the Sun-Worshippers.

At last the village of Pegwaomi was reached, and, oh, we were not sorry, for the havoc of the jiggers in our feet was getting terrible! The keen-eyed inhabitants caught sight of us while we were still distant, and when we reined up, Timoteo's aged mother tremblingly said, "Yoape" ("Come here") to him, and she wept as she embraced her boy. Truly, there was no sight so sweet to "mother" as that of her ragged, travel-stained son; and Timoteo, the strong man, wept. The fatted calf was then killed a few yards from the doorstep, by having its throat cut. Offal littered up the doorway, and the children in their glee danced in the red blood. The dogs' tails and the women's tongues wagged merrily, making us feel that we were joined on to the world again. I was surprised to find that we were days out of reckoning; I had been keeping Sunday on Thursday!

During this stay at Pegwaomi I nearly lost Old Stabbed Arm. The day after we returned our hostess very seriously asked me if he might marry her daughter. Thinking he had sent her to ask, I consented. It was a surprise to learn afterwards that he knew nothing at all of the matter.

Although Pegwaomi gained no new inhabitant, I secured what proved to be one of the truest and most faithful friends of my life--a little monkey. His name was Mr. Pancho. With him it was love at first sight, and from that time onward, I believe, he had only two things in his mind--his food and his master. He would cry when I left him, and hug and kiss me on my return. Pancho rode the pack-mare into the village of Concepcion, and busied himself on the way catching butterflies and trying to grasp the multi-colored humming-birds hovering over the equally beautiful passion-flowers growing in the bushes on each side of the path.

Surely a stranger sight was never seen on the streets of Concepcion than that of a tired, dusty pack-horse bearing a live monkey, a dead god, and an equally dead devil on his back! Mrs. Sorrows was overjoyed to see me return, and earnestly told me that my first duty was to hurry down to the store and buy two colored candles to burn before her saint, who had brought me back, even though I was a heretic, which fact she greatly lamented. We had been given up as lost months before, for word came down that I had been killed by Indians. Here I was, however, safe and fairly well, saving that the ends of two of my toes had rotted off with jiggers, and fever burned in my veins! Mrs. Dolores doctored my feet with tobacco ashes as I reclined in a hammock under the lime trees surrounding her hut. I did not buy the candles, but she did; and while I silently thanked a Higher Power, and the *ta-tas* burned to *her* deity, she informed me that my countryman, the prodigal, had been carried to the "potters' field." Not all prodigals reach home again; some are buried by the swine-troughs.

For some time I was unable to put my feet to the ground; but Pancho, ever active, tied in a fig tree, helped himself to ripe fruit, and took life merrily. Pancho and I were eventually able to bid good-bye to Mrs. Sorrows, and, thousands of miles down life's pathway, this little friend and I journeyed together, he ever loving and true. I took him across the ocean, away from his tropical home, and--he died. I am not sentimental--nay, I have been accused of hardness--but I make this reference to Pancho in loving memory. Unlike some friends of my life, *he* was constant and true. [From letters awaiting me at the post-office, I learned, with intense sorrow and regret, that my strange patron had gone "the way of all flesh" The land I had been to explore, along-with a bequest of $250,000, passed into the hands of the Baptist Missionary Society, to the Secretary of which Society all my reports were given.]

CHAPTER XI.
CHACO SAVAGES.

The Gran Chaco, an immense region in the interior of the continent, said to be 2,500,000 square miles in extent, is, without doubt, the darkest part of "The Darkest Land." From time immemorial this has been given up to the Indians; or, rather, they have proved so warlike that the white man has not dared to enter the vast plain. The Chaco contains a population of perhaps 3,000,000 of aborigines. These are divided into many tribes, and speak numerous languages. From the military outposts of Argentina at the south, to the Fort of Olimpo, 450 miles north, the country is left entirely to the savage. The former are built to keep back the Tobas from venturing south, and the latter is a Paraguayan fort on the Brazilian frontier. Here about one hundred soldiers are quartered and some fifty women banished, for the Paraguayan Government sends its female convicts there. [The women are not provided with even the barest necessities of life. Here they are landed and, perforce, fasten themselves like leeches on the licentious soldiery. I speak from personal knowledge, for I have visited the "hell" of Paraguay.] Between these forts and Bolivia, on the west, I have been privileged to visit eight different tribes of Indians, all of them alike degraded and sunken in the extreme; savage and wild as man, though originally made in the image of God, can be.

The Chaco is a great unknown land. The north, described by Mr. Minchin, Bolivian Government Explorer, as "a barren zone--an almost uninterrupted extent of low, thorny scrub, with great scarcity of water," and the centre and south, as I have seen in exploring journeys, great plains covered with millions of palm trees, through which the astonished traveller can ride for weeks without seeing any limit. In the dry season the land is baked by the intense heat of the tropical sun, and cracked into deep fissures. In the rainy season it is an endless marsh--a veritable dead man's land.

During a 200-mile ride, 180 lay through water with the sun almost vertical. All this country in past ages must have been the bed of a great salt sea.

As I have said, the Chaco is peculiarly Indian territory, into which the white man steps at his peril. I accepted a commission, however, to examine and report on certain parts of it, so I left the civilized haunts of men and set foot on the forbidden ground.

My first introduction to the savages in Chaco territory was at their village of Teepmuckthlawhykethy (The Place Where the Cows Arrived). They were busy devouring a dead cow and a newly-born calf, and I saw their naked bodies through such dense clouds of mosquitos that in one clap of the hands I could kill twenty or thirty. This Indian *toldo* consists of three large wigwams, in which live about eighty of the most degraded aborigines to be found on earth. When they learned I was not one of the **Christians** from across the river, and that I came well introduced, they asked: Did I come across the **big water** in a dug-out? Was it a day's journey? Would I give them some of "the stuff that resembles the eggs of the ant?" (their name for rice).

I was permitted to occupy a palm hut without a roof, but I slept under a tiger's skin, and that kept off dew and rain. They reserved the right to come and go in it as they pleased. The women, with naked babies astride their hips, the usual way of carrying them, were particularly annoying. A little girl, however, perhaps ten years old, named Supupnik (Sawdust), made friends with me, and that friendship lasted during all my stay with them. Her face was always grotesquely painted, but she was a sweet child.

These Indians are of normal stature, and are always erect and stately, perhaps because all burdens are borne by straps on the forehead. The expression of the savage is peculiar, for he pulls out all the hair on his face, even the eyelashes and eyebrows, and seems to think the omission of that act would be a terrible breach of cleanliness. These same individuals will, however, frequently be seen with their whole body so coated with dirt that it could easily be scraped off with a knife in cakes, as the housewife would scrape a burnt loaf! The first use to which the women put the little round tin looking-glasses, which I used for barter, was to admire their pretty (?) faces; but the men, with a sober look, would search for the detested hair on lip or chin. That I was so lost to decency as to suffer a moustache to cover my lip was to them a constant puzzle and wonder, for in every other respect the universal opinion was that I was a civilized kind of "thing." I write *thing* advisedly, for the white man is to them an inferior creation--not a *person*.

In place of a beard or moustache, the inhabitant of the Chaco prefers to paint his face, and sometimes he makes quite an artistic design.

These wild inhabitants of Central South America generally wear a skin around the loins, or a string of ostrich feathers. Some tribes, as, for example, the Chamacocos, dispense with either. The height of fashion is to wear strings of tigers' teeth, deer's hoofs, birds' bills, etc., around the neck. Strings of feathers or wool are twisted around ankles and wrists, while the thickly matted hair is adorned with plumes, standing upright.

The men insert round pieces of wood in the lobe of the ear. Boys of tender age have a sharp thorn pushed through the ear, where more civilized nations wear earrings. This hole is gradually enlarged until manhood, when a round piece, two inches in diameter and one and a half inches thick, can be worn, not depending from the ear, but in the gristle of it. The cartilage is thus so distended that only a narrow rim remains around the ornament, and this may often be seen broken out. Sometimes three or four rattles from the tail of the rattlesnake also hang from the ear on to the shoulder.

These tribes of the Chaco were all vassals of the Inca at the advent of the Spaniards. They had been by them reclaimed from savagery, and taught many useful arts, one or two of which, such as the making of blankets and string, they still retain. The Inca used the ear ornaments of solid gold, but made in the form of a wheel. The nearest approach to this old custom is when the wooden ear-plug is painted thus, as are some in the author's possession.

I was fortunate in gaining the favor of the tribe living near the river, and because of certain favors conferred upon them, was adopted into the family. My face was painted, my head adorned with ostrich plumes, and I was given the name of Wanampangapthling ithma (Big Cactus Red Mouth). Because of this formal initiation, I was privileged to travel where I chose, but to the native Paraguayan or Argentine the Chaco is a forbidden land. The Indian describes himself as a *man*; monkeys are *little men*; I was a *thing*; but the Paraguayans are *Christians*, and that is the lowest degree of all. The priests they see on the other side of the river are **Yankilwana** (neither man nor woman); and a **Yankilwana**, in his distinctive garb, could never tread this Indian soil. So abhorrent to them is the name of Christian, that the missionaries have been compelled to use another word to describe their converts, and they are called "Followers of Jesus." All the members of some large expeditions have been massacred just because they were **Christians**. Surely this is convincing corroboration of my remarks regarding the state of Roman Catholicism in those dark lands.

A few miserable-looking, diminutive sheep are kept by some tribes, and the blankets referred to are made from the wool, which is torn off the sheep with a sharp shell, or, if near the coast, with a knife. The blankets are woven by hand across two straight branches of tree, and they are sometimes colored in various shades. A bulbous root they know of dyes brown, the cochineal insect red, and the bark of a tree yellow. String is made from the fibre of the *caraguatai* plant, and snail shells are used to extract the fibre. This work is, of course, done by the women, as is also the making of the clay pots they use for cooking. The men only hunt.

All sleep on the ground, men, women, children and dogs, promiscuously. The wigwams are nothing more than a few branches stuck in the ground and tied at the top. The sides are left open. Very often even this most primitive of dwellings is dispensed with, and the degraded beings crawl under the shelter of the bushes. Furniture of any kind they are, of course, wit-out, and their destitution is only equalled by the African pigmy or the Australian black.

The Chaco is essentially a barren land, and the Indians' time seems almost fully taken up in procuring food. The men, with bows and arrows, hunt the deer, ostrich, fox, or wolf, while the women forage for roots and wild fruit.

One tribe in the north of the Chaco are cannibals, and they occasionally make war on their neighbors just to obtain food.

A good vegetable diet is the cabbage, which grows in the heart of certain palms, and weighs three or four pounds. To secure this the tree has perforce to be cut down. To the Indian without an axe this is no light task. The palm, as is well known, differs from other trees by its having the seat of life in the head, and not in the roots; so when the cabbage is taken out the tree dies.

Anything, everything, is eaten for food, and a roasted serpent or boiled fox is equally relished. During my stay among them I ceased to ask of what the mess was composed; each dish was worse than the former. Among the first dishes I had were mandioca root, a black carrion bird, goat's meat, and fox's head. The puma, otter, ant-bear, deer, armadillo, and ostrich are alike eaten, as is also the jaguar, a ferocious beast of immense size. I brought away from those regions some beautiful skins of this animal, the largest of which measures nearly nine feet from nose to tail.

In the sluggish, almost salt, streams, fish are numerous, and these are shot by the Indian with arrows, to which is attached a string of gut. Lakes and rivers are also filled with hideous-looking alligators of all sizes. These grow to the length of twelve or fifteen feet in these warm waters, and the tail is considered quite a delicacy. Besides these varied dishes, there is the electric eel; and, sunk in a yard depth of mud, is the ***lollock***, of such interest to naturalists The lollock is a fish peculiar to the Chaco. Though growing to the length of three and four feet, it has only rudimentary eyes, and is, in consequence, quite blind; it is also unable to swim. The savage prods in the mud with a long notched lance, sometimes for hours, until he sticks the appetizing fish.

The steamy waters are so covered with aquatic plants that in some places I have been able to walk across a living bridge. Once, when out hunting, I came upon a beautiful forest glade, covered with a carpet of green. Thinking it a likely place for deer, I entered, when lo, I sank in a fotid lake of slime. Throwing my gun on to the bank, I had quite a difficulty to regain dry land.

In my journeyings here and there I employed one or another of the braves to accompany me. All they could eat and some little present was the pay. No sooner was the gift in their hand, however, after supper, than they would put it back in mine and say, "Give me some more food?" I was at first accompanied by Yantiwau (The Wolf Rider). Armed with a bow and arrows, he was a good hunter for me, and a faithful servant, but his custom of spitting on my knife and spoon to clean them I did not like. When my supplies were getting low, and I went to the river for a wash, he would say: "There's no ***kiltanithliacack*** (soap)--only ***clupup*** (sand)." Yantiwau was interested in pictures; he would gaze with wondering eyes at photos, or views of other lands, but he looked at them ***the wrong side up***, as they all invariably do. While possessed of a profound respect for me in some ways, he thought me very lacking in common knowledge. While I was unable to procure game, through not seeing any, he could call the bird to him in a "ducky, ducky, come and be killed" kind of way; and my tongue was parched when he would scent water. This was sometimes very easy to smell, however, for it was almost impossible to drink out of a waterhole without holding the nose and straining the liquid through my closed teeth. Chaco water at best is very brackish, and on drying off the ground a white coat of salt is left.

My Indian's first and last thought was of his stomach. While capable of passing two or three days without eating, and feeling no pangs of hunger, yet, when food was to hand, he gorged himself, and could put away an incredible amount. Truly, his make-up was a constant wonder to me. Riding through the "hungry belt" I would be famishing, but to my question: "Are you hungry?" he would answer, "No." After a toilsome journey, and no supper at the end: "Would you like to eat?" "No." But let an ostrich or a deer come in sight, and he could not live another minute without food! Another proof to Yantiwau of my incapacity was the fact that when my matches were all used I could not light the fire. He, by rubbing a blunt-pointed hard stick in a groove of soft wood, could cause such a friction that the dust would speedily ignite, and set fire to the dry twigs which he was so clever in collecting. Although such a simple process to the Indian, I never met a white man who could use the firesticks with effect.

Sitting by the camp-fire in the stillness of evening, my guide would draw attention to a shooting star. "Look! That is a bad witch doctor," he would say. "Did you notice he went to the west? Well, the Toothlis live there. He has gone for vengeance!"

The wide palm plains are almost uninhabited; I have journeyed eighty miles without sighting human being or wigwam. In the rainy season the trees stand out of a sea-like expanse of steaming water, and one may wade through this for twenty miles without finding a dry place for bivouac. Ant hills, ten and fifteen feet high, with dome-shaped roofs, dot the wild waste like pigmy houses, and sometimes they are the only dry land found to rest on. The horses flounder through the mire, or sink up to the belly in slime, while clouds of flies make the life of man and beast a living death. Keys rust in the pocket, and boots mildew in a day. At other seasons, as I know by painful experience, the hard-baked ground is cracked up into fissures, and not a drop of water is to be found in a three days' journey. The miserable savages either sit in utter dejection on logs of wood or tree roots, viewing the watery expanse, or roam the country in search of ***yingmin*** (water).

Whereas the Caingwas may be described as inoffensive Indians, the inhabitants of the Chaco are ***savages***, hostile to the white man, who only here and there, with their permission, has settled on the river bank. Generally a people of fine physique and iron constitution, free from disease of any kind, they are swept into eternity in an incredibly short space of time if ***civilized*** diseases are introduced. Even the milder ones, such as measles, decimate a whole tribe; and I have known communities swept away as autumn leaves in a strong breeze with the ***grippe***. I was informed that the hospital authorities at Asuncion gave them the cast-off fever clothing of their patients during an epidemic to sweep them off the face of the earth!

The Indians have been ill-treated from the beginning. Darwin relates that, in their eagerness to exterminate the red men, the Argentine troops have pursued them for three days without food. On the frontier they are killed in hundreds; by submitting to the white man they die in thousands. Latin civilization is more terrible to them than war. Sad to state, their only hope is to fight, and this the savage affirms he will do for ever and ever.

Francia, the Dictator of Paraguay, ordered every Indian found--man, woman or child--to be put to death! Lopez, a later ruler, took sport in hunting Indians like deer. We are told that on one occasion he was so successful as to kill forty-eight! The children he captured and sold into slavery at fifteen and twenty dollars each. The white settler considers himself very brave if he kills the savage with a rifle sighted at five hundred yards, while well out of range of the Indians' arrows, and I have known them shot just "for fun"! The Indians retaliate by ***cutting off the heels*** of their white captives, or leaving them, ***in statu naturae***, bound with thongs on an anthill; and a more terrible death could not be devised by even the inquisitor, Torquemada, of everlasting execration. The Indian is hard and cruel, indifferent to pain in himself or others. A serpent may sting a comrade, and he takes no notice; but let one find food and there is a general scamper to the spot. The Chaco savage is barbarous in the extreme. The slain enemies are often eaten, and the bones burnt and scattered over their food. The children of enemies are traded off to other tribes for more food.

The Chaco Indian is a born warrior. Sad to say, his only hope is to fight against the Latin paleface.

Most of us have at times been able to detect a peculiar aroma in the negro. The keen-scented savage detects that something in us, and we "smell" to them. Even I, **Big Cactus Red Mouth**, was not declared free from a subtle odor, although I washed so often that they wondered my skin did not come off. *They never wash*, and in damp weather the dirt peels from them in cakes. Of course they *don't* smell!

When a man or woman is, through age, no longer capable of looking after the needs of the body, a shallow grave is dug, the aged one doubled up until the knees are pressed into the hollow cheeks, and the back is broken. This terrible work done, the undesired one is dragged by one leg to the open tomb. Sometimes the face and whole body is so mangled, by being pulled through thorns and over uneven ground, that it is not recognizable, and the nose has at times been actually torn off. While sometimes still alive, the body is covered up with mother earth. Frequently the grave is so shallow that the matted hair may be seen coming out at the top. The burial is generally made near a wood, and, if passible, under the *holy wood tree*, which, in their judgment, has great influence with evil spirits. Wild beasts, attracted by the odor of the corpse, soon dig up the remains, and before next day it is frequently devoured.

An *ordinary* burial service may be thus described: A deep cut is first made in the stomach of the departed one. Into this incision a stone, some bone ash, and a bird's claw are introduced. The body is then placed over the grave on two sticks, a muttering incantation is said by the witch doctor, and the sticks are roughly knocked from under the body, so as to permit it to fall in a sitting posture. A bow and arrows, and some food and cooking utensils, are dropped into the grave. All shooting stars, according to the Indian belief, are flying stones; hence the custom of placing a stone in the stomach of the dead. It is supposed to be able to mount heavenward, and, assuming its true character, become the avenging adversary, and destroy the one who caused the death--always a bad witch doctor. The bird's claw scratches out the enemy's heart, and the ashes annihilate the spirit. One of the missionaries in the Lengua tribe stated that he assisted at the burial of a woman where the corpse fell head foremost into the grave, the feet remaining up. Four times the attempt to drop her in right was made, with similar results, and finally the husband deliberately broke his dead wife's neck, and bent the head on to the back; then he broke her limbs across his knee, and so the ghastly burial was at last completed!

Truly, "the dark places of the earth are full of the habitations of cruelty." Let the one whose idea is to "leave the pagan in his innocency" visit these savages, and, if he lives to tell it, his ideas will have undergone a great change. They are ***lost!*** and millions have not yet heard of the "Son of Man," who "came to seek and to save that which was lost."

At the death of any member, the ***toldo*** in which he lived is burnt, all his possessions are destroyed, and the people go into mourning. The hair of both sexes is cut short or pulled out, and each one has the face blackened with a vegetable dye, which, from experience, I know hardly ever wears off again. As I have said, everything the man owned in life is burnt and the village is deserted; all move right away to get out of the presence of the death-giving spirit. To me the ***toldo*** would not only seem abandoned, but the people gone without leaving a trace of their path; but not so to Wolf Rider, my guide. By the position of the half-burnt wood of the fire, he could tell the direction they had taken, and the number gone--although each steps in the other's footprints--whether they were stopping to hunt on the way, and much more he would never tell me. Some of the missionaries have spent ten years in the Chaco, but cannot get the savage to teach them this lesson of signs.

In some tribes the aged ones are just *"left to die"* sitting under a palm-leaf mat. All the members of the tribe move away and leave them thus. Many are the terrible things my eyes have witnessed, but surely the most pathetic was the sight of an old woman sitting under the mat. I was one day riding alone, but had with me two horses, when I caught sight of the palm-leaf erection and the solitary figure sitting under it. Getting down from my horse, I approached the woman and offered to take her to a place of safety, promising to feed her and permit her to live as long as she chose. Would she come with me? I begged and entreated, but the poor woman would not so much as lift her eyes to mine. The law of her tribe had said she must die, and the laws are to them unalterable. Most reluctantly, I left her to be eaten later on by the wild beasts.

Terrible as this custom is, other tribes kill and eat their aged parents "as a mark of respect." Another tribe will not permit one member to go into the spirit world alone, so they hang another one, in order that there may be two to enter together.

Whereas the Caingwas are a religious people, even attributing their custom of piercing the lip to divine commandment, the Chaco aborigines have no god and no religion. Missionaries in the solitary station I have referred to, after ten years' probing, have been unable to find any approach to worship in their darkened minda. "The miserable wretches who inhabit that vast wilderness are so low in the scale of reasoning beings that one might doubt whether or not they have human souls." [Washburn's "History of Paraguay."] These "lost sheep" have no word to express God, and have no idols. "The poverty of the Indian dialects of the Chaco is scarcely surpassed by that of the dumb brutes."

These wretched tribes have perfect community of goods; what is secured by one belongs equally to all. A piece of cloth is either torn up and distributed, or worn in turns by each one. The shirt which I gave my guide, Yantiwau, for much arduous toil, was worn by one and another alternately. Much as the savage at first desires to possess some garment, it does not take long for him to tire of it. All agree with Mark Twain, that "the human skin is the most comfortable of all costumes," and, clothed in the sunlight, the human form divine is not unlovely.

Sometimes the Indians of the interior take skins, etc., to the Paraguayan towns across the river. Not knowing the use of money, their little trading is done by barter. Their knowledge of value is so crude that on one occasion they refused a two-dollar axe for an article, but gladly accepted a ten-cent knife. The Chaco Indian, however, is seldom seen in civilization. His home is in the interior of an unknown country, which he wanders over in wild freedom. While the Caingwas are home-keeping, these savages are nomadic, and could not settle down. The land is either burnt up or inundated, so they do not plant, but live only by the chase. So bold and daring are they that a man, armed only with a lance, will attack a savage jaguar; or, diving under an alligator, he will stab it with a sharpened bone. The same man will run in abject terror if he thinks he hears *spirits*.

Though not religious, the savages are exceedingly superstitious, afraid of ghosts and evil spirits, and the fear of these spectral visitants pursues them through life. During a storm they vigorously shake their blankets and mutter incantations to keep away supernatural visitors.

All diseases are caused by evil spirits, or the moon; and a comet brings the measles. The help of the witch doctor has to be sought on all occasions, for his special work is to drive away the evil spirit that has taken possession of a sick one. This he does by rattling a hollow calabash containing stones. That important person will perform his mystic *hocus pocus* over the sick or dying, and charm away the spirits from a neighborhood. I have known an Indian, when in great pain through having eaten too much, send for the old fakir, who, after examination of the patient and great show of learning, declared that the suffering one *had two tigers in his stomach*. A very common remedy is the somewhat scientific operation of bleeding a patient, but the manner is certainly uncommon--the witch doctor sucks out the blood. One I was acquainted with, among the Lengua tribe, professed to suck three cats out of a man's stomach. His professional name was thereafter "Father of Kittens." The doctor's position is not one to be envied, however, for if three consecutive patients die, he must follow them *down the dark trail!*

These medicine-men are experts in poisons, and their enemies have a way of dying suddenly. It cannot be denied that the Indians have a very real knowledge of the healing virtues of many plants. The writer has marvelled at the cures he has seen, and was not slow to add some of their methods to his medical knowledge. Not a few who have been healed, since the writer's return to civilization, owe their new life to the knowledge there learned.

Infanticide is practised in every tribe, and in my extensive wanderings among eight *toldos*, I never met a family with more than two children. The rest are killed! A child is born, and the mother immediately knocks it on the head with a club! After covering the baby with a layer of earth, the woman goes about as if nothing had occurred. One chief of the Lengua tribe, that I met, had himself killed nineteen children. An ironwood club is kept in each *toldo* for this gruesome work. Frequently a live child is buried with a dead parent; but I had better leave much of their doings in the inkpot.

When a girl enters the matrimonial market, at about the age of twelve or thirteen, her face is specially colored with a yellow paint, made from the flower of the date palm, and the aspirant to her hand brings a bundle of firewood, neatly tied up, which he places beside her earthen bed at early morning. As the rising sun gilds the eastern sky, the girl awakes out of her sleep, rubs her eyes,--and sees the sticks. Well does she know the meaning of it, and a glad light flashes in her dark eyes as she cries out, "Who brought the sticks?" All men, women and children, take up the cry, and soon the whole encampment resounds with, "Who brought the sticks?" The medicine-man, who sleeps apart from the "common herd" under an incense-tree, hears the din, and, quickly donning his head-dress, hurries down to the scene. With an authoritative voice, which even the chief himself does not use, he demands, "Who brought the sticks?" until a young brave steps forward in front of him and replies, "Father of Kittens, I brought the sticks." This young man is then commanded to stand apart, the girl is hunted out, and together they wait while the witch-doctor X-rays them through and through. After this close scrutiny, they are asked: "Do you want this man?" "Do you want this girl?" To which they reply, "Yes, Father of Kittens, I do." Then, with great show of power, the medicine-man says, "Go!" and off the newly-married pair start, to live together until death (in the form of burial) does them part.

It may be a great surprise to the reader to learn that these savages are exceedingly moral. Infidelity between man and wife is punished with death, but in all my travels I only heard of one such case. A man marries only one wife, and although any expression of love between them is never seen, they yet seem to think of one another in a tender way, and it is especially noticeable that the parents are kind to their children.

One evening I rode into an encampment of savages who were celebrating a feast. About fifty specially-decked-out Indians were standing in a circle, and one of the number had a large and very noisy rattle, with which he kept time to the chant of Ha ha ha ha ha! u u u u u! o o o oo! au au au au au! The lurid lights of the fires burning all around lit up this truly savage scene. The witch-doctor, the old fakir named "Father of Kittens," came to me and looked me through and through with his piercing eyes. I was given the rattle, and, although very tired, had to keep up a constant din, while my wild companions bent their bodies in strange contortions. In the centre of the ring was a woman with a lighted pipe in her hand. She passed this from one to another and pushed it into the mouth of each one, who had "a draw." My turn came, and lo! the pipe was thrust between my teeth, and the din went on: Ha ha! u u! o o! au au! This feast lasted three nights and two days, but the music was not varied, and neither man nor woman seemed to sleep or rest. Food was cooking at the different fires, attended by the women, but my share was only a ***roasted fox's head!*** The animal was laid on the wood, with skin, head and legs still attached, and the whole was burnt black. I was very hungry, and ate my portion thankfully. Christopher North said: "There's a deal of fine confused feeding about a sheep's head," and so I found with the fox's. Truly, as the Indian says, "hunger is a very big man."

At these feasts a drum, made by stretching a serpent's skin over one of their clay pots, is loudly beaten, and the thigh-bone of an ostrich, with key-holes burned in, is a common musical instrument. From the *algarroba* bean an intoxicating drink is made, called *ang- min*, and then yells, hellish sounds and murderous blows inspire terror in the paleface guest. "It is impossible to conceive anything more wild and savage than the scene of their bivouac. Some drink till they are intoxicated, others swallow the steaming blood of slaughtered animals for their supper, and then, sick from drunkenness, they cast it up again, and are besmeared with gore and filth."

After the feast was over I held a service, and told how sin was *injected* into us by the evil spirit, but that all are invited to the heavenly feast. My address was listened to in perfect silence, and the nodding heads showed that some, at least, understood it. When I finished speaking, a poor woman, thinking she must offer something, gave me her baby--a naked little creature that had never been washed in its life. I took it up and kissed it, and the poor woman smiled. Yes, a savage woman can smile.

As already stated, many different tribes of Indians dwell in the Chaco, and each have their different customs. In the Suhin tribe the rite of burial may be thus described. "The digger of the grave and the performer of the ceremony was the chief, who is also a witch- doctor, and I was told that he was about to destroy the witch-doctor who had caused the man's death. A fire was lit, and whilst the digging was in progress a stone and two pieces of iron were being heated. Two bones of a horse, a large bird's nest built of sticks, and various twigs were collected. The skin of a jaguar's head, a tooth, and the pads of the same animal were laid out. A piece of wax and a stone were also heated; and in a heap lay a hide, some skins for bedding, and a quantity of sheep's wool. The grave being finished, the ceremony began by a wooden arrow being notched in the middle and waxed, then plunged into the right breast of the corpse, when it was snapped in two at the notch, and the remaining half was flung into the air, accompanied with a vengeful cry, in the direction of the Toothli tribe, one of whose doctors, it was supposed, had caused the man's death. Short pointed sticks, apparently to represent arrows, were also daubed with wax, two being plunged into the throat and one into the left breast, the cry again accompanying each insertion. One of the jaguar's pads was next taken, and the head of the corpse torn by the claws, the growl of the animal being imitated during the process. An incision was next made in the cheek, and the tooth inserted; then the head and face were daubed with the heated wax. The use of the wax is evidently to signify the desire that both arrows and animal may stick to the man if he be attacked by either. The arrows were plunged, one into the right breast downwards, and another below the ribs, on the same side, but in an upward direction, a third being driven into the right thigh. They also spoke about breaking one of the arms, but did not do so. An incision being made in the abdomen, the heated stone was then placed within the body. They place most reliance upon the work of the stone. The ceremony is known by the name of 'Mataimang' stone, and all the other things are said to assist it. Meteorites, when seen to pass along the sky, are regarded with awe; they are believed to be these stones in passage. The body was placed in the grave with the head to the west, the jaguar's head and pads being first placed under it. A bunch of grass, tied together, was placed upon the body; then the bird's nest was burned upon it. The bones were next thrown in, and over all the various articles before mentioned were placed. These were to accompany the soul in its passage to the west. In this act the idea of a future state is more distinctly seen than ever it has been seen amongst the Lenguas, who burn all a man's possessions at his death. The ceremony finished, the grave was covered in, logs and twigs being carelessly thrown on the top, apparently simply to indicate the existence of a grave. The thing which struck me most was the intense spirit of vengeance shown."

Notwithstanding such terrible savagery, however, the Indian has ideas of right and wrong that put Christian civilization to shame. The people are perfectly **honest** and **truthful**. I believe they **cannot lie**, and stealing is entirely unknown among them.

Many are the experiences I have had in the Chaco. Some of them haunt me still like ghostly shadows. The evening camp-fire, the glare of which lit up and made more hideous still my savage followers, gorging themselves until covered with filth and gore. The times when, from sheer hunger, I have, like them, torn up bird or beast and eaten it raw. The draughts of water from the Indian hole containing the putrefying remains of some dead animal; my shirt dropping off in rags and no wash for three weeks. The journeys through miles of malarial swamps and pathless wilderness. The revolting food, and the want of food. Ah! the memory is a bad dream from which I must awake.

The other side, you say? Yes, there is another. A cloudless blue sky overhead. The gorgeous air-flowers, delicate and fragrant. Trees covered with a drapery of orchidaceae. The loveliest of flowers and shrubs. Birds of rainbow beauty, painted by the hand of God, as only He can. Flamingoes, parrots, humming-birds, butterflies of every size and hue. Arborescent ferns; cacti, thirty feet high, like huge candelabra. Creeping plants growing a hundred feet, and then passing from the top of one ever-vernal tree to another, forming a canopy for one from the sun's rays. Chattering monkeys. Deer, with more beautiful eyes than ever woman had since Eve fell. The balmy air wafting incense from the burning bush; and last, but oh, not least, the joy in seeing the degraded aborigine learning to love the "Light of the World"! Yes, there are delights; but "life is real, life is earnest," and a meal of *algarroba* beans (the husks of the prodigal son of Luke XV.) is not any more tempting if eaten under the shade of a waving palm of surpassing beauty.

The mission station previously referred to lies one hundred miles in from the river bank, three hundred miles north of Asuncion, among the Lengua Indians. As far as I am aware, no Paraguayan has ever visited there. The missionaries wish their influence to be the only one in training the Indian mind. The village bears the strange name of Waikthlatemialwa (The Place Where the Toads Arrived). At the invitation of the missionaries, I was privileged to go there and see their work. A trail leads in from the river bank, but it is so bad that bullock carts taking in provisions occupy ten and twelve days on the journey. Tamaswa (The Locust Eater), my guide, led me all during the first day out through a palm forest, and at night we slept on the hard ground. The Indian was a convert of the mission, and although painted, feathered and almost naked, seemed really an exemplary Christian. The missionaries labored for eleven years without gaining a single convert, but Tamaswa is not the only "follower of Jesus" now. During the day we shot a deer, and that evening, being very hungry, I ate perhaps two pounds of meat. Tamaswa finished the rest! True, it was only a small deer, but as I wish to retain my character for veracity, I dare not say how much it weighed. This meal concluded, we knelt on the ground. I read out of the old Book: "I go to prepare a place for you," and Locust Eater offered a simple prayer for protection, help and safety to the God who understands all languages.

My blanket was wet through and through with the green slime through which we had waded and splashed for hours, but we curled ourselves up under a beer barrel tree and tried to sleep. The howling jaguars and other beasts of prey in the jungle made this almost impossible. Several times I was awakened by my guide rising, and, by the light of a palm torch, searching for wood to replenish the dying fire, in the smoke of which we slept, as a help against the millions of mosquitos buzzing around. Towards morning a large beast of some kind leaped right over me, and I rose to rekindle the fire, which my guide had suffered to die out, and then I watched until day dawned. As all the deer was consumed, we started off without breakfast, but were fortunate later on in being able to shoot two wild turkeys.

That day we rode on through the endless forest of palms, and waded through a quagmire at least eight miles in extent, where the green slime reached up to the saddle-flaps. On that day we came to a sluggish stream, bearing the name of "Aptikpangmakthlaingwainkyapaimpangkya" (The Place Where the Pots Were Struck When They Were About to Feast). There a punt was moored, into which we placed our saddles, etc., and paddled across, while the horses swam the almost stagnant water. Saddling up on the other side, we had a journey of thirty miles to make before arriving at a waterhole, where we camped for the second night. I don't know what real nectar is, but that water was nectar to me, although the horses sniffed and at first refused to drink it.

At sunset on the third day we emerged from the palm forest and endless marshes, and by the evening of the fourth day the church, built of palm logs, loomed up on the horizon. Many of the Indians came out to meet us, and my arrival was the talk of the village. The people seemed happy, and the missionaries made me at home in their roughly-built log shanties. Next morning I found a gift had been brought me by the Indians. It was a beautiful feather headdress, but it had just been left on the step, the usual way they have of making presents. The Indian expects no thanks, and he gives none. The women received any present I handed them courteously but silently. The men would accept a looking-glass from me and immediately commence to search their face for any trace of "dirty hairs," probably brought to their mind by the sight of mine, but not even a grunt of satisfaction would be given. No Chaco language has a word for "thanks."

There is, among the Lenguas, an old tradition to the effect that for generations they have been expecting the arrival of some strangers who would live among them and teach them about the spirit-world. These long-looked-for teachers were called *The Imlah*. The tradition says that when the Imlah arrive, all the Indians must obey their teaching, and take care that the said Imlah do not again leave their country, for if so they, the Indians, would disappear from the land. When Mr. Grubb and his helpers first landed, they were immediately asked, "Are you the Imlah?" and to this question they, of course, answered yes. Was it not because of this tradition that the Indian who later shot Mr. Grubb with a poisoned arrow was himself put to death by the tribe?

About twenty boys attend the school established at Waikthlatemialwa, and strange names some of them bear; let Haikuk (Little Dead One) serve as an example. It is truly a cheering sight to see this sign of a brighter day. When these boys return to their distant *toldos* to tell "the news" to their dark-minded parents, the most wonderful of all to relate is "Liklamo ithnik nata abwathwuk enthlit God; hingyahamok hiknata apkyapasa apkyitka abwanthlabanko. Aptakmilkischik sat ankuk appaiwa ingyitsipe sata netin thlamokthloho abyiam." [John 3:16]

Well might the wondering mother of "Dark Cloud" call her next-born "Samai" (The Dawn of Day).

The Indian counts by his hands and feet. Five would be one hand, two hands ten, two hands and a foot fifteen, and a specially clever savage could even count "my two hands and my two feet." Now Mr. Hunt is changing that: five is *thalmemik*, ten *sohok-emek*, fifteen *sohokthlama-eminik*, and twenty *sohok-emankuk*.

When a boy in school desires to say eighteen, he must first of all take a good deep breath, for *sohok-emek-wakthla-mok-eminick- antanthlama* is no short word. This literally means: "finished my hands--pass to my other foot three."

At the school I saw the skin of a water-snake twenty-six feet nine inches long, but a book of pictures I had interested the boys far more.

The mission workers have each a name given to them by the Indians, and some of them are more than strange. Apkilwankakme (The Man Who Forgot His Face) used to be called Nason when he moved in high English circles; now he is ragged and torn-looking; but the old Book my mother used to read says: "He that loseth his life for My sake shall find it." Some of us have yet to learn that if we would remember *His face* it is necessary for us to forget our own. If the unbeliever in mission work were to go to Waik-thlatemialwa, he would come away a converted man. The former witch-doctor, who for long made "havoc," but has since been born again, would tell him that during a recent famine he talked to the Unseen Spirit, and said: "Give us food, God!" and that, when only away a very short while, his arrows killed three ostriches and a deer. He would see Mrs. Mopilinkilana walking about, clothed and in her right mind. Who is she? The murderess of her four children--the woman who could see the skull of her own boy kicking about the *toldo* for days, and watch it finally cracked up and eaten by the dogs. Can such as she be changed? The Scripture says: "Every one that believeth."

The Lengua language contains no word for God, worship, praise, sacrifice, sin, holiness, reward, punishment or duty, but their meanings are now being made clear.

The church at Waikthlatemialwa has no colored glass windows--old canvas bags take their place. The reverent worshippers assemble morning and evening, in all the pride of their paint and feathers, but there is no hideous idol inside; nay! they worship the invisible One, whom they can see even with closely shut eyes. To watch the men and women, with erect bearing, and each walking in the other's footsteps, enter the church, is a sight well worth the seeing. They bow themselves, not before some fetish, as one might suppose, but to the One whom, having not seen, some of them are learning to love.

One of the missionaries translated my simple address to the dusky congregation, who listened with wondering awe to the ever-new story of Jesus. As the Lengua language contains no word for God, the Indians have adopted our English word, and both that name and Jesus came out in striking distinctness during the service, and in the fervent prayer of the old ex-witch-doctor which followed. With the familiar hymn, "There is a green hill far away," the meeting concluded. The women with nervous air silently retired, but the men saluted me, and some even went so far as to shake hands--with the left hand. Would that similar stations were established all over this neglected land! While churches and mission buildings crowd each other in the home lands, the Chaco, with an estimated population of three millions, must be content with this one ray of light in the dense night.

On that far-off "green hill" we shall meet some even from the Lengua tribe.

Christ said: "I am the door; by Me if **any** man enter in, he shall be saved." But oh, "Painted Face," you spoke truth; the white "thing" **is** selfish, and keeps this wondrous knowledge to himself.

PART IV.
BRAZIL

"There can be no more fascinating field of labor than Brazil, notwithstanding the difficulty of the soil and the immense tracts of country which have to be traversed. It covers half a continent, and is *three times the size of British India*. Far away in the interior there exist numerous Indian tribes with, as yet, no written language, and consequently no Bible. Thrust back by the white man from their original homes, these children of the forest and the river are, perhaps, the most needy of the tribes of the earth. For all that these millions know, the Gospel is non-existent and Jesus Christ has never visited and redeemed the world." [The Neglected Continent]

BRAZIL

The Republic of Brazil has an area of 3,350,000 square miles. From north to south the country measures 2,600 miles, and from east to west 2,500 miles. While the Republic of Bolivia has no sea coast, Brazil has 3,700 miles washed by ocean waves. The population of this great empire is twenty-two millions. Out of this perhaps twenty millions speak the Portuguese language.

"If Brazil was populated in the same proportion as Belgium is per square mile, Brazil would have a population of 1,939,571,699. That is to say, Brazil, a single country in South America, could hold and support the entire population of the world, and hundreds of millions more, the estimate of the earth's population at the beginning of the twentieth century being 1,600,000,000." [Bishop Neely's "South

America."]

Besides the millions of mules, horses and other animals, there are, in the republic, twenty-five millions of cattle.

Brazil is rich in having 50,000 miles of navigable waterways. Three of the largest rivers of the world flow through its territory. The Orinoco attains a width of four miles, and is navigable for 1,400 miles. The Amazon alone drains a basin of 2,500,000 square miles.

Out of this mighty stream there flows every day three times the volume of water that flows from the Mississippi. Many a sea-captain has thought himself in the ocean while riding its stormy bosom. That most majestic of all rivers, with its estuary 180 miles wide, is the great highway of Brazil. Steamboats frequently leave the sea and sail up its winding channels into the far interior of Ecuador--a distance of nearly 4,000 miles. All the world knows that both British and American men-of-war have visited the city of Iquitos in Peru, 2,400 miles up the Amazon River. The sailor on taking soundings has found a depth of 170 feet of water at 2,000 miles from the mouth. Stretches of water and impenetrable forest as far as the eye can reach are all the traveller sees.

Prof. Orton says: "The valley of the Amazon is probably the most sparsely populated region on the globe," and yet Agassiz predicted that "the future centre of civilization of the world will be in the Amazon Valley." I doubt if there are now 500 acres of tilled land in the millions of square miles the mighty river drains. Where cultivated, coffee, tobacco, rubber, sugar, cocoa, rice, beans, etc., freely grow, and the farmer gets from 500 to 800-fold for every bushel of corn he plants. Humboldt estimated that 4,000 pounds of bananas can be produced in the same area as 33 pounds of wheat or 99 pounds of potatoes.

The natural wealth of the country is almost fabulous. Its mountain chains contain coal, gold, silver, tin, zinc, mercury and whole mountains of the very best iron ore, while in forty years five million carats of diamonds have been sent to Europe. In 1907 Brazil exported ten million dollars' worth of cocoa, seventy million dollars' worth of rubber; and from the splendid stone docks of Santos, which put to shame anything seen on this northern continent, either in New York or Boston, there was shipped one hundred and forty-two million dollars' worth of coffee. Around Rio Janeiro alone there are a hundred million coffee trees, and the grower gets two crops a year.

Yet this great republic has only had its borders touched. It is estimated that there are over a million Indians in the interior, who hold undisputed possession of four-fifths of the country. Three and a quarter million square miles of the republic thus remains to a great extent an unknown, unexplored wilderness. In this area there are over a million square miles of virgin forest, "the largest and densest on earth." The forest region of the Amazon is twelve hundred miles east to west, and eight hundred miles north to south, and this sombre, primeval woodland has not yet been crossed. [Just as this goes to press the newspapers announce that the Brazilian Government has appropriated $10,000 towards the expenses of an expedition into the interior, under the leadership of Henry Savage Landor, the English explorer.]

Brazil's federal capital, Rio de Janeiro, stands on the finest harbor of the world, in which float ships from all nations. Proudest among these crafts are the large Brazilian gunboats. "It is a curious anomaly," says the *Scientific American*, "that the most powerful Dreadnought afloat should belong to a South American republic, but it cannot be denied that the *Minas Geraes* is entitled to that distinction." This is one of the vessels that mutinied in 1910.

Brazil is a strange republic. Fanatical, where the Bible is burned in the public plaza whenever introduced, yet, where the most obscene prints are publicly offered for sale in the stores. Where it is a "mortal sin" to listen to the Protestant missionary, and *not* a sin to break the whole Decalogue. Backward--where the villagers are tied to a post and whipped by the priest when they do not please him. Progressive-- in the cities where religion has been relegated to women and children and priests.

Did I write the word religion? Senhor Ruy Barbosa, the most conspicuous representative of South America at the last Hague Conference, and a candidate for the Presidency of Brazil, wrote of it: "Romanism is not a religion, but a political organization, the most vicious, the most unscrupulous, and the most destructive of all political systems. The monks are the propagators of fanaticism, the debasers of Christian morals. The history of papal influence has been nothing more nor less than the story of the dissemination of a new paganism, as full of superstition and of all unrighteousness as the mythology of the ancients--a new paganism organized at the expense of evangelical traditions, shamelessly falsified and travestied by the Romanists. The Romish Church in all ages has been a power, religious scarcely in name, but always inherently, essentially and untiringly a political power." As Bishop Neely of the M. E. Church was leaving Rio, Dr. Alexander, one of Brazil's most influential gentlemen, said to him: "It is sad to see my people so miserable when they might be so happy. Their ills, physical and moral, spring from lack of religion. They call themselves Catholics, but the heathen are scarcely less Christian!" Is it surprising that the Italian paper *L'Asino* (The Ass), which exists only to ridicule Romanism, has recently been publishing much in praise of what it calls authentic Christianity?

"Rio Janeiro, the beautiful," is an imperial city of imposing grandeur. It is the largest Portuguese city of the world--greater than Lisbon and Oporto together. It has been called "the finest city on the continents of America,--perhaps in the world, with unqualifiedly the most beautiful street in all the world, the Avenida Central." [Clark. "Continent of Opportunity."] That magnificent avenue, over a mile long and one hundred and ten feet wide, asphalt paved and superbly illuminated, is lined with costly modern buildings, some of them truly imposing. Ten people can walk abreast on its beautiful black and white mosaic sidewalks. The buildings which had to be demolished in order to build this superb avenue cost the government seven and a half millions of dollars, and they were bought at their *taxed* value, which, it was estimated, was only a third of the actual. ["But as a wonderful city, the crowning glory of Brazil--yes of the world, I believe--is Rio de Janeiro."--C. W. Furlong, in "The World's Work."]

Some years ago I knew a thousand people a day to die in Rio Janeiro of yellow fever. It is now one of the healthiest of cities, with a death-rate far less than that of New York.

Rio Janeiro, as I first knew it, was far behind. Oil lamps shed fitful gleams here and there on half-naked people. Electric lights now dispel the darkness of the streets, and electric streetcars thread in and out of the "Ruas." There is progress everywhere and in everything.

To-day the native of Rio truthfully boasts that his city has "the finest street-car system of any city of the world."

A man is not permitted to ride in these cars unless he wears a tie, which seems to be the badge of respectability. To a visitor these exactions are amusing. A friend of mine visited the city, and we rode together on the cars until it was discovered that he wore no tie. The day was hot, and my friend (a gentleman of private means) had thought that a white silk shirt with turn-down collar was enough. We felt somewhat humiliated when he was ignominiously turned off the car, while the black ex-slaves on board smiled aristocratically. If you visit Rio Janeiro, by all means wear a tie. If you forget your shirt, or coat, or boots, it will matter little, but the absence of a tie will give the negro cause to insult you.

Some large, box-like cars have the words "Descalcos e Bagagem" (literally, "For the Shoeless and Baggage") printed across them. In these the poorer classes and the tieless can ride for half-price. And to make room for the constantly inflowing people from Europe, two great hills are being removed and "cast into the sea."

Rio Janeiro may be earth's coming city. It somewhat disturbs our self-complacency to learn that they have spent more for public improvements than has any city of the United States, with the exception of New York. Municipal works, involving an expenditure of $40,000,000, have contributed to this.

Rio Janeiro, however, is not the only large and growing city Brazil can boast of. Sao Paulo, with its population of 300,000 and its two- million-dollar opera house, which fills the space of three New York blocks, is worthy of mention. Bahia, founded in 1549, has 270,000 inhabitants, and is the centre of the diamond market of Brazil. Para, with its population of 200,000, who export one hundred million dollars' worth of rubber yearly and keep up a theatre better than anything of the kind in New York, is no mean city. Pernambuco, also, has 200,000 inhabitants, large buildings, and as much as eight million dollars have recently been devoted to harbor improvements there.

Outside of these cities there are estates, quite a few of which are worth more than a million dollars; one coffee plantation has five million trees and employs five thousand people.

With its Amazon River, six hundred miles longer than the journey from New York to Liverpool, England, with its eight branches, each of which is navigable for more than a thousand miles, Brazil's future must be very great.

CHAPTER XII.
A JOURNEY FROM RIO JANEIRO TO THE INLAND TOWN OF CORUMBA.

Brazil has over 10,000 miles of railway, but as it is a country larger than the whole of Europe, the reader can easily understand that many parts must be still remote from the iron road and almost inaccessible. The town of Cuyaba, as the crow flies, is not one thousand miles from Rio, but, in the absence of any kind of roads, the traveller from Rio must sail down the one thousand miles of sea- coast, and, entering the River Plate, proceed up the Parana, Paraguay, and San Lorenzo rivers to reach it, making it a journey of 3,600 miles.

"In the time demanded for a Brazilian to reach points in the interior, setting out from the national capital and going either by way of the Amazon or Rio de la Plata systems of waterways, he might journey to Europe and back two or three times over." [Sylvester Baxter, in The Outlook, March, 1908.]

The writer on one occasion was in Rio when a certain mission called him to the town of Corumba, distant perhaps 1,300 miles from the capital. Does the reader wish to journey to that inland town with him?

Boarding an ocean steamer at Rio, we sail down the stormy sea-coast for one thousand miles to Montevideo. There we tranship into the Buenos Ayres boat, and proceed one hundred and fifty miles up the river to that city. Almost every day steamers leave that great centre for far interior points. The "Rapido" was ready to sail for Asuncion, so we breasted the stream one thousand miles more, when that city was reached. There another steamer waited to carry us to Corumba, another thousand miles further north.

The climate and scenery of the upper reaches of the Paraguay are superb, but our spirits were damped one morning when we discovered that a man of our party had mysteriously disappeared during the night. We had all sat down to dinner the previous evening in health and spirits, and now one was missing. The All-seeing One only knows his fate. To us he disappeared forever.

Higher up the country--or lower, I cannot tell which, for the river winds in all directions, and the compass, from pointing our course as due north, glides over to northwest, west, southwest, and on one or two occasions, I believe, pointed due south--we came to the first Brazilian town, Puerto Martinho, where we were obliged to stay a short time. A boat put off from the shore, in which were some well- dressed natives. Before she reached us and made fast, a loud report of a Winchester rang out from the midst of those assembled on the deck of our steamer, and a man in the boat threw up his arms and dropped; the spark of life had gone out. So quickly did this happen that before we had time to look around the unfortunate man was weltering in his own blood in the bottom of the boat! The assassin, an elderly Brazilian, who had eaten at our table and scarcely spoken to anyone, stepped forward quietly, confessing that he had shot one of his old enemies. He was then taken ashore in the ship's boat, there to await Brazilian justice, and later on, to appear before a higher tribunal, where the accounts of all men will be balanced.

Such rottenness obtains in Brazilian law that not long since a judge sued in court a man who had bribed him and sought to evade paying the bribe. Knowing this laxity, we did not anticipate that our murderous fellow-traveller would have to suffer much for his crime. The **News**, of Rio Janeiro, recently said: "The punishment of a criminal who has any influence whatever is becoming one of the forgotten things."

After leaving Puerto Martinho, the uniform flatness of the river banks changes to wild, mountainous country. On either hand rise high mountains, whose blue tops at times almost frowned over our heads, and the luxuriant tropical vegetation, with creeping lianas, threatened to bar our progress. Huge alligators sunned themselves on the banks, and birds of brilliant plumage flew from branch to branch. *Carpinchos*, with heavy, pig-like tread, walked among the rushes of the shore, and made more than one good dish for our table. This water-hog, the largest gnawing animal in the world, is here very common. Their length, from end of snout to tail, is between three and four feet, while they frequently weigh up to one hundred pounds.

The girth of their body will often exceed the length by a foot. For food, they eat the many aquatic plants of the river banks, and the puma, in turn, finds them as delicious a morsel as we did. The head of this amphibious hog presents quite a ludicrous aspect, owing to the great depth of the jaw, and to see them sitting on their haunches, like huge rabbits, is an amusing sight. The young cling on to the mother's back when she swims.

Farther on we stopped to take in wood at a large Brazilian cattle establishment, and a man there assured us that "there were no venomous insects except tigers," but these killed at least fifteen per cent. of his animals. Not long previously a tiger had, in one night, killed five men and a dog. The heat every day grew more oppressive. On the eighth day we passed the Brazilian fort and arsenal of Cuimbre, with its brass cannon shining in a sun of brass, and its sleepy inhabitants lolling in the shade.

Five weeks after leaving Rio Janeiro we finally anchored in Corumba, an intensely sultry spot. Corumba is a town of 5,000 inhabitants, and often said to be one of the hottest in the world. It is an unhealthy place, as are most towns without drainage and water supply. In the hotter season of the year the ratio on a six months' average may be two deaths to one birth. It is a place where dogs at times seem more numerous than people, a town where justice is administered in ways new and strange. Does the reader wish an instance? An assassin of the deepest dye was given over by the judge to the tender mercies of the crowd. The man was thereupon attacked by the whole population in one mass. He was shot and stabbed, stoned and beaten until he became almost a shapeless heap, and was then hurried away in a mule cart, and, without coffin, priest or mourners, was buried like a dog.

Perhaps the populace felt they had to take the law into their own hands, for I was told that the Governor had taken upon himself the responsibility of leaving the prison gates open to thirty-two men, who had quietly walked out. These men had been incarcerated for various reasons, murder, etc., for even in this state of Matto Grosso an assassin who cannot pay or escape suffers a little imprisonment. The excuse was, "We cannot afford to keep so many idle men--we are poor." What a confession for a Brazilian! I do not vouch for the story, for I was not an eye-witness to the act, but it is quite in the range of Brazilian possibilities. The only discrepancy may be the strange way of Portuguese counting. A man buys three horses, but his account is that he has bought twelve feet of horses. He embarks a hundred cows, but the manifest describes the transaction as four hundred feet. The Brazilian is in this respect almost a Yankee-- little sums do not content him. Why should they, when he can truthfully boast that his territory is larger than that of the United States? His mile is longer than that of any other nation, and the ***bocadinho***, or extra "mouthful," which generally accompanies it, is endless. Instead of having one hundred cents to the dollar, he has two thousand, and each cent is called a "king." The sound is big, but alas, the value of his money is insignificantly small!

The child is not content with being called John Smith. "Jose Maria Jesus Joao dois Sanctos Sylva da Costa da Cunha" is his name; and he recites it, as I, in my boyhood's days, used to "say a piece" while standing on a chair. There is no school in the town. In Brazil, 84 per cent. of the entire population are illiterate.

Corumba contains a few stores of all descriptions, but it would seem that the stock in trade of the chemist is very low, for I overheard a conversation between two women one day, who said they could not get this or that--in fact, "he only keeps cures for stabs and such like things." In the ***armazems*** liquors are sold, and rice, salt and beans despatched to the customer by the pint. Why wine and milk are not sold by the pound I did not enquire.

One is not to ask too much in Brazil, or offence is given. When seated at table one day with a comrade, who had the misfortune to swallow a bone, I quietly "swallowed" the remedy a Brazilian told us of. He said their custom was for all to turn away their heads, while the unfortunate one revolved his plate around three times to the left, and presto! the bone disappeared. My friend did not believe in the cure; consequently, he suffered for several days.

I have said that dogs are numerous. These animals roam the streets by day and night in packs and fight and tear at anyone or anything. Some days before we arrived there were even more, but a few pounds of poison had been scattered about the streets--which, by the way, are the worst of any town I have ever entered--and the dog population of the world decreased nine hundred. This is the Corumba version. Perhaps the truth is, nine hundred feet, or, as we count, two hundred and twenty-five dogs. In the interests of humanity, I hope the number was nine hundred heads. Five carts then patrolled the streets and carried away to the outskirts those dead dogs, which were there burnt. I, the writer, find the latter part of the story hardest to believe. Why should a freeborn Brazilian lift dogs out of the street? In what better place could they be? They would fill up the holes and ruts, and, in such intense heat, why do needless work?

Corumba is a typical Brazilian town. Little carts, drawn by a string of goats or rams, thread their way through the streets. Any animal but the human must do the work. As the majority of the people go barefooted, the patriarchal custom prevails of having water offered on entering a house to wash the feet. At all hours of the day men, women and children seek to cool themselves in the river, which is here a mile wide, and with a depth of 20 feet in the channel. While on the subject of bathing, I might mention that a wooden image of the patron saint of the town is, with great pomp, brought down at the head of a long procession, once every year, to receive his annual "duck" in the water. This is supposed to benefit him much. After his immersion, all the inhabitants, men, women and children, make a rush to be the first to dip in the "blessed water," for, by doing this, all their sins are forgiven them for a year to come. The sick are careful to see that they are not left in the position of the unfortunate one mentioned in the Gospel by John, who "had no one to put him into the pool."

I have also known the Virgin solemnly carried down to the water's edge, that she might command it to rise or fall, as suited the convenience of the people. While she exercised her power the natives knelt around her on the shingly beach in rapturous devotion. At such times the "Mother of Heaven" is clothed in her best, and the jewels in her costume sparkle in the tropical sun.

What the Nile is to Egypt, the Paraguay River is to these interior lands, and what Isis was to the Egyptians, so is the Virgin to these people. Once, when the waters were low, it is related the Virgin came down from heaven and stood upon some rocks in the river bed. To this day the pilot tells you how her footprints are to be clearly seen, impressed in the stone, when the water is shallow. Strange that Mahomet does not rise from his tomb and protest, for that miracle we must concede to him, because his footprints have been on the sacred rocks at Mecca for a thousand years. Does he pass it over, believing, with many, that imitation is the sincerest form of flattery?

Whatever Roman Catholicism is in other parts of the world, in South America it is pure Mariolatry. The creed, as we have seen, reads: "Mary must be our first object of worship, Saint Joseph the second." Along with these, saints, living and dead, are numberless.

A traveller in South Brazil thus writes of a famous monk: "There, in a shed at the back of a small farm, half sitting, half reclining on a mat and a skin of some wild animal, was a man of about seventy years of age, in a state of nudity. A small piece of red blanket was thrown over his shoulders, barely covering them. His whole body was encrusted with filth, and his nails had grown like claws. His vacant look showed him to be a poor, helpless idiot. Beside him a large wood fire was kept burning. The ashes of this fire, strewn around him for the sake of cleanliness, are carried away for medicinal purposes by the thousands of pilgrims who visit him. Men and women come from long distances to see him, in the full persuasion that he is a holy man and has miraculous powers." ["The Neglected Continent"] Romanism is thus seen to be in a double sense "a moral pestilence."

The church is, of course, very much in evidence in Corumba, for it is a very religious place. A *missa cantata* is often held there, when a noisy brass band will render dance music, often at the moat solemn parts. The drums frequently beat until the worshippers are almost deafened.

In the town of Bom Fim, a little further north, the priest runs a "show" opposite his church, and over it are printed the words, "Theatre of the Holy Ghost."

Think, O intelligent reader, how dense must be the darkness of Papal America when a church notice, which anyone may see affixed to the door, reads:

RAFFLE FOB SOULS.

A raffle for souls will be held at this Church on January 1st, at which four bleeding and tortured souls will be released from purgatory to heaven, according to the four highest tickets in this most holy lottery. Tickets, $1.00. To be had of the father in charge. Will you, for the poor sum of one dollar, leave your loved ones to burn in purgatory for ages?

At the last raffle for souls, the following numbers obtained the prize, and the lucky holders may be assured that their loved ones are forever released from the flames of purgatory: Ticket 41.--The soul of Madame Coldern is made happy for ever. Ticket 762.--The soul of the aged widow, Francesca de Parson, is forever released from the flames of purgatory. Ticket 841.--The soul of Lawyer Vasquez is released from purgatory and ushered into heavenly joys. ["Gospel Message."]

But, my reader asks, "Do the people implicitly believe all the priest says?" No, sometimes they say, "Show us a sign." This was especially true of the people living on the Chili-Bolivian border. The wily, yet progressive, priest there made a number of little balloons, which on a certain day of the year were sent up into the sky, bearing away the sins of the people. Of course, when the villagers saw their sins float away before their own eyes, enclosed in little crystal spheres, such as *could not be earthly*, they believed and rejoiced. Yes, reader, the South American priest is alive to his position after all, and even "patents" are requisitioned. In some of the larger churches there is the "slot" machine, which, when a coin is inserted, gives out *"The Pope's blessing."* This is simply a picture representing his Holiness with uplifted hands.

The following is a literal translation, from the Portuguese, of a "notice" in a Rio Janeiro newspaper:

FESTIVAL IN HONOR OF THE LADY OF NAZARETH.

"The day will be ushered in with majestic and deafening fireworks, and the 'Hail Mary' rendered by the beautiful band of the----Infantry regiment. There will be an intentional mass, grand vocal and instrumental music, solemn vespers, the Gospel preached, and ribbons, which have been placed round the neck of the image of St. Broz, distributed.

"The square, tastefully decorated and pompously illuminated, will afford the devotees, after their supplications to the Lord of the Universe, the following means of amusement,-----the Chinese Pavilion, etc.,-----. Evening service concluded, there will be danced in the Flora Pavilion the *fandango a pandereta*. In the same pavilion a comic company will act several pieces. On Sunday, upon the conclusion of the Te Deum, the comic company will perform," etc.

The spiritual darkness is appalling. If the following can be written of Pernambuco, a large city of 180,000 inhabitants, on the sea coast, the reader can, in a measure, understand the priestly thraldom of these isolated towns. A Pernambuco newspaper, in its issue of March 1st, 1903, contains an article headed, "Burning of Bibles," which says:

"As has been announced, there was realized in the square of the Church of Penha, on the 22nd ult., at nine o'clock in the morning, in the presence of more than two thousand people, the burning of two hundred and fourteen volumes of the

Protestant Bible, amidst enthusiastic cheers for the Catholic religion, the immaculate Virgin Mary, and the High Priest Leo XIII.--cheers raised spontaneously by the Catholic people." [Literal translation from the Portuguese.]

A colporteur, known to me, when engaged selling Bibles in a Brazilian town, reports that the fanatical populace got his books and carried them, fastened and burning, at the end of blazing torches, while they tramped the streets, yelling: "Away with all false books!" "Away with the religion of the devils!" A recent Papal bull reads: "Bible burnings are most Catholic demonstrations."

Is it cause for wonder that the Spanish-American Republics have been so backward?

I have seen a notice headed "SAVIOUR OF SOULS," making known the fact that at a certain address a *Most Holy Reverend Father* would be in attendance during certain hours, willing to save the soul of any and every applicant on payment of so much. That revelation which tells of a Saviour without money or price is denied them.

Corumba is a strange, lawless place, where the ragged, barefooted night policeman inspires more terror in the law-abiding than the professional prowler. The former has a sharp sword, which glitters as he threatens, and the latter has often a kind heart, and only asks "mil reis" (about thirty cents).

How can a town be governed properly when its capital is three thousand miles distant, and the only open route thither is, by river and sea, a month's journey? Perhaps the day is not far distant when Cuyaba, the most central city of South America, and larger than Corumba, lying hundreds of miles further up the river, will set up a head of its own to rule, or misrule, the province. Brazil is too big, much too big, or the Government is too little, much too little.

The large states are subdivided into districts, or parishes, each under an ecclesiastical head, as may be inferred from the peculiar names many of them bear. There are the parishes of:

"Our Lady, Mother of God of Porridge."

"The Three Hearts of Jesus."

"Our Lady of the Rosary of the Pepper Tree."

"The Souls of the Sand Bank of the River of Old Women."

"The Holy Ghost of the Cocoanut Tree."

"Our Lady Mother of the Men of Mud."

"The Sand Bank of the Holy Ghost."

"The Holy Spirit of the Pitchfork."

The Brazilian army, very materially aided by the saints, is able to keep this great country, with its many districts, in tolerable quietness. Saint Anthony, who, when young, was ***privileged to carry the toys of the child Jesus***, is, in this respect, of great service to the Brazilians. The military standing of Saint Anthony in the Brazilian army is one of considerable importance and diversified service. According to a statement of Deputy Spinola, made on the 13th of June, the eminent saint's feast day, his career in the military service of Brazil has been the following: By a royal letter of the 7th of April, 1707, the commission of captain was conferred upon the image of Saint Anthony, of Bahia. This image was promoted to be a major of infantry by a decree of September 13th, 1819. In July, 1859, his pay was placed upon the regular pay-roll of the Department of War.

The image of St. Anthony in Rio de Janeiro, however, outranks his counterpart of Bahia, and seems to have had a more brilliant military record. His commission as captain dates from a royal letter of March 21st, 1711. He was promoted to be major of infantry in July, 1810, and to be lieutenant-colonel in 1814. He was decorated with the Grand Cross of the Order of Christ also, in 1814, and his pay as lieutenant-colonel was made a permanent charge on the military list in 1833.

The image of St. Anthony of Ouro Preto attained the rank and pay of captain in 1799. His career has been an uneventful one, and has been confined principally to the not unpleasant task of drawing $480 a month from the public treasury. The salaries of all these soldiery images are drawn by duly constituted attorneys. [Rio News]

Owing to bubonic plague, my stay in Corumba was prolonged. I have been in the city of Bahia when an average of 200 died every day from this terrible disease, so Brazil is beginning to be more careful.

Though steamers were not running, perspiration was. Oh, the heat! In my excursions in and around the town I found that even the mule I had hired, acclimatized as it was to heat and thirst and hunger, began to show signs of fatigue. Can man or beast be expected to work when the temperature stands at 130 degrees Fahrenheit in the shade?

As the natives find bullocks bear the heat better than mules, I procured one of these saddle animals, but it could only travel at a snail's pace. I was indeed thankful to quit the oven of a town when at last quarantine was raised and a Brazilian steamboat called.

Rats were so exceedingly numerous on this packet that they would scamper over our bodies at night. So bold were they that we were compelled to take a cudgel into our berths! A Brazilian passenger declared one morning that he had counted three hundred rats on the cabin floor at one time! I have already referred to Brazilian numbering; perhaps he meant three hundred feet, or seventy-five rats.

With the heat and the rats, supplemented by millions of mosquitos, my Corumba journey was not exactly a picnic.

In due time we arrived again at Puerto Martinio, only to hear that our former fellow-passenger, the assassin, had regained his freedom and could be seen walking about the town. But then--well, he was rich, and money does all in Brazil--yea, the priest will even tell you it purchases an entrance into heaven! In worldly matters the people *see* its power, and in spiritual matters they **believe** it. If the priest has heard of Peter's answer to Simon--"Thy money perish with thee, because thou hast thought that the gift of God may be purchased with money"--he keeps it to himself. How can he live if he deceives not? Strange indeed is the thought that, three hundred years before the caravels of Portuguese conquerors ever sailed these waters, the law of the Indian ruler of that very part of the country read: "Judges who receive bribes from their clients are to be considered as thieves meriting death." And a clause in the Sacred Book read: "He who kills another condemns his own self." Has the interior of South America gone forward or backward since then? Was the adoration of the Sun more civilizing than the worship of the Virgin?

When we got down into Argentine waters I began to feel cold, and donned an overcoat. Thinking it strange that I should feel thus in the latitude which had in former times been so agreeable, I investigated, and found the thermometer 85 degrees Fah. in the shade. After Corumba that was *cold*.

PART V.
URUGUAY
THE LONE TRAIL.

And sometimes it leads to the desert and the tongue swells
out of the mouth,
And you stagger blind to the mirage, to die in the mocking
drouth.
And sometimes it leads to the mountain, to the light of the
lone camp-fire,
And you gnaw your belt in the anguish of the hunger-goaded
desire.

--Robert W. Service.

The Republic of Uruguay has 72,210 square miles of territory, and is the smallest of the ten countries of South America. Its population is only 1,103,000, but the Liebig Company, "which manufactures beef tea for the world, owns nearly a million acres of land in Uruguay. On its enormous ranches over 6,000,000 head of cattle have passed through its hands in the fifty years of its existence." [Clark. "Continent of Opportunity."]

The republic seems well governed, but, as in all Spanish-American countries, the ideas of right and wrong are strange. While taking part in a religious procession, President Borda was assassinated in 1897. A man was seen to deliberately walk up and shoot him. The Chief Executive fell mortally wounded. This cool murderer was condemned to two years' imprisonment for *insulting* the President.

In 1900, President Arredondo was assassinated, but the murderer was acquitted on the ground that "he was interpreting the feelings of the people."

Uruguay is a progressive republic, with more than a thousand miles of railway. On these lines the coaches are very palatial. The larger part of the coach, made to seat fifty-two passengers, is for smokers, the smaller compartment, accommodating sixteen, is for non-smokers, thus reversing our own practice. Outside the harbor of the capital a great sea-wall is being erected, at tremendous cost, to facilitate shipping, and Uruguay is certainly a country with a great future.

The capital city occupies a commanding position at the mouth of the great estuary of the Rio de la Plata; its docks are large and modern, and palatial steamers of the very finest types bring it in daily communication with Buenos Ayres. The Legislative Palace is one of the finest government buildings in the world. The great Solis Theatre, where Patti and Bernhardt have both appeared, covers nearly two acres of ground, seats three thousand people and cost three million dollars to build. The sanitary conditions and water supply are so perfect that fewer people die in this city, in proportion to its size, than in any other large city of the world.

The Parliament of Uruguay has recently voted that all privileges hitherto granted to particular religious bodies shall be abrogated, that the army shall not take part in religious ceremonies, that army chaplains shall be dismissed, that the national flag shall not be lowered before any priest or religious symbol. So another state cuts loose from Rome!

The climate of the country is such that grapes, apricots, peaches, and many other fruits grow to perfection. Its currency is on a more stable basis than that of any other Spanish republic, and its dollar is actually worth 102 cents. The immigrants pouring into Uruguay have run up to over 20,000 a year; the population has increased more than 100 per cent in 12 years; so we shall hear from Uruguay in coming years more than we have done in the past.

CHAPTER XIII.
SKETCHES OF A HORSEBACK RIDE THROUGH THE REPUBLIC.
I CROSS THE SILVER RIVER.

I left Buenos Ayres for Uruguay in an Italian *polacca*. We weighed anchor one Sunday afternoon, and as the breeze was favorable, the white sails, held up by strong ropes of rawhide, soon wafted us away from the land. We sailed through a fleet of ships from all parts of the world, anchored in the stream, discharging and loading cargoes. There, just arrived, was an Italian emigrant ship with a thousand people on board, who had come to start life afresh. There was the large British steamer, with her clattering windlass, hoisting on board live bullocks from barges moored alongside. The animals are raised up by means of a strong rope tied around their horns, and as the ship rocks on the swell they dangle in mid-air. When a favorable moment arrives they are quickly dropped on to the deck, completely stupefied by their aerial flight.

As darkness fell, the wind dropped, and we lay rocking on the bosom of the river, with only the twinkling lights of the Argentine coast to remind us of the solid world. The shoreless river was, however, populous with craft of all rigs, for this is the highway to the great interior, and some of them were bound to Cuyaba, 2,600 miles in the heart of the continent. During the night a ship on fire in the offing lit up with great vividness the silent waste of waters, and as the flames leaped up the rigging, the sight was very grand. Owing to calms and light winds, our passage was a slow one, and I was not sorry when at last I could say good-bye to the Italians and their oily food. Three nights and two days is a long time to spend in crossing a river.

MONTEVIDEO.

Montevideo, the capital of Uruguay, is "one of the handsomest cities in all America, north or south." Its population is over 350,000. It is one of the cleanest and best laid-out cities on the continent; it has broad, airy streets and a general look of prosperity. What impresses the newcomer most is the military display everywhere seen. Sentry boxes, in front of which dark-skinned soldiers strut, seem to be at almost every corner. Although Uruguay has a standing army of under 3,500 men, yet gold-braided officers are to be met with on every street. There are twenty-one generals on active service, and many more living on pension. More important personages than these men assume to be could not be met with in any part of the world.

The armies of most of these republics are divided into sections bearing such blasphemous titles as "Division of the Son of God," "Division of the Good Shepherd," "Division of the Holy Lancers of Death" and "Soldiers of the Blessed Heart of Mary." These are often placed under the sceptre of the Sacred Heart of Jesus as the national emblem.

Boys of seven and old men of seventy stand on the sidewalks selling lottery tickets; and the priest, with black beaver hat, the brim of which has a diameter of two feet, is always to be seen. One of these priests met a late devotee, but now a follower of Christ through missionary effort, and said: "Good morning, *Daughter of the Evil One*!" "Good morning, *Father*," she replied.

The cemetery is one of the finest on the continent, and is well worth a visit. Very few of Montevideo's dead are *buried*. The coffins of the rich are zinc-lined, and provided with a glass in the lid. All caskets are placed in niches in the high wall which surrounds the cemetery. These mural niches are six or eight feet deep in the wall, and each one has a marble tablet for the name of the deposited one. By means of a large portable ladder and elevator combined, the coffins are raised from the ground. At anniversaries of the death the tomb is filled with flowers, and candles are lit inside, while a wreath is hung on the door. A favorite custom is to attend mass on Sunday morning, then visit the cemetery, and spend the afternoon at the bull-fights.

NATIVE HOUSES AND HABITS.

Uruguay is essentially a pastoral country, and the finest animals of South America are there raised. It is said that "Uruguay's pasture lands could feed all the cattle of the world, and sheep grow fat at 50 to the acre." In 1889, when I first went there, there were thirty- two millions of horned cattle grazing on a thousand hills. Liebig's famous establishments at Fray Bentos, two hundred miles north of Montevideo, employs six hundred men, and kills one thousand bullocks a day.

Uruguay has some good roads, and the land is wire-fenced in all directions. The rivers are crossed on large flat-bottomed boats called **balsas**. These are warped across by a chain, and carry as many as ten men and horses in one trip. The roads are in many places thickly strewn with bones of dead animals, dropped by the way, and these are picked clean by the vultures. No sooner does an animal lie down to die than, streaming out of the infinite space, which a moment before has been a lifeless world of blue ether, there come lines of vultures, and soon white bones are all that are left.

On the fence-posts one sees many nests of the **casera** (housebuilder) bird, made of mud. These have a dome-shaped roof, and are divided by a partition inside into chamber and ante-chamber. By the roadside are hovels of the natives not a twentieth part so well-built or rain- tight. Fleas are so numerous in these huts that sometimes, after spending a night in one, it would have been impossible to place a five-cent piece on any part of my body that had not been bitten by them. Scorpions come out of the wood they burn on the earthen floor, and monster cockroaches nibble your toes at night. The thick, hot grass roofs of the ranches harbor centipedes, which drop on your face as you sleep, and bite alarmingly. These many-legged creatures grow to the length of eight or nine inches, and run to and fro with great speed. Well might the little girl, on seeing a centipede for the first time, ask: "What is that queer-looking thing, with about a million legs?" Johnny wisely replied: "That's a millennium. It's something like a centennial, only its has more legs."

After vain attempts to sleep, you rise, and may see the good wife cleaning her only plate for you by rubbing it on her greasy hair and wiping it with the bottom of her chemise. Ugh! Proceeding on the journey, it is a common sight to see three or four little birds sitting on the backs of the horned cattle getting their breakfast, which I hope they relish better than I often did.

A WAKE, AND HOW TO GET TO HEAVEN.

During my journey I was asked: Would I like to go to the wake held that night at the next house, three miles away? After supper, horses were saddled up and away we galloped. Quite a number had already gathered there. We found the dead man lying on a couple of sheepskins, in the centre of a mud-walled and mud-floored room. "No useless coffin enclosed his breast," nor was he wound in either sheet or shroud. There he lay, fully attired, even to his shoes. Four tallow candles lighted up the gloom, and these were placed at his head and feet. His clammy hands were reverently folded over his breast, whilst entwined in his fingers was a bronze cross and rosary, that St. Peter, seeing his devotion, might, without questioning, admit him to a better world. The scene was weird beyond description. Outside, the wind moaned a sad dirge; great bats and black moths, the size of birds, flitted about in the midnight darkness. These, ever and anon, made their way inside and extinguished the candles, which flickered and dripped as they fitfully shone on the shrunken features of the corpse. He had been a reprobate and an assassin, but, luckily for him, a pious woman, not wishing to see him die "in his sins," had sprinkled *Holy Water* on him. The said "Elixir of Life" had been brought eighty miles, and was kept in her house to use only in extreme cases. The poor woman had paid the price of a cow for the bottle of water, but the priest had declared that it was an effectual soul-saver, and they never doubted its efficacy. Around the corpse was a throng of women, and they all chattered as women are apt to do. The men, standing around the door, talked of their horse-races, fights or anything else. For some hours I heard no allusion to the dead, but as the night wore on the prophetess of the people came forth.

If my advent among them had caused a stir, the entrance of this old woman caused a bustle; even the dead man seemed to salute her, or was it only my imagination--for I was in a strangely sensitive mood--that pictured it? As she slowly approached, leaning heavily on a rough, thick staff, all the females present bent their knees. Now prayers were going to be offered up for the dead, and the visible woman was to act as interceder with the invisible one in heaven. After being assisted to her knees, the old woman, in a cracked, yet loud, voice, began. "Santa Maria, ruega por nosotros, ahora, y en la hora de nuestra muerte!" (Holy Mary pray for us now, and in the hour of our death!) This was responded to with many gesticulations and making of crosses by the numerous females around her. The prayers were many and long, and must have lasted perhaps an hour; then all arose, and mate and cigars were served. Men and women, even boys and girls, smoked the whole night through, until around the Departed was nothing but bluish clouds.

The natives are so fond of wakes that when deaths do not occur with great frequency, the bones of "grandma" are dug up, and she is prayed and smoked over once more. The digging up of the dead is often a simple matter, for the corpse is frequently just carried into the bush, and there covered with prickly branches.

THE SNAKE'S HISTORY.

I met with a snake, of a whitish color, that appeared to have two heads. Never being able to closely examine this strange reptile, I cannot positively affirm that it possesses the two heads, but the natives repeatedly affirmed to me that it does, and certainly both ends are, or seem to be, exactly alike. In the Book of Genesis the serpent is described as "a beast," but for its temptation of Eve it was condemned to crawl on its belly and become a reptile. A strange belief obtains among the people that all serpents must not only be killed, but ***put into a fire***. If there is none lit, they will kindle one on purpose, for it must be burned. As the outer skin comes off, it is declared, the four legs, now under it, can be distinctly seen.

A GIRL'S NEW BIRTH AND TRANSLATION.

At Rincon I held a series of meetings in a mud hut. Men and women, with numerous children, used to gather on horseback an hour before the time for opening. A little girl always brought her three-legged stool and squatted in front of me.

The rest appropriated tree-trunks and bullocks' skulls. The girl referred to listened to the Gospel story as though her life depended upon it, as indeed it did! When at Rincon only a short time, the child desired me to teach her how to pray, and she clasped her hands reverently. "Would Jesus save *me*?" she asked. "Did He die for me--me? Will He save me now?" The girl **believed**, and entered at once into the family of God.

One day a man on horseback, tears streaming down his cheeks, galloped up to my hut. It was her father. His girl was dead. She had gone into the forest, and, feeling hungry, had eaten some berries; they were poisonous, and she had come home to die. Would I bury her? Shortly afterwards I rode over to the hovel where she had lived. Awaiting me were the broken-hearted parents. A grocery box had been secured, and this rude coffin was covered with pink cotton. Four horses were yoked in a two-wheeled cart, the parents sat on the casket, and I followed on horseback to the nearest cemetery, sixteen miles away. There, in a little enclosure, we lowered the girl into her last earthly resting- place, in the sure and certain hope of a glorious resurrection. She had lived in a house where a cow's hide served for a door, but she had now entered the "pearly gates." The floor of her late home was mother earth; what a change to be walking the "streets of gold!" Some day, "after life's fitful fever," I shall meet her again, not a poor, ragged half-breed girl, but glorified, and clothed in His righteousness.

HOW I DID NOT LOSE MY EYES.

One day I was crossing a river, kneeling on my horse's back, when he gave a lurch and threw me into the water. Gaining the bank, and being quite alone, I stripped off my wet clothes and waited for the sun to dry them. The day was hot and sultry, and, feeling tired, I covered myself up with the long grass and went to sleep. How long I lay I cannot tell, but suddenly waking up, I found to my alarm that several large vultures, having thought me dead, were contemplating me as their next meal! Had my sleep continued a few moments longer, the rapacious birds would have picked my eyes out, as they invariably do before tearing up their victim. All over the country these birds abound, and I have counted thirty and forty tearing up a living, quivering animal. Sometimes, for mercy's sake, I have alighted and put the suffering beast out of further pain. Before I got away they have been fighting over it again in their haste to suck the heart's blood.

A BACHELOR RABBIT.

The pest of Australia is the rabbit, but, strange to say, I never found one in South America. In their place is the equally destructive *viscacha* or prairie dog--a much larger animal, probably three or four times the size, having very low, broad head, little ears, and thick, bristling whiskers. His coat is gray and white, with a mixture of black. To all appearance this is a ferocious beast, with his two front tusk-like teeth, about four inches long, but he is perfectly harmless. The viscacha makes his home, like the rabbit, by burrowing in the ground, where he remains during daylight. The faculty of acquisition in these animals must be large, for in their nightly trips they gather and bring to the mouth of their burrow anything and everything they can possibly move. Bones, manure, stones and feathers are here collected, and if the traveller accidentally dropped his watch, knife or handkerchief, it would be found and carried to adorn the viscacha's doorway, if those animals were anywhere near.

The lady reader will be shocked to learn that the head of the viscacha family, probably copying a bad example from the ostrich, his neighbor, is also very unamiable with his "better half," and inhabits bachelor's quarters, which he keeps all to himself, away from his family. The food of this strange dog-rabbit is roots, and his powerful teeth are well fitted to root them up. At the mouth of their burrows may often be seen little owls, which have ejected the original owners and themselves taken possession. They have a strikingly saucy look, and possess the advantage of being able to turn their heads right around while the body remains immovable. Being of an inquisitive nature, they stare at every passer-by, and if the traveller quietly walks around them he will smile at the grotesque power they have of turning their head. When a young horse is especially slow in learning the use of the reins, I have known the cowboy smear the bridle with the brains of this clever bird, that the owl's facility in turning might thus be imparted to it.

Another peculiar animal is the **comadreka**, which resembles the kangaroo in that it is provided with a bag or pouch in which to carry its young ones. I have surprised these little animals (for they are only of rabbit size) with their young playing around them, and have seen the mother gather them into her pouch and scamper away.

DRINKING WATER, SAINTS AND THE VIRGIN.

In Uruguay it is the custom for all, on approaching a house, to call out, "Holy Mary the Pure!" and until the inmate answers: "Conceived without sin!" not a step farther must be made by the visitor. At a hut where I called there was a baby hanging from the wattle roof in a cow's hide, and flies covered the little one's eyes. On going to the well for a drink I saw that there was a cat and a rat in the water, but the people were drinking it! When smallpox breaks out because of such unsanitary conditions, I have known them to carry around the image of St. Sebastian, that its divine presence might chase away the sickness. The dress of the Virgin is often borrowed from the church, and worn by the women, that they may profit by its healing virtues. A crucifix hung in the house keeps away evil spirits.

The people were very **religious**, and no rain having fallen for five months, had concluded to carry around a large image of the Virgin they had, and show her the dry crops. I rode on, but did not get wet!

NO NEED OF THE DOCTOR OR VET.

"A poor girl got very severely burnt, and the remedy applied was a poultice of mashed ears of **viscacha**. The burn did not heal, and so a poultice of pig's dung was put on. When we went to visit the girl, the people said it was because they had come to our meetings that the girl did not get better. A liberal cleansing, followed by the use of boracic acid, has healed the wound. Another case came under our notice of a woman who suffered from a gathering in the ear, and the remedy applied was a negro's curl fried in fat."

To cure animals of disease there are many ways. Mrs. Nieve boasted that, by just saying a few cabalistic words over a sick cow, she could heal it. A charm put on the top of the enclosure where the animals are herded will keep away sickness. To cure a bucking horse all that is necessary is to pull out its eyebrows and spit in its face. Let a lame horse step on a sheepskin, cut out the piece, and carry it in your pocket; if this can't be done, make a cross with tufts of grass, and the leg will heal. For ordinary sickness tie a dog's head around the horse's neck. If a horse has pains in the stomach, let him smell your shirt.

A RACE FOR INFORMATION.

Uruguay is said to have averaged a revolution every two years for nearly a century, so in times of revolutionary disturbance the younger children are often set to watch the roads and give timely warning, that the father or elder brother may effect an escape. The said persons may then mount their fleetest horse and be out of sight ere the recruiting sergeant arrives. Being one day perplexed, and in doubt whether I was on my right road, I made towards a boy I had descried some distance away, to ask him. No sooner did the youth catch sight of me than he set off at a long gallop away from me; why, I could not tell, as they are generally so interested at the sight of a stranger. Determined not to be outdone, and feeling sure that without directions I could not safely continue the journey, I put spurs to my horse and tried to overtake him. As I quickened my pace he looked back, and, seeing me gain upon him, urged his horse to its utmost speed. Down hill and up hill, through grass and mud and water, the race continued. A sheepskin fell from his saddle, but he heeded it not as he went plunging forward. Human beings in those latitudes were very few, and if I did not catch him I might be totally lost for days; so I went clattering on over his sheepskin, and then over his wooden saddle, the fall of which only made his horse give a fresh plunge forward as he lay on its neck. Thus we raced for at least three miles, until, tired out and breathless, I gave up in despair.

Concluding that my fleet-footed but unamiable young friend had undoubtedly some place in view, I continued in the same direction, but at a more respectable pace. Shortly afterwards I arrived at a very small hut, built of woven grass and reeds, which I presumed was his home. Making for the open door, I clapped my hands, but received no answer. The hut was certainly inhabited--of that I saw abundant signs--but where were the people? I dare not get down from my horse; that is an insult no native would forgive; so I slowly walked around the house, clapping my hands and shouting at the top of my voice. Just as I was making the circuit for the third time, I descried another and a larger house, hidden in the trees some distance away, and thither I forthwith bent my steps. There I learned that I had been taken for a recruiting sergeant, and the inhabitants had hidden themselves when the boy galloped up with the message of my approach.

I FIND DIAMONDS.

"For one shall grasp and one resign.
One drink life's rue, and one its wine;
And God shall make the balance good."

Encamped on the banks of the Black River, idly turning up the soil with the stock of my riding-whip, I was startled to find what I believed to be real diamonds! Beautifully white, transparent stones they were, and, rising to examine them closely in the sunlight, I was more than ever convinced of the richness of my find. Was it possible that I had unwittingly discovered a diamond field? Could it be true that, after years of hardship, I had found a fortune? I was a rich man--oh, the enchanting thought! No need now to toil through scorching suns. I could live at ease. As I sat with the stones glistening in the light before my eyes, my brain grew fevered. Leaving my hat and coat on the ground, I ran towards my horse, and, vaulting on his bare back, wildly galloped to and fro, that the breezes might cool my fevered head. Rich? Oh, how I had worked and striven! Life had hitherto been a hard fight. When I had gathered together a few dollars, I had been prostrated with malarial or some other fever, and they had flown. After two or three months of enforced idleness I had had to start the battle of life afresh with diminished funds. Now the past was dead; I could rest from strife. Rest! How sweet it sounded as I repeated aloud the precious word, and the distant echoes brought back the word, Rest!

I was awakened from my day dreams by being thrown from my horse! Hope for the future had so taken possession of me that the present was forgotten. I had not seen the caves of the prairie dog, but my horse had given a sudden start aside to avoid them, and I found myself licking the dust. Bather a humiliating position for a man to be in who had just found unlimited wealth; Somewhat subdued, I made my way back to my solitary encampment.

Well, how shall I conclude this short but pregnant chapter of my life? Suffice it to say that my idol was shattered! The stones were found to be of little worth.

"The flower that smiles to-day,
To-morrow dies;
All that we wish to stay
Tempts, and then flies."

A MAN WITH TWO NOSES AND TWO MOUTHS.

I was lost one day, and had been sitting in the grass for an hour or more wondering what I should do, when the sound of galloping hoofs broke the silence. On looking around, to my horror, I saw a ***something*** seated on a fiery horse tearing towards me! What could it be? Was it human? Could the strange-looking being who suddenly reined up his horse before me be a man? A man surely, but possessing two noses, two mouths, and two hare-lips. A hideous sight! I shuddered as I looked at him. His left eye was in the temple, and he turned it full upon me, while with the other he seemed to glance toward the knife in his belt. When he rode up I had saluted him, but he did not return the recognition. Feeling sure that the country must be well known to him, I offered to reward him if he would act as my guide. The man kept his gleaming eye fixed upon me, but answered not a word. Beginning to look at the matter in rather a serious light, I mounted my horse, when he grunted at me in an unintelligible way, which showed me plainly that he was without the power of speech. He turned in the direction I had asked him to take, and we started off at a breakneck speed, which his fiery horse kept up. I cannot say he followed his nose, or the reader might ask me which nose, but he led me in a straight line to an eminence, from whence he pointed out the estancia I was seeking. The house was still distant, yet I was not sorry to part with my strange guide, who seemed disinclined to conduct me further. I gave him his fee, and he grunted his thanks and left me to pursue my journey more leisurely. A hut I came to had been struck by lightning, and a woman and her child had been buried in the debris. Inquiring the particulars, I was informed that the woman was herself to blame for the disaster. The saints, they told me, have a particular aversion to the *ombu* tree, and this daring Eve had built her house near one. The saints had taken *spite* at this act of bravado, and destroyed both mother and daughter. Moral: Heed the saints.

A FLEET-FOOTED DEER.

One day an old man seriously informed me that in those parts there was a deer which neither he nor any other one had been able to catch. Like the Siamese twins, it was two live specimens in one. When I asked why it was impossible to catch the animal, he informed me that it had eight legs with which to run. Four of the legs came out of the back, and, when tired with using the four lower ones, it just turned over and ran with the upper set. I did not see this freak, so add the salt to your taste, O reader.

I SLEEP WITH THE RATS.

Hospitality is a marked and beautiful feature of the Uruguayan people. At whatever time I arrived at a house, although a stranger and a foreigner, I was most heartily received by the inmates. On only one occasion, which I will here relate, was I grudgingly accommodated, and that was by a Brazilian living on the frontier. The hot sun had ruthlessly shone on me all day as I waded through the long arrow grass that reached up to my saddle. The scorching rays, pitiless in their intensity, seemed to take the energy from everything living. All animate creation was paralyzed. The relentless ball of fire in the heavens, pouring down like molten brass, appeared to be trying to set the world on fire; and I lay utterly exhausted on my horse's neck, half expecting to see all kindled in one mighty blaze! I had drunk the hot, putrid water of the hollows, which did not seem to quench my thirst any, but perhaps did help to keep me from drying up and blowing away. My tongue was parched and my lips dried together. Fortunately, I had a very quiet horse, and when I could no longer bear the sun's burning rays I got down for a few moments and crept under him.

Shelter there was none. The copious draughts of evil-smelling water I had drunk in my raging thirst brought on nausea, and it was only by force of will that I kept myself from falling, when on an eminence I joyfully sighted the Brazilian estancia. Hope then revived in me. My knowing horse had seen the house before me, and without any guidance made straight towards it at a quicker pace. Well he knew that houses in those desolate wastes were too far apart to be passed unheeded by, and I thoroughly concurred in his wisdom. As I drew up before the lonely place my tongue refused to shout "Ave Maria," but I clapped my perspiring hands, and soon had the satisfaction of hearing footsteps within. Visions of shade and of meat and drink and rest floated before my eyes when I saw the door opened. A coal-black face peeped out, which, in a cracked, broken voice, I addressed, asking the privilege to dismount. Horror of horrors, I had not even been answered ere the door was shut again in my face! Get down without permission I dare not. The house was a large edifice, built of rough, undressed stones, and had a thick, high wall of the same material all around.

Were the inmates fiends that they let me sit there, knowing well that there was no other habitation within miles? As the minutes slowly lengthened out, and the door remained closed, my spirits sank lower and lower. After a silence of thirty-five minutes, the man again made his appearance, and, coming right out this time, stared me through and through. After this close scrutiny, which seemed to satisfy him, but elicited no response to a further appeal from me, he went to an outlying building, and, bringing a strong hide lasso, tied it around my horse's neck. Not until that was securely fastened did he invite me to dismount. Presuming the lasso was lent me to tie out my horse, I led him to the back of the house. When I returned, my strange, unwilling host was again gone, so I lay down on a pile of hides in the shade of the wall, and, utterly tired out, with visions of banquets floating before my eyes, I dropped off to sleep.

Perhaps an hour afterwards, I awoke to find a woman, black as night, bending over me. Not seeing a visitor once in three months, her feminine curiosity had impelled her to come and examine me. Seemingly more amiable than her husband, she spoke to me, but in a strange, unmusical language, which I could not understand; and then she, too, left me. As evening approached, another inmate of the house made his appearance. He was, I could see, of a different race, and, to my joy, I found that he spoke fluently in Spanish. Conducting me to the aforementioned outhouse, a place built of canes and mud, he told me that later on a piece of meat would be given me, and that I could sleep on the sheepskins. I got the meat, and I slept on the skins. Fatigued as I was, I passed a wretched night, for dozens of huge rats ran over my body, bit my hands, and scratched my face, the whole night long. Morning at last dawned, and, with the first streaks of coming day, I saddled my horse, and, shaking the dust of the Brazilian estancia off my feet, resumed my journey.

THE BURSTING OF A MAN.

A friend of mine came upon an ostrich's nest. The bird was not near, so, dismounting, he picked up an egg and placed it in an inside pocket of his coat. Continuing the journey, the egg was forgotten, and the horse, galloping along, suddenly tripped and fell. The rider was thrown to the ground, where he lay stunned. Three hours afterwards consciousness returned. As his weary eyes wandered, he noticed, with horror, that his chest and side were thickly besmeared. With a cry of despair, he lay back, groaning, "I have burst!" The presence of the egg he had put in his pocket had quite passed from his mind!

I FIND A LONE SCOTSMAN.

One evening after a long day's journey, I reached a house, away near the Brazilian frontier, and was surprised indeed to see that the owner was a real live Scotsman. Great was my astonishment and pleasure at receiving such a warm Scotch welcome. He was eighty miles away from any village--alone in the mountains--and at the sight of me he wept like a child. Never can I forget his anguish as he told me

that his beloved wife had died just a few days before, and that he had buried her--
"there in the glen." At the sight of a British face he had completely broken down;
but, pulling himself together, he conducted me through into the courtyard, and the
difficulty of my journey was forgotten as we sat down to the evening meal. Being
anxious to hear the story of her who had presided at his board, I bade him recount
to me the sad circumstances.

She was a "bonnie lassie," and he had "lo'ed her muckle." There they had lived
for twelve years, shut out from the rest of the world, yet content. Hand in hand
they had toiled in joy and sorrow, when no rain fell for eight long months, and
their cattle died; or when increase was good, and flocks and herds fat. Side by side
they had stood alone in the wild tangle of the wilderness. And now, when riches
had been gathered and comfort could be had, his "lassie" had left him, and "Oh!
he grudged her sair to the land o' the leal!" Being so far removed from his fellows,
he had been compelled to perform the sacred offices of burial himself. Surrounded
by kind hearts and loving sympathizers, it is sad indeed to lose our loved ones. But
how inexpressibly more sad it is when, away in loneliness, a man digs the cold clay
tomb for all that is left of his only joy! When our dear ones sleep in "God's acre"
surrounded by others it is sad. But how much more heartbreaking is it to bury the
darling wife in the depths of the mountains alone, where a strong stone wall must
be built around the grave to keey the wild beasts from tearing out the remains! Only
those who have been so situated can picture the solemnity of such a scene.

At his urgent request, I promised I would accompany him to the spot-- sancti-
fied by his sorrow and watered by his tears--where he had laid his dear one. Early
the following morning a native servant saddled two horses, and we rode in silence
towards the hallowed ground. In about thirty minutes we came in view of the quiet
tomb. Encircling the grave he had built a high stone wall. When he silently opened
the gate, I saw that, although all the pasture outside was dry and withered, that on
the mound was beautifully green and fresh. Had he brought water from his house,
for there was none nearer, or was it watered by his tears? His greatest longing was,
as he had explained to me the previous night, that she should have a Christian burial, and if I would read some chapter over her grave he would feel more content, he
said. As with bared heads we reverently knelt on the mound, I now complied with
his request. Then, for the first time in the world's history, the trees that surrounded

us listened to the Christian doctrine of a resurrection from the dead. "It is sown in corruption, it is raised in incorruption." And the leaves whispered to the mountains beyond, which gave back the words: "It is sown a natural body, it is raised a spiritual body."

Never have I seen a man so broken with grief as was that lone Scotsman. There were no paid mourners or idle sightseers. There was no show of sorrow while the heart remained indifferent and untouched. It was the spectacle of a lone man who had buried his all and was left--

"To linger when the sun of life,
The beam that gilds its path, is gone--
To feel the aching bosom's strife,
When Hope is dead and Love lives on."

As we knelt there, I spoke to the man about salvation from sin, and unfolded God's plan of inheritance and reunions in the future life. The Lord gave His blessing, and I left him next day rejoicing in the Christ who said: "I am the resurrection and the life; he that believeth in Me, though he were dead, yet shall he live."

As the world moves forward, and man pushes his way into the waste places of the earth, that lonely grave will be forgotten. Populous cities will be built; but the doctrine the mountains then heard shall live when the gloomy youth of Uruguay is forgotten.

THE WORD OF GOD CONTRASTED WITH THAT OF THE R. C. CHURCH.

"Thou shalt worship the Lord thy God, and Him only shalt thou serve."--The Christ.

"Mary must be the first object of our worship, St. Joseph the second."--Roman Catholic Catechism.

"Thou shalt not make unto thee any graven image or any likeness of anything that is in heaven above, or that is in the earth beneath, or that is in the water under the earth. Thou shalt not bow down thyself to them, nor serve them, for I the Lord thy God am a jealous God."

"I most firmly assert that the images of Christ and of the mother of God, ever virgin, and also of the other saints, are to be had and retained, and that due honor and veneration are to be given to them."--Creed of Pope Pius IV.

"My glory will I not give to another, neither my praise to graven images."--Jehovah.

"The saints reigning together with Christ are to be honored and invocated; ... they offer prayers to God for us... their relics are to be venerated."--Creed of Pope Pius IV.

"For there is one God, and one mediator between God and men--the man Christ Jesus."--Paul.

"Mary is everything in heaven and earth, and we should adore her."-- The South American Priest.

"Who changed the truth of God into a lie and worshipped and served the creature more than the Creator, who is blessed for ever."--Paul

"All power was given to her."--Peter Damian, Cardinal of Rome.

"Search the Scriptures."--The Christ.

"All who read the Bible should be stoned to death."--Pope Innocent III.

PART VI.
MARIOLATRY AND IMAGE WORSHIP.

CHAPTER XIV.
MARIOLATRY AND IMAGE WORSHIP.

Before the light of Christianity dawned on ancient Rome, the Pantheon contained goddesses many and gods many. Chief of these deities to receive the worship of the people seems to have been Diana of the Ephesians, a goddess whose image fell down from Jupiter; the celestial Venus of Corinth, and Isis, sister to Osiris, the god of Egypt. These popular images, so universally worshipped, were naturally the aversion of the early followers of Christ. "The primitive Christians were possessed with an unconquerable repugnance to the use and abuse of images. The Jewish disciples were especially bitter against any but the triune God receiving homage, but, by a slow, though inevitable, progression, the honors of the original were transferred to the copy, the devout Christian prayed before the image of a saint, and the pagan rites of genuflexion, luminaries, and incense stole into the Christian Church." [Gibbons' "Rome."]

Having Paul's masterly epistle to the Romans, in the first chapter of which he so distinctly portrays man's tendency to change "the glory of the uncorruptible God into an image made like to corruptible man," and worship and serve the creature more than the Creator, who is blessed forever, they were careful to remember that "God is a spirit," and to be worshipped only in spirit. Peter, in his epistle to them, also wrote of the One "whom having not seen ye love." As time wore on, however, the original inclination of man to worship a god he could see and feel (a trait seen all down the pages of history) asserted itself, and Mary, the mother of Christ, took the place in the eye and the heart previously occupied by her predecessors. [Just as this work goes to press, the dally papers of the world announce that the oldest idol ever discovered has just been unearthed. The idol is a goddess, who is holding an infant in her arms.] Being in possession of the Acts of the Apostles, which plainly declares that Mary herself met with the rest of the disciples "for prayer and supplication," and, knowing from the four Gospels that no worship had been at first given to her, the innovation was slow to find favor; but, in the year 431, the Council of Ephesus decided that Mary was equal with God.

"After the ruin of paganism they were no longer restrained by the apprehension of an odious parallel" in the idol worship. Symptoms of degeneracy may be observed even in the first generations which adopted and cherished this pernicious innovation. "The worship of images had stolen into the Church by insensible degrees, and each petty step was pleasing to the superstitious mind, as productive of comfort and innocent of sin. But, in the beginning of the eighth century, in the full magnitude of the abuse, the more timorous Greeks were awakened by an apprehension that, under the mask of Christianity, they had restored the religion of their fathers. They heard with grief and impatience the name of 'idolaters,' the incessant charge of the Jews and Mahometans, who derived from the Law and the Koran an immortal hatred to graven images and all the relative worship." [Gibbons' "Rome."]

It should be a most humiliating fact to the Romanists to have it recorded as authentic history that "the great miracle-working Madonna of Rome, worshipped in the Church of St. Augustina, is only a pagan statue of the wicked Agrippina with her infant Nero in her arms. Covered with jewels and votive offerings, her foot encased in gold, because the constant kissing has worn away the stone, this haughty and evil-minded Roman matron bears no possible resemblance to the pure Virgin Mary; yet crowds are always at her feet, worshipping her. The celebrated bronze statue of St. Peter, which is adored in the great Church, and whose feet are entirely kissed away by the lips of devotees, is but an antique statue of Jupiter, an idol of paganism. All that was necessary to make the pagan god a Christian saint was to turn the thunderbolt in his uplifted right hand to two keys, and put a gilded halo around his head. Yet, on any Church holiday, you will see thousands passing solemnly before this image (arrayed in gorgeous robes, with the Pope's mitre on its head), and after bowing before it, rise on their toes and repeatedly kiss its feet." [Vickers' "Rome"]

This method of receiving heathen deities as saints has been common all over South America, and many Indian idols may be seen in the churches, now adored as Roman Catholic saints, while the worship of Mary has grown to an alarming extent. In Lima's largest church, printed right over the chancel, is the motto, "Glory to Mary."

In Cordoba, the Argentine seat of learning--a city so old that university degrees were being given there when the Pilgrim Fathers landed on the shores of New England--charms, amulets and miniature images of the Virgin are manufactured in large numbers. These are worn around the neck, and are supposed to work great wonders. As may be understood, the workers in these crafts stand up for Romanism, and are willing to cry themselves hoarse for Mary, just as the people of old cried for Diana of the Ephesians.

It is often told of the Protestant worker that he keeps behind his door an image of the Blessed Virgin, and, when entering or leaving the house, he spits in her face. No pains are spared to stamp out any dissenting work, and the missionary is made a by-word of opprobrium. I have repeatedly had the doors and windows of my preaching places broken and wrecked. The priests have incited the vulgar crowd to hoot and yell at me, and on these occasions I have been both shot at and stoned.

In Cordoba, there is a very costly image of Mary. Once every year it is brought out into the public square, while all the criminals from the state prison stand in line. By a move of her head she is supposed to point out the one whom she thinks should be given his liberty.

From Goldsmith's "Rome" we learn that the ***vestal virgins*** possessed the power to pardon any criminal whom they met on the road to execution. Thus does Romanism follow paganism. With the Virgin is often the image of St. Peter. The followers of this saint affirm that they are always warned, three days before they die, to prepare for death. St. Peter comes in person and knocks on the wall beside their bed.

As the virgin, Diana, was the guardian of Ephesus, so the Virgin Mary protects Argentina.

The Bishop of Tucuman, in a recent speech, said: "Argentina is now safe against possible invasion. The newly-crowned ***Lady of the Miracles*** defends the north, and the *Lady of Lujan* guards the south."

A writer in *The Times of Argentina* naively asks: "If these can safely defy and defeat all comers, is there any further necessity for public expenditure in military matters?"

South America groans under the weight of a mediaeval religion which has little to do with spiritual life. In Spain and Portugal, perhaps the two most deluded of European lands, I have seen great darkness, but even there the priest is often good, and at least puts on a veneer of piety. In South America this is not generally considered necessary. Frequently he is found to be the worst man in the village. If you speak to him of his dissolute life, he may tell you that he, being a priest, may do things you, a layman, must not. In Spain, Portugal and Italy, next door to highly enlightened countries, the priest cannot, for very shame, act as he is free to do in South America. That great continent has been ruled and governed only by Roman Catholics, without outside interference, and Romanists in other lands do not, and would not, believe the practices there sanctioned.

"You ask about this nation and the Roman Catholic Church," said the American Minister in one South American capital. "Well, the nation is rotten, thanks to the Church and to Spain. The Church has taught lies and uncleanness, and been the bulwark of injustice and wrong for 300 years. How could you expect anything else?" "Lies," said a priest to a friend, who told the remark to us, "what do lies have to do with religion." ["Missions In South America," Robt. E. Speer.]

A missionary writes: "Recently the Roman bishop and several other priests visited the various towns. It was a business trip, for they charged a good price for baptisms, confirmations, etc., and carried away thousands of dollars. In Santa Cruz a disgraceful scene was publicly enacted in the church by the resident priest and one of the visitors. Both saw a woman drop a twenty-five cent piece into the pan; each grabbed for it, and then they fought before the people! The village priest wanted me to take his photo, but he was so drunk I had to help him put on his official robes. He was taken standing in the doorway of the church beside an image of the Virgin."

"There wan a feast in honor of the image of the Holy Spirit in the church. This is a figure of a man with a beard; beside it sits a figure of Christ, and between them a dove. Great crowds of people attend these feasts to buy, sell and drink. On a common in the town a large altar was erected, and another image of the Holy Spirit placed, and before it danced Indians fantastically dressed to represent monkeys, tigers, lions and deer. Saturday, Sunday and Monday were days of debauchery. Men, women and children were intoxicated; the jails were full, and extravagances of all kinds were practised by masked Indians. The vessels in the church are of gold and silver, and the images each have a man to care for them. The patron saint is a large image of the Virgin, dressed in clothing that cost $2,500."

Since returning to more civilized lands, I have been asked: But do they really worship the Virgin, or God, through her? I answer that in enlightened countries where Roman Catholicism prevails, the latter may be true, but that in South America, discovered and governed by Romanists from the earliest times, millions of people worship the Virgin without any reference to God. She is the great goddess of the people, and while one may see her image in every church, it is seldom indeed that God is honored with a place--then He may be seen as an old man with a long white beard. What kind of God they think He is may be seen from the words of Missionary F. Glass: "I found a 'festa' in full swing, called the 'Feast of the Divine Eternal Father,' and a drunken crowd were marching round, with trumpets, drums and a sacred banner, collecting alms professedly on His behalf." ["Through the Heart of Brazil"]

Mary is the one to whom the vast majority of people pray. They have been taught to address supplications to her, and, being a woman, her heart is considered more tender than a man's could be. During a drought their earnest prayer for rain was answered in an unexpected way, for not only did she send it, but with such accompanying violence that it washed away the church!

In some churches the mail-box stands in a corner, and *"Letters to the Virgin"* is printed over it. There are always many young women to be seen before the image of St. Anthony, for he is the patron of marriages, and many a timid confession of love is dropped into the letter-box, and it often happens that a marriage is arranged as a result. The superstitious maiden believes that her letter goes directly to the Virgin or to the saint in his heavenly mansion, and she has no suspicion that it is read by the parish priest.

Saints are innumerable and their powers extraordinary. When travelling in Entre Rios, I learned that St. Ramon was an adept in guiding the path of the thunderbolt. A terrific storm swept across the country, and a woman, afraid for her house, placed his image leaning against the outside wall, that he might be able to see and direct the elements. The tempest raged, and as though to show the saint's utter helplessness, the end of the house was struck by lightning and set on fire. Little damage was done, but I smiled when the indignant woman, after the storm ceased, soundly thrashed the image for not attending to its duty.

While preaching in the town of Quilmes, a poor deluded worshipper of Rome "turned from idols to serve the living and true God." He had been a sincere believer in St. Nicolas, and implicitly believed the absurd account of that saint having raised to life three children who had been brutally murdered by their father and secreted in a barrel. He brought me a picture of this wonder-worker tapping the barrel, and the little ones in the act of coming out alive and well.

One familiar with Romanism in South America has said: "It is amazing to hear men who have access to the Word of God and the facts of history and of the actual state of the Romish world attempt to apologize for or even defend Romanism. Romanism is not Christianity."

The Church deliberately lies about the Ten Commandments, entirely omitting the second and dividing the tenth in order to make the requisite number. Can a Church which deceives the people teach them true religion? Is the preaching of Mary the preaching of Christ? ["Mission In South America," Robert B. Speer.]

"There is not an essential truth which is not distorted, covered up, neutralized, poisoned, and completely nullified by the doctrines of the Romish system." [Bishop Neely's "South America."]

A missionary in Cartago writes: "I must tell you about the annual procession of the wonderful miracle-working image called 'Our Lady Queen of the Angels,' through the principal streets of the town. Picture to yourselves, if you can, hundreds of people praying, worshipping, and doing homage to this little stone idol, for which a special church has been built. To this image many people come with their diseases, for she is supposed to have power to cure all. On a special day of the procession, people receive pardon for particular sins if they only carry out the bidding of 'Our Lady,' She seems to order some extraordinary things, such as crawling in the streets with big rocks on the head after the procession, or painting one's self all the colors of the rainbow. One man was painted black, while others wore wigs and beards of a long parasitic grass which grows from the trees. Some were dressed in sackcloth, and all were doing penance for some sin or crime. This little image was carried by priests, incense was burned before her, and at intervals in the journey she was put on lovely altars, on which sat little girls dressed in blue and green, with wings of white, representing angels. Some weeks ago 'Our Lady' was carried through the streets to collect money for the bull-fights got up in her honor. She is said to be very fond of these fights, which are immoral and full of bloody cruelty. This year the bulls were to kill the men, or the men the bulls, and the awful drunkenness I cannot describe. After this collection the bishop came over here, and is said to have taken away some of the money. Soon after he died, and the people here say that 'Our Lady' was angry with him."

From a recent list of prayers used in the Church of Rome I select the following expressions:

"Queen of heaven and earth, Mother of God,
my Sovereign Mistress, I present myself before
you as a poor mendicant before a mighty Queen.

"All is subject to Mary's empire, even God
Himself. Jesus has rendered Mary omnipotent:
the one is omnipotent by nature, the other
omnipotent by grace.

"You, O Holy Virgin, have over God the authority
of a mother.

"It is impossible that a true servant of Mary
should be damned.

"My soul is in the hands of Mary, so that if
the Judge wishes to condemn me the sentence
must pass through this clement Queen, and she
knows how to prevent its execution.

"We, Holy Virgin, hope for grace and salvation
from you.

"Dispensatrix of Divine Grace."

How history repeats itself! How hard paganism is to kill! The ancient Egyptians worshipped the "Queen of Heaven." Jeremiah, as far back as 587 B.C., prophesied desolation to Judah for having "burned incense to the Queen of Heaven," and poured out "drink offerings" unto her, and "made cakes to worship her."--Jer. xliv. 17-19.

Of the *wise* men (Matthew ii.) we read: "And when they were come into the house, they saw the young child with Mary, His mother, and fell down and worshipped *Him*."

The South American version of Matthew 11:28, as may be seen carved on a stone of the Jesuit Church in Cuzco, is: "Come to MARY, all you who are laden with works, and weary beneath the weight of your sins, and *she* will alleviate you," A literal translation of one of the prayers offered to her reads: "Yes, beloved Mother! of thee I supplicate all that is necessary for the salvation of my soul. Of whom should I ask this grace but of Thee? To whom should a loving son go but to his beloved Mother? To whom the weak sheep cry but to its divine shepherdess? Whom seek the sick, but the celestial doctor? Whom invoke those in affliction but the mother of consolation? Hear me then, Holy Queen!"

The statues of the "Queen of Heaven" are often of great magnificence, the dress of one which I know having cost $2,000. In the poor Indian churches a bag of maize leaves, tied near the top to make a neck, and above that an Indian physiognomy, painted with some vegetable dye, serves the same purpose. The Bishop of La Serena, in Chili, has received as much as $40,000 a year for keeping up the revered image in that church, and these images *are worshipped*. Bequests are often left to them, and a popular one will receive many legacies annually.

To be just, I must mention that in the arms of this "Mother of God" there is, almost invariably, the child Jesus, but I must also state that to tens of thousands this baby never grew to manhood, but went up to heaven in His mother's arms. What a caricature of Christianity! Paul said: "If Christ be not risen, then is our preaching vain, and your faith is also vain." "Make Jesus a perpetual child, and Mariolatry becomes lower than Chinese ancestral worship." If He, as a child, was translated to heaven, then He never died and rose again. Mary is, to them, the Saviour. The child Jesus happened to be her son, and, as she was the great divine one, He, through her, partook of divinity. *La Cruz*, a weekly paper, published in Tucuman, Argentina, in its issue of September 3rd, 1899, had the following article:

THE BIRTH OF MARY.

"Chroniclers say that such was the fury that possessed the devils in hell, at the moment of the birth of the Most Blessed Virgin, that they nearly broke loose.

"There was sounded in heaven the first cannon shot in salutation of such a happy event. Lucifer gave such a jump that he got his horns caught in the moon, and there, it is said, he remained hanging all the day, like the insignificant fellow he is, to the great amusement of the blessed ones above, who laughed to see such an uncommon sight.

"The other devils, who could not jump so high, remained below screaming and kicking!, and tearing their apology for beards, when not otherwise occupied in scratching and biting and burning the unfortunate condemned ones.

"And all this because... it had been foretold that... a woman, yes, a woman, should one day bruise their heads... and, according to all appearances, this was the woman... and that she was that bright and morning star that announces the appearance of the Sun.

"Why should we not therefore rejoice, as the angels in heaven rejoiced, over that moat happy event--the birth of Mary."

From this it is clear that in Tucuman, at any rate--and this, by the way, is an important city, of at least 75,000 inhabitants--they believe that Mary, not Christ, came to bruise the serpent's head. The Roman Catholic translation of Gen. 3:15 is: "She shall bruise the serpent's head." Thus, the reader sees, at the very commencement of God's Word, and in the very first promise of a Saviour for fallen men, the eyes of seeking souls are turned by Romanists from the Creator to the creature.

How these words are understood by Romanists is plainly seen by the pictures of Mary trampling on the serpent, which are found everywhere in Romish lands.

Under pictures of the Virgin, circulated everywhere, are the words: "We have seen the star and are come to adore her." The prayers of adoration run, "To the holiest birth of Mary, that in death it may bring about our birth to eternal glory. Ave Maria!" "To the anguish of Mary, that we may be made predestined children of her sorrows. Ave Maria!"

The veneration with which the Virgin Mary is regarded, and the power with which she is invested, are thus told by many a priest: "Once God was so angry with the world that He determined to destroy it, and was about to execute His design when Mary said to Him: 'Give me back first the milk with which I fed you, and then you can do so!' In this way she averted the impending destruction."

"Millions in Brazil look upon the Virgin Mary as their Saviour. A book widely circulated throughout northern Brazil says that Mary, when still a mere child, went bodily to heaven and begged God to send Christ, through her, into the world. Further on it says that Mary went again to heaven to plead for sinners; and at the close Mary's will is given, disposing of the whole world, and God the Father, Son, and Holy Spirit--the Trinity--act as the three witnesses to the will. How many good Christians at home think Brazil is a Christian country?" [W. C. Porter.]

If the Bible were in circulation throughout South America, the populace would be enabled to see that Christ is not the remorseless Judge but the loving Saviour, and that it was He who purchased redemption for us. Mary, according to Luke 1:47, was herself in need of a Saviour, and her only recorded command was to do as He, the Christ, enjoined (See John 2:5). Not only Protestants, but not even Roman Catholics born in Protestant countries, can understand what Romanism is in South America.

Christ said: "Search the Scriptures." Rome has done her best to destroy the sacred volume. Papal bulls, said to have been **dictated by the Holy Ghost**, have been issued by several Popes. Rome sometimes burned the martyrs with a Bible hanging around their necks. Romanists showed their hatred against Wycliffe, the first translator of the New Testament into English, by unearthing his crumbling remains and burning them to ashes. I have often seen the same spirit shown in South America.

A colporteur, writing of Scripture circulation in the Argentine, says: "Many of the people are trying to get us ejected from the city. One, to whom a Bible was offered, became so infuriated that he said: 'If it were not such a public place? I would drown you in the river.'" A missionary writes: "A young fellow called out after me, 'I renounce you, Satan,' but as that is not my name, I did not turn back. During the meeting on Sunday evening, the priest came riding up to the window, and shouted that he would soon put a stop to us. Today he has had a number of bills printed, warning his parishioners to have nothing to do with us. To-night one of the bills was pasted on the door. Br. Arena took it off, and no sooner had he the door shut than two shots were fired, but they did no more harm than to pierce the door-- thank God! I have been informed that a number of young men will either beat or shoot me, and that as I am the only one left they are going to make me leave, too, by foul or by fair means. The following is a translation of the priest's warning:

"To the faithful of Candelaria. Beware.
This parish has been invaded by one of the
wicked sects of Protestantism, and, having the
sacred duty of warning my parishioners, I give
them to understand that should any one of
them attend, even from mere curiosity, to hear
the false and pernicious propaganda, or accept
tracts or books that come from the propagators
of Protestantism, he will be excommunicated
from the true and only Church of Jesus Christ,
Catholic, Apostolic, and Roman, wherein resides
the infallible authority. Beware, then, oh, ye
faithful, and listen to your parish priest, who
advises you of the danger of your souls."

Yet with all this darkness and error, the majority are well contented, and quite willing to obey "warnings" like this and the following, published in *Los Principios*, of Cordoba:

"It has come to our knowledge that there are
amongst us various Protestant ministers, that
distribute with profusion leaflets containing their
erroneous doctrines and calumnies against the
Catholic Church. Some of these leaflets and booklets

have fallen into our hands, and in them we
have found confirmation of what we say above.
In one of these leaflets, for example, they treat
as idolatry the worship that we Catholics tribute
to the Mother of God. They treat as superstition
the veneration they have in Rome for the holy
staircase by which our Lord Jesus Christ went
up to the judgment hall of Pilate. They combat
the worship of images, relics, and things of that
description.

"Catholics ought to know that it is not lawful
for them to read these leaflets, nor the Sacred
Bible distributed by the Protestants, because it
has been falsified by them, accommodating its
texts to their errors. The Church has prohibited
its children many times these pernicious readings.
Let us reject, according to the counsel
of St. Paul, these ravenous wolves that come in
sheep's clothing, for they come to kill and to
destroy souls, thrusting them into the ways of
error, being separated from the true Church of
Jesus Christ, from which Luther, Calvin,
Zuinglio, Henry VIII, and others separated
themselves, of whom Cobbell, the Protestant
historian, himself has said: 'Never has the
world seem gathered into one century so many
perverse men as Luther, Zuiniglio, Calvin,' etc."

One acquainted with Spanish-American Romanism will smile at the reference
in the above article to the Bible having been falsified by us. If the text of any version
extant is compared with those which are painted on the walls of the church in Cel-
aya, there surely will be found a great discrepancy. The following are translations:

"MARY, my mother, in thee I hope; save me from those that persecute me."--Psalm vii. 1.

"Be thou exalted, O MARY, above the heavens, and thy glory above all the earth."--Psalm lvii. 5.

'I will sing to MARY while I live."--Psalm civ. 33.

"Serve MARY with love, and rejoice in her with trembling."--Psalm ii. 11.

"Offer sacrifices of righteousness and trust in MARY."--Psalm iv. 5.

"Let everything that hath breath praise OUR LADY," etc., etc.

Protestant Christians pay almost all the entire cost of circulating Roman Catholic translations of the Scriptures over the world. In the versions of De Saci (French), Martini (Italian), Scio (Spanish), Pereira (Portuguese), and Wuyka (Polish), we find in Matthew 3: 2, and thirty-four other places, instead of "repent ye" the words, "do penance," while in Matthew 3: 8, and some twenty other places, the word that should be translated "repentance," is rendered *penance.* In the following light way "penance" can be done, while "repentance" is not thought of.

For sins against the Church the priest will often condemn the culprit to wear a hideous garment for hours, or days, according to the gravity of the offence, but this punishment can be worn by proxy. There are always those who, for a consideration, will don the badge of disgrace.

What is called "Holy Week" gives proofs of the shallowness of Rome's piety. Priests and people alike can weep, fast and faint, because their God is suffering and dying; all traffic can stop because, they say, "God has died"; but as soon as the death of Judas is announced, at noon on Saturday, the noise of guns, pistols, squibs, etc., takes the place of the death-like quiet that had reigned. After an hour or two silence again prevails till Sunday morning, when all restraint is removed, and people seem to make up for lost time. Drinking and kindred evils run riot, and it is no uncommon thing on the Sunday night to see the people drinking and dancing by the light of the candles they were burning to their favorite virgin or saint.

In the large city of Lima, for centuries a very stronghold of image worship, the interest in the Church has of late years been waning. Perhaps one reason for this is the changing nature of the native population of the city, for the deaths there exceed the births. Seeing this falling away from the Church, the priests announced that they had decided to send for the *Sacred Heart of the Virgin*, and trusted that the presence of this holy relic would promote the more faithful attendance of the flock. The *heart* arrived and was with great solemnity hung from the roof of the cathedral as the incentive to piety. Thousands flocked into the sacred building with reverent awe. The women gazed upon the heart with tearful eyes, and as they thought of Mary's sufferings and goodness they were emulated to deeper acts of love and piety. One day the wind blew very strongly through the open doorway, and the *Sacred Heart* began to sway to and fro. Getting more and more momentum with every oscillation, the heart finally struck against a sharp cornice, when lo--all the sawdust fell out of the canvas bag they had worshipped as the heart of flesh of their goddess. How they reconciled the existence of the heart of the Virgin with their belief that she ascended to heaven in a bodily form I do not pretend to imagine. It may be remarked that this is surely Romanism corrupted. Nay, it is rather Romanism developed.

"Andacilli is a hamlet, at which there is an image of the Virgin. Every year pilgrims resort thither, and a great feast to the Virgin is celebrated, the most important day being December 26th. During the last few years there has been a falling off in the number of pilgrims, especially those of the better class, but this last year the clerical authorities have left no stone unturned in order to get together more people than ever. Six bishops were advertised to come, and they were to crown the Virgin with a crown which cost thousands of dollars. These proceedings rouse an incredible enthusiasm in the people." ["Regions Beyond."]

Sometimes Mary's image is baptized in the river, while men and women line the bank, ready to leap into the *holy water* when she is lifted out. Afterwards the water in which she was immersed is sold as a cure for bodily ills. Sometimes the earth from under the building where she is kept is also sold for the same purpose.

Imagine a church like that in Tucuru! "It consists of a palm-leaf hut, with a bare floor and no furniture whatever. Round the sides stand twelve life-size figures, made of canvas and stuffed with husks of corn, which some one of the Indian worshippers has painted with the features and dress of his own race. When I went in two women lay prostrate on the floor, and one of them screamed in agonizing tones, 'My Lords, send the rod of your power to heal him!'--evidently praying to these apostles on behalf of some sick relative. Here, once a year, a priest celebrates mass, and when he last came he stuck a paper over the entrance, which read: *Hoec*

est Domus Del et Porta Coeli (' This is the House of God and the Gate of Heaven.')
In San Jose we have the four walls of a new church, consecrated to the 'Virgin,'
where, recently, a raffle was held on behalf of the projected edifice. As we enter,
the first thing seen is an inscription, professing to be a message to each visitor from
the Virgin, which says, 'My son, behold me without a temple. Come, help in building it, and I shall reward thee with Eternal Life." [Report of the British and Foreign
Bible Society.]

Christ said: "I give unto My sheep eternal life"; but the record of that saying is
jealously kept from them.

When the early colonists left Spain for the New World, they took with them
the Creed of Pius IV. That creed expressly states that the Bible is not for the people.
"Whoever will be saved must *renounce* it. It is a forbidden book."

"In 1850, when the Christian world was first being roused to the darkness of
South America, and philanthropic men were desirous of sending Bibles there, Pope
Pius IX. wrote an Encyclical letter in which he spoke of Bible study as 'poisonous
reading,' and urged all his venerable brethren with vigilance and solicitude to put
a stop to it. Thus has South America been denied the revelation of God. The priest
has, because of this ignorance, been able to 'lord it over God's heritage.'" [Guiness's
"Romanism and the Reformation."]

With an open Bible, Spanish America would have progressed as North America
has done. Without the enlightening influences of that Word, behold the darkness!
Could anything be more eloquent than the prosperity of the land of the Pilgrim
Fathers in proclaiming the value of the open Bible?

Mr. Hudson Taylor, of the China Inland Mission, speaking on a recent occasion, said: "I always pray for South America. It is a most needy part of the world,
and wants your prayers as well as mine. The workers there have great difficulties to
contend with, and of the same sort as we have in China, from Roman Catholicism-
-the most God- dishonoring system in the world. The heathen need your prayers,
but the Roman Catholic needs them ten times more. He is ten times as much in the
dark as the heathen themselves are."

The *Missionary Review of the World* describes South America as "Earth's
darkest land." Do you not think, O reader, the words are most truly applied?

"There are in South America eight hundred missionaries, men and women, from

Great Britain, the Continent of Europe, Canada and the United States. In Canada and the United States there is on an average one Protestant minister for every 514 persons. In South America each missionary has a constituency of about fifty thousand, indicating a need in proportion of population one hundred times as great as in the Protestant countries of North America." [Bishop Neely's "South America."]

Yet, One called Jesus, whom we say we love, said: "Go ye into all the world and preach the Gospel to every creature."

The Codes Of Hammurabi And Moses
W. W. Davies

QTY

The discovery of the Hammurabi Code is one of the greatest achievements of archaeology, and is of paramount interest, not only to the student of the Bible, but also to all those interested in ancient history...

Religion   ISBN: *1-59462-338-4*   **Pages:132**
MSRP $12.95

The Theory of Moral Sentiments
Adam Smith

QTY

This work from 1749. contains original theories of conscience amd moral judgment and it is the foundation for systemof morals.

Philosophy ISBN: *1-59462-777-0*   **Pages:536**
MSRP $19.95

Jessica's First Prayer
Hesba Stretton

QTY

In a screened and secluded corner of one of the many railway-bridges which span the streets of London there could be seen a few years ago, from five o'clock every morning until half past eight, a tidily set-out coffee-stall, consisting of a trestle and board, upon which stood two large tin cans, with a small fire of charcoal burning under each so as to keep the coffee boiling during the early hours of the morning when the work-people were thronging into the city on their way to their daily toil...

Pages:84

Childrens   ISBN: *1-59462-373-2*   *MSRP $9.95*

My Life and Work
Henry Ford

QTY

Henry Ford revolutionized the world with his implementation of mass production for the Model T automobile. Gain valuable business insight into his life and work with his own auto-biography... "We have only started on our development of our country we have not as yet, with all our talk of wonderful progress, done more than scratch the surface. The progress has been wonderful enough but..."

Pages:300

Biographies/   ISBN: *1-59462-198-5*   *MSRP $21.95*

www.bookjungle.com *email: sales@bookjungle.com fax: 630-214-0564 mail: Book Jungle PO Box 2226 Champaign, IL 61825*

The Art of Cross-Examination
Francis Wellman

QTY

I presume it is the experience of every author, after his first book is published upon an important subject, to be almost overwhelmed with a wealth of ideas and illustrations which could readily have been included in his book, and which to his own mind, at least, seem to make a second edition inevitable. Such certainly was the case with me; and when the first edition had reached its sixth impression in five months, I rejoiced to learn that it seemed to my publishers that the book had met with a sufficiently favorable reception to justify a second and considerably enlarged edition. ..

Pages:412

Reference   **ISBN: *1-59462-647-2***   *MSRP $19.95*

On the Duty of Civil Disobedience
Henry David Thoreau

QTY

Thoreau wrote his famous essay, On the Duty of Civil Disobedience, as a protest against an unjust but popular war and the immoral but popular institution of slave-owning. He did more than write—he declined to pay his taxes, and was hauled off to gaol in consequence. Who can say how much this refusal of his hastened the end of the war and of slavery ?

Law   **ISBN: *1-59462-747-9***   **Pages:48**

MSRP $7.45

Dream Psychology Psychoanalysis for Beginners
Sigmund Freud

QTY

Sigmund Freud, born Sigismund Schlomo Freud (May 6, 1856 - September 23, 1939), was a Jewish-Austrian neurologist and psychiatrist who co-founded the psychoanalytic school of psychology. Freud is best known for his theories of the unconscious mind, especially involving the mechanism of repression; his redefinition of sexual desire as mobile and directed towards a wide variety of objects; and his therapeutic techniques, especially his understanding of transference in the therapeutic relationship and the presumed value of dreams as sources of insight into unconscious desires.

Pages:196

Psychology   **ISBN: *1-59462-905-6***   *MSRP $15.45*

The Miracle of Right Thought
Orison Swett Marden

QTY

Believe with all of your heart that you will do what you were made to do. When the mind has once formed the habit of holding cheerful, happy, prosperous pictures, it will not be easy to form the opposite habit. It does not matter how improbable or how far away this realization may see, or how dark the prospects may be, if we visualize them as best we can, as vividly as possible, hold tenaciously to them and vigorously struggle to attain them, they will gradually become actualized, realized in the life. But a desire, a longing without endeavor, a yearning abandoned or held indifferently will vanish without realization.

Pages:360

Self Help   **ISBN: *1-59462-644-8***   *MSRP $25.45*

QTY

The Rosicrucian Cosmo-Conception Mystic Christianity *by Max Heindel*   ISBN: *1-59462-188-8* **$38.95**
The Rosicrucian Cosmo-conception is not dogmatic, neither does it appeal to any other authority than the reason of the student. It is: not controversial, but is: sent forth in the, hope that it may help to clear...   *New Age/Religion Pages 646*

Abandonment To Divine Providence *by Jean-Pierre de Caussade*   ISBN: *1-59462-228-0* **$25.95**
"The Rev. Jean Pierre de Caussade was one of the most remarkable spiritual writers of the Society of Jesus in France in the 18th Century. His death took place at Toulouse in 1751. His works have gone through many editions and have been republished...   *Inspirational/Religion Pages 400*

Mental Chemistry *by Charles Haanel*   ISBN: *1-59462-192-6* **$23.95**
Mental Chemistry allows the change of material conditions by combining and appropriately utilizing the power of the mind. Much like applied chemistry creates something new and unique out of careful combinations of chemicals the mastery of mental chemistry...   *New Age Pages 354*

The Letters of Robert Browning and Elizabeth Barret Barrett 1845-1846 vol II   ISBN: *1-59462-193-4* **$35.95**
by Robert Browning and Elizabeth Barrett   *Biographies Pages 596*

Gleanings In Genesis (volume I) *by Arthur W. Pink*   ISBN: *1-59462-130-6* **$27.45**
Appropriately has Genesis been termed "the seed plot of the Bible" for in it we have, in germ form, almost all of the great doctrines which are afterwards fully developed in the books of Scripture which follow...   *Religion/Inspirational Pages 420*

The Master Key *by L. W. de Laurence*   ISBN: *1-59462-001-6* **$30.95**
In no branch of human knowledge has there been a more lively increase of the spirit of research during the past few years than in the study of Psychology, Concentration and Mental Discipline. The requests for authentic lessons in Thought Control, Mental Discipline and...   *New Age/Business Pages 422*

The Lesser Key Of Solomon Goetia *by L. W. de Laurence*   ISBN: *1-59462-092-X* **$9.95**
This translation of the first book of the "Lernegton" which is now for the first time made accessible to students of Talismanic Magic was done, after careful collation and edition, from numerous Ancient Manuscripts in Hebrew, Latin, and French...   *New Age/Occult Pages 92*

Rubaiyat Of Omar Khayyam *by Edward Fitzgerald*   ISBN:*1-59462-332-5* **$13.95**
Edward Fitzgerald, whom the world has already learned, in spite of his own efforts to remain within the shadow of anonymity, to look upon as one of the rarest poets of the century, was born at Bredfield, in Suffolk, on the 31st of March, 1809. He was the third son of John Purcell...   *Music Pages 172*

Ancient Law *by Henry Maine*   ISBN: *1-59462-128-4* **$29.95**
The chief object of the following pages is to indicate some of the earliest ideas of mankind, as they are reflected in Ancient Law, and to point out the relation of those ideas to modern thought.   *Religion/History Pages 452*

Far-Away Stories *by William J. Locke*   ISBN: *1-59462-129-2* **$19.45**
"Good wine needs no bush, but a collection of mixed vintages does. And this book is just such a collection. Some of the stories I do not want to remain buried for ever in the museum files of dead magazine-numbers an author's not unpardonable vanity..."   *Fiction Pages 272*

Life of David Crockett *by David Crockett*   ISBN: *1-59462-250-7* **$27.45**
"Colonel David Crockett was one of the most remarkable men of the times in which he lived. Born in humble life, but gifted with a strong will, an indomitable courage, and unremitting perseverance...   *Biographies/New Age Pages 424*

Lip-Reading *by Edward Nitchie*   ISBN: *1-59462-206-X* **$25.95**
Edward B. Nitchie, founder of the New York School for the Hard of Hearing, now the Nitchie School of Lip-Reading, Inc, wrote "LIP-READING Principles and Practice". The development and perfecting of this meritorious work on lip-reading was an undertaking...   *How-to Pages 400*

A Handbook of Suggestive Therapeutics, Applied Hypnotism, Psychic Science   ISBN: *1-59462-214-0* **$24.95**
by Henry Munro   *Health/New Age/Health/Self-help Pages 376*

A Doll's House: and Two Other Plays *by Henrik Ibsen*   ISBN: *1-59462-112-8* **$19.95**
Henrik Ibsen created this classic when in revolutionary 1848 Rome. Introducing some striking concepts in playwriting for the realist genre, this play has been studied the world over.   *Fiction/Classics/Plays 308*

The Light of Asia *by sir Edwin Arnold*   ISBN: *1-59462-204-3* **$13.95**
In this poetic masterpiece, Edwin Arnold describes the life and teachings of Buddha. The man who was to become known as Buddha to the world was born as Prince Gautama of India but he rejected the worldly riches and abandoned the reigns of power when...   *Religion/History/Biographies Pages 170*

The Complete Works of Guy de Maupassant *by Guy de Maupassant*   ISBN: *1-59462-157-8* **$16.95**
"For days and days, nights and nights, I had dreamed of that first kiss which was to consecrate our engagement, and I knew not on what spot I should put my lips..."   *Fiction/Classics Pages 240*

The Art of Cross-Examination *by Francis L. Wellman*   ISBN: *1-59462-309-0* **$26.95**
Written by a renowned trial lawyer, Wellman imparts his experience and uses case studies to explain how to use psychology to extract desired information through questioning.   *How-to/Science/Reference Pages 408*

Answered or Unanswered? *by Louisa Vaughan*   ISBN: *1-59462-248-5* **$10.95**
Miracles of Faith in China   *Religion Pages 112*

The Edinburgh Lectures on Mental Science (1909) *by Thomas*   ISBN: *1-59462-008-3* **$11.95**
This book contains the substance of a course of lectures recently given by the writer in the Queen Street Hall, Edinburgh. Its purpose is to indicate the Natural Principles governing the relation between Mental Action and Material Conditions...   *New Age/Psychology Pages 148*

Ayesha *by H. Rider Haggard*   ISBN: *1-59462-301-5* **$24.95**
Verily and indeed it is the unexpected that happens! Probably if there was one person upon the earth from whom the Editor of this, and of a certain previous history, did not expect to hear again...   *Classics Pages 380*

Ayala's Angel *by Anthony Trollope*   ISBN: *1-59462-352-X* **$29.95**
The two girls were both pretty, but Lucy who was twenty-one who supposed to be simple and comparatively unattractive, whereas Ayala was credited, as her Bombwhat romantic name might show, with poetic charm and a taste for romance. Ayala when her father died was nineteen...   *Fiction Pages 484*

The American Commonwealth *by James Bryce*   ISBN: *1-59462-286-8* **$34.45**
An interpretation of American democratic political theory. It examines political mechanics and society from the perspective of Scotsman James Bryce   *Politics Pages 572*

Stories of the Pilgrims *by Margaret P. Pumphrey*   ISBN: *1-59462-116-0* **$17.95**
This book explores pilgrims religious oppression in England as well as their escape to Holland and eventual crossing to America on the Mayflower, and their early days in New England...   *History Pages 268*

www.**bookjungle**.com *email: sales@bookjungle.com fax: 630-214-0564 mail: Book Jungle PO Box 2226 Champaign, IL 61825*

QTY

The Fasting Cure *by Sinclair Upton*   ISBN: *1-59462-222-1* **$13.95**

In the Cosmopolitan Magazine for May, 1910, and in the Contemporary Review (London) for April, 1910, I published an article dealing with my experiences in fasting. I have written a great many magazine articles, but never one which attracted so much attention... New Age/Self Help/Health Pages 164

Hebrew Astrology *by Sepharial*   ISBN: *1-59462-308-2* **$13.45**

In these days of advanced thinking it is a matter of common observation that we have left many of the old landmarks behind and that we are now pressing forward to greater heights and to a wider horizon than that which represented the mind-content of our progenitors...   Astrology Pages 144

Thought Vibration or The Law of Attraction in the Thought World   ISBN: *1-59462-127-6* **$12.95**

by William Walker Atkinson   *Psychology/Religion Pages 144*

Optimism *by Helen Keller*   ISBN: *1-59462-108-X* **$15.95**

Helen Keller was blind, deaf, and mute since 19 months old, yet famously learned how to overcome these handicaps, communicate with the world, and spread her lectures promoting optimism. An inspiring read for everyone...   Biographies/Inspirational Pages 84

Sara Crewe *by Frances Burnett*   ISBN: *1-59462-360-0*   **$9.45**

In the first place, Miss Minchin lived in London. Her home was a large, dull, tall one, in a large, dull square, where all the houses were alike, and all the sparrows were alike, and where all the door-knockers made the same heavy sound...   Childrens/Classic Pages 88

The Autobiography of Benjamin Franklin *by Benjamin Franklin*   ISBN: *1-59462-135-7* **$24.95**

The Autobiography of Benjamin Franklin has probably been more extensively read than any other American historical work, and no other book of its kind has had such ups and downs of fortune. Franklin lived for many years in England, where he was agent...   Biographies/History Pages 332

Name	
Email	
Telephone	
Address	
City, State ZIP	

☐ **Credit Card**   ☐ **Check / Money Order**

Credit Card Number	
Expiration Date	
Signature	

Please Mail to: Book Jungle
PO Box 2226
Champaign, IL 61825
or Fax to: 630-214-0564

ORDERING INFORMATION

web*: www.bookjungle.com*
email*: sales@bookjungle.com*
fax*: 630-214-0564*
mail*: Book Jungle PO Box 2226 Champaign, IL 61825*
or PayPal *to sales@bookjungle.com*

Please contact us for bulk discounts

DIRECT-ORDER TERMS

**20% Discount if You Order
Two or More Books**
Free Domestic Shipping!
Accepted: Master Card, Visa,
Discover, American Express